B
BERKLEY

$9.99 USA
$12.99 CAN

W9-BMP-286

EAN

ISBN 978-1-9848-0290-3

9 781984 802903

5 0 9 9 9

KAY HOOPER

HIDDEN SALEM

A BISHOP/SPECIAL CRIMES UNIT NOVEL

Titles by Kay Hooper

Bishop / Special Crimes Unit Novels

HAVEN

HOSTAGE

HAUNTED

FEAR THE DARK

WAIT FOR DARK

HOLD BACK THE DARK

HIDDEN SALEM

The Bishop Files

THE FIRST PROPHET

A DEADLY WEB

FINAL SHADOWS

HIDDEN SALEM

KAY HOOPER

JOVE
New York

A JOVE BOOK
Published by Berkley
An imprint of Penguin Random House LLC
penguinrandomhouse.com

Copyright © 2020 by Kay Hooper

A JOVE BOOK, BERKLEY, and the BERKLEY & B colophon
are registered trademarks of Penguin Random House LLC.

ISBN: 9781984802903

Berkley hardcover edition / April 2020
Jove premium edition / March 2021

Printed in the United States of America
1 3 5 7 9 10 8 6 4 2

Cover design by Rita Frangie
Village skyline by Artem Hvozdkov / Shutterstock
Typography by Anna Zasimova / Shutterstock

HIDDEN
SALEM

PROLOGUE

Salem

Do it.

  Do it now.

Mark Summers could hear the command, but not out loud. His head hurt horribly, and he had the hazy idea that the commands that kept ringing out were actually inside his head, as clear as one of his own thoughts, but . . . savage. It blocked out everything else, the people circling him, the almost overpowering scent of some kind of herb or incense, the low sounds they had been making—not exactly a chant but a weird sort of hum.

Before he'd closed his eyes, they had only been shadowy shapes flickering in the candlelight, but he'd felt their demand, like the one in his mind, insistent. Every beat of it hurt, and he had the dim sense that they had . . . done things . . . to his body. That they had hurt him, over and over.

And always the questions, the demands that hurt even more, that seemed to wrench at something inside his very skull.

"I don't understand," he managed to whisper, wondering vaguely what he was lying on, because it felt like solid stone. And he couldn't move his arms or legs, even though he didn't think he was tied down. No, there was . . . something holding him still. And he felt something else . . . wet . . . underneath him, and flowing out of him.

Do it. You know. Deep down inside you, you know.

"No . . . I don't understand." He felt appallingly weak, even though they'd been feeding him, more or less. Since he'd stopped on his way into Salem to help a stranded traveler and—and he didn't remember much after that.

Summers opened his eyes for a moment, then shut them again, dizzy, because the flickering candles were moving now, all around him, and that hum grew louder, more of a chant now, and he still didn't understand.

"Please," he murmured. "Please let me go. I won't tell anyone. I just want to go . . . home."

Hot breath on his face, smelling faintly of something he almost recognized, and then a harsh voice said, "You *are* home, Mark. You know it's true. You've come back to Salem. Back to your family."

"I don't have a family," he whispered.

"Your family called you here, Mark. And now it's time for you to do what you were born to do."

He wanted to question, to protest, but there was a pres-

sure building in his mind, something . . . powerful . . .
pressing against the bone of his skull, and he knew, suddenly, that he would never be able to contain all that
strength, all that power. It was too big for him, too much
for him . . . too much . . .

He was fading, losing consciousness, but even as the
blackness closed over him he identified the smell of that
hot, harsh breath.

Brimstone.

ONE

He passed her on one of the backstreets of downtown Salem, and if Geneva Raynor hadn't been relaxing her shield for a bit so she could send out a few cautiously probing telepathic tendrils, she would have completely missed him. A hunter, recently down from the mountains even though it was still very early, and . . .

Oh, God, oh, Jesus, what coulda done that? I never seen so much blood, so much . . . What kind of animal coulda . . . And all that on the rocks . . . all them symbols or signs, like witchcraft . . . but in blood, I know it was in blood . . .

His horror was such that Geneva could hardly sort through and try to get a location from his scattered thoughts, and what she got was maddeningly uncertain, a vague direction at best.

Still, she waited only until he was well past, then wandered in the opposite direction, pausing now and again, against every instinct screaming at her to hurry, in order to point her camera and click to capture a beautiful bit of scenery.

Or whatever. She didn't give a damn about the scenery.

She didn't want to take the time to go back to the B and B and lose her camera; for one thing, she'd need it. And for another, from everything she'd heard before and since arriving in Salem, the town militia was uncanny in how swiftly and thoroughly they "took care" of little problems. Like a murdered and mutilated human body.

Possibly, she reminded herself, knowing that whatever the hunter had seen might have been something else. Maybe.

But probably he'd seen just what he thought he had. Hunters knew what dead game looked like, after all, even if it had been torn to shreds.

There had been three dead human bodies to date, if her information was correct; she had no reason to doubt that info and every reason to trust it. And she had certainly found no trace of the three missing persons she'd been sent here to ferret out. She was very good at her job; if they had been here, she would have found them, likely in the first few days but certainly in the last two weeks. They were gone. And by now, Geneva didn't expect to find them, alive or dead.

But this one . . . if this was a fourth missing person . . . then she had the chance to see at least what the hunter had seen, get a step or two ahead of all this for once.

So she made her way from town, her pace lazy as she looked around, as usual, for what might make a good shot. She was casual when she began to follow one of the trails that led seemingly straight up a mountain, as she had done fairly often in the last couple of weeks. But this time Geneva didn't remain on the trail long; she didn't want to be observed by anyone in town heading in a particular direction. And she was very much aware that as soon as the hunter calmed down, or perhaps sooner, he'd be reporting to a person in authority what he'd seen—and then the militia would be on the job.

Forcing herself to think slowly and clearly even as she used saplings and sometimes harsh bushes that didn't spare her hands to help her climb the slope, her legs already starting to burn despite a superbly conditioned body, Geneva wondered if a fourth person had, in fact, gone missing while she'd been here in Salem. There would have been no way for Bishop to let her know. Not, at least, until he sent her partner in.

Friday or Saturday, most likely.

Until then, she was on her own. Today was Tuesday.

Geneva kept looking around, trying to find the landmarks she had gotten somewhat fuzzily from the hunter. She was able to pick out one giant boulder and another odd-shaped tree, and as soon as she knew she was in the right general area, she concentrated and opened up the lone spider sense she could claim.

At first there was nothing, and Geneva silently cursed the camera that seemed to be catching on every branch and bit of undergrowth, knowing it was a distraction she didn't need. She paused a moment in the steep climb toward . . .

Blood.

The spider senses varied within the members of Bishop's unit, some able to enhance all their normal senses, and some only one or two. For Geneva it had always been scent. No matter how hard she tried, she could not enhance her sight or hearing. But her scent . . . that she could do.

With a vengeance.

Blood . . . blood . . . blood . . .

She tried to breathe through her mouth, which was easy in one way because she was getting winded from the long, steep climb, and more difficult in another way because the smell of blood was so strong she could taste it now, thick and coppery. And even without enhanced senses she could hear the buzzing of flies . . .

Geneva closed her mind to that. She kept climbing grimly, until the sapling she'd grasped to help pull her along snapped forward and propelled her into a small clearing so quickly she was barely able to keep to her feet.

Blessed with a cast-iron stomach and being a seasoned agent besides, Geneva didn't immediately lose her breakfast. But her enhanced sense of smell told her the hunter had, and she tried not to think about that, tried, now, to shut down the spider sense.

Not that she could. Once triggered, it was a wayward thing with a mind of its own, the team members who used it had decided. Unlike the truly psychic senses, which could usually be cut off by erecting a shield, the spider senses were just . . . there. Once turned on, they were impossible to turn off. They were just raw nerves exposed to the air, gradually ebbing over minutes. Or hours.

Grimly, Geneva breathed through her mouth, trying to ignore the thick feeling of scent even there, and stood right where she was, studying the scene carefully.

A dump site. Not a murder scene; for all the blood and viscera, and there was a lot of both, the ground around the . . . remains . . . wasn't soaked, and that told her this victim had been killed somewhere else.

The worst of the butchery had been done afterward, and here, long after his heart had stopped pumping blood.

Victim. Male; he was naked, and nothing had been done to mutilate his genitals. She noted that dispassionately, just as she mentally checked the box beside NOT SEXUALLY MOTIVATED.

Young but no child; from what she could see of bony shoulders and upper chest, her guess would be in his twenties. After that . . . all she could do was note details. Arms and legs had been slashed repeatedly, some shallow cuts and some showing white bone. His chest and midsection had been opened, the breastbone and ribs broken outward, and with great force. That could be done by an expert with the right tools, she knew, but this . . . this didn't look like anything she'd seen, not in textbooks, not at the body farm, and not at any crime scene or dump site she'd witnessed until now.

Almost as if he'd swallowed some kind of explosive device, though she saw no signs of other damage such a device would cause. Just those outward-bent, splintered ribs and breastbone.

Virtually all of his organs appeared undamaged yet had been cut free of the body and now lay alongside it in a way that looked to her eye more hurried than carefully staged.

And his head . . . his skull . . . looked as if it had somehow . . . burst open under the same extreme force that had broken the breastbone and ribs outward. Shards and fragments of bone from the skull were also angled outward, some bent, some broken, white in the morning sunlight with only a patch or two of scalp still clinging to bone.

His brain was gone.

Just gone.

It was difficult to remain dispassionate at that, but she mentally checked another box in her head: SOMETHING I'VE NEVER SEEN BEFORE; NO IDEA WHAT CAUSED IT.

Geneva forced herself to look carefully, still not moving closer, and saw no sign of that organ anywhere.

There were several boulders not much larger than basketballs around the body that looked as if they had been rolled from somewhere else and placed there, a few clearly pried loose from dark earth still clinging to them. Placed carefully, she thought, to surround the body. *That much was staged. A hasty effort to make this look like something occult or satanic?* And on bared areas of gray granite, probably in the victim's blood, were signs and symbols. Like an ancient language. Or the scribbling of a toddler.

Geneva didn't recognize a single one of them as having any kind of meaning, occult or otherwise. And though she might not be *the* SCU's expert on the occult, she was more than familiar with the basics, as all primary agents were.

The clock in her head was ticking away the minutes she likely had before the militia arrived. And it was ticking fast. She grabbed at the camera, grateful for it now, and began skillfully photographing the scene.

She was no crime scene tech, but like all of Bishop's people, she had spent some time working with the best specialized teams at Quantico in order to learn the skills she might need in the field. And that practice of their unit chief's, arming his people with as much knowledge and experience as possible in a wide variety of skills, had come in handy more times than any of them could count. Because you never knew what you would need in the field until you were there.

She moved as carefully as possible, trying to leave no evidence that she had been there, circling the scene but staying well back, placing her feet wherever possible on rock or some other surface that would not leave traces.

They don't use dogs to track. I don't think they use dogs. Never heard of that, and I would have. I think. Surely would have picked up on it somehow. Maybe. Dammit.

Two weeks here and she knew so *little*.

It probably took no more than five minutes, though alarm bells were already screaming in her mind, before Geneva finished to her satisfaction. Then she carefully backed away, chose a different direction that would take her well away from the town before she'd have to angle back toward it, and began to make her way back down the mountain. She went cautiously, leaning on all the woodcraft she knew, pausing now and then to listen, to strain her eyes looking around through the dim forest. And then she went on.

The smell of blood she'd resolutely closed her mind to had gradually faded away. As for the rest . . . she didn't need to see the pictures she'd taken to remember every horrific detail.

She was perhaps fifteen minutes and quite a distance from the dump site before she paused near a thicket of brambles, used a piece of dead limb to dig a hole in the ground, and lost her breakfast. When she was done, she carefully scraped the dirt back over the hole, then pulled a thicket of brambles over it.

She stood back, studying the area critically for a long moment to make certain there were no signs of her passing this way. And then Geneva adjusted the camera strap on her shoulder and continued to angle on down the mountain, toward one of the narrow but well-used trails that would take her to the town of Salem.

IT WAS STORMING. The storm had come out of no-where, according to the bewildered weather guy on TV, and seemed isolated over a very small area. No snow, but a sporadic icy rain mixed with sleet. And thunder, which was rare with winter storms. He couldn't understand it. Nellie Cavendish turned him off with a faint sigh. Of course it was storming.

It always stormed when she was upset.

Especially *this* upset.

She left the light on in the bathroom because she hated the dark, and lay back in the surprisingly comfortable bed. Leo licked her hand, and she gently pulled at her dog's short, silky ears as he lay alongside her. He knew she was upset.

It was storming, after all.

"I won't dream," she murmured, to him or to herself. "Not tonight. I'm so close now. Surely I won't dream."

Leo whined.

Maybe he knew she would dream. Nellie didn't have the sort of connection with Leo to be sure what he knew or didn't know except when it was obvious. It stormed when she was very upset, very nervous, or very anxious. After five years with her he knew that and tended to stick even closer than usual.

He knew they were on a trip, and normally Leo enjoyed travel. Exploring new places with new things to smell was fun; that was the sense she got from him. But not this time. He had been uncharacteristically subdued all the way here.

Then again, maybe it was just this motel.

She had spent the last two nights at this very unsettling and weirdly familiar roadside motel about ten miles away from Salem, trying to get up her nerve to actually drive into town. It had been the closest lodging she'd been able to find not actually in the town—the only lodging, really, within at least thirty miles, which was weird.

No weirder than the rest of this, she supposed, but . . .

Weird.

It was almost as if the town wanted to be hidden.

Almost.

Her car's GPS system hadn't had a clue, and neither had the maps app on her cell, so she'd had to rely on some pretty old, many-folded maps of the kind still sold at most gas stations. And even then she'd found herself stopping often to ask where she was on them (since roads and highways had been added everywhere since the maps had been printed) and how to find Salem. The directions she had followed had consisted entirely of physical land-marks such as an ancient tumbledown barn just off the highway, a lone pancake house that appeared to have gone out of business a considerable time previously, and, at the off-ramp itself, what looked like a truckers' gas station and café actually called Mama's Good Food.

Mama's cooking didn't appear to be a very strong draw. Nellie hadn't seen a single truck or, for that matter, a car at the café, even though a blinking red neon sign in the window, a few dim places in its tubing adding to the weirdness, had declared the place to be open.

It was hardly inviting. Nellie hadn't been tempted to stop.

Miles off the highway ramp she had been somewhat reassured to discover that her interim destination, rec-ommended by a helpful man at a gas station several hours before, was neat and in good repair. The neon sign indi-cating the Raven Lodge had not been missing any of its illumination, blue letters shining brightly, functioning as the beacon it was no doubt designed to be to draw in weary travelers for a brief respite from their adventures in the middle of godforsaken nowhere.

A single crow had been perched on the sign and had watched Nellie's arrival with bright eyes. Weirdly appropriate, even though it was a crow and not a raven. And she didn't even know if she could have explained the difference. Just that she knew this was a crow, because she saw them all the time.

She had deliberately avoided looking at it as she checked in and parked near her room, carrying in her bags herself. And she hadn't looked out to see if the crow lingered.

They almost never did once she got inside.

Almost never.

Since then, she had mostly stayed inside. A couple of other guests had come and gone for a single night, which had been reassuring, but not very; Nellie had seen them only in passing, and they'd had the glazed-eyed look of exhausted travelers just looking for a place to rest for a few hours before moving on in their journey from somewhere to somewhere else.

It was a lonely place. Still, Nellie really wasn't all that worried about anyone bothering her. She had her gun. And Leo. Not many people were willing to mess with a ninety-pound Pit bull.

Or even a little woman holding a gun with very expert ease.

No, the Raven Lodge, despite its somewhat eerie isolation, was to all appearances safe enough, neatly kept and maintained as though someone cared; she'd seen a gardener working, and there were at least two maids who took care of the rooms.

So. It was a place to pause for a day or three and think about this, which was why she had stopped instead of pushing on when she was so close. To think. To walk Leo—always within sight of the motel—and to ask herself again and again if she was making the biggest mistake of her life.

A place to pause and consider—that's what she had needed. And never mind that there was always a crow visible somewhere when she took Leo out. Sometimes more than one, always watching her with their small, black, eerily intelligent eyes.

She ignored them.

Because this was a good place to stop and think, without distractions, feathered or otherwise.

It had this fairly comfortable bed, after all, complete with a snowy white duvet cover freshly bleached instead of the mystery bedspread of many hotels and motels made infamous by unpleasant stains hidden by dark, busy floral prints. There were plenty of good pillows and warm blankets, plenty of hot water in the shower, and plenty of towels. The heating system worked efficiently without sounding like a jet taking off just outside the window. Both the satellite TV on a seemingly brand-new flat-screen and the Wi-Fi password she'd been given at check-in for her laptop worked with no problem at all as long as she remembered not to rest her fingers or hands on the laptop for any longer than necessary.

They tended to go dead on her if she wasn't careful.

Even if they were plugged into an electrical outlet. Even if she wore her gloves.

There was no food service or restaurant on-site or nearby, but there were vending machines in a central niche where the ice machine lived, and a fair selection of those, even providing sandwiches and microwavable soup and other meals. She had both a coffeemaker and a microwave in her room. And, anyway, it beat driving all the way back to Mama's.

So a good place to pause. To think.

But she had still dreamed the first night here. And last night. The same horrible, inexplicable dream that woke her with a scream of terror tangled in her throat, locked behind her gritted teeth. And so tonight it was storming, the rumble of thunder rolling and rolling and rolling as if seeking a particular path through these old mountains and valleys. Or a particular thing.

Hunting.

Hunting her.

Dumb. Dumb thought. Turn out the lights, the TV, listen to the storm—and imagine it's hunting you. Oh, yeah, that'll lead to a restful night.

Leo licked her hand again, and Nellie murmured to him soothingly, then closed her eyes in determination. The storm was *not* hunting her. This little motel was perfectly ordinary and perfectly safe, and she could sleep easily.

She *could*.

She told herself that over and over.

And she almost believed herself.

————

IT WAS NEVER the same, Nellie's dream—and yet it was. The same terror and shame and confusion. The same overwhelming sense that this wasn't *her*, that she was watching someone else do these inexplicable, sickening, unspeakable things.

It was always in the woods, dense woods like those that surrounded this isolated motel. There was always a big fire, a bonfire, with shadowy figures she could never quite make out throwing more branches onto the fire to keep it burning high and hot.

She could never tell if it was a mist or smoke that made it difficult for her to see clearly, but she never could. The brightness of the bonfire, the shifting human shapes of shadows. Smoke or mist swirling, distorting everything.

There was always chanting. Words she could never make out, or maybe a language she didn't know. Or maybe she just didn't want to understand what they were saying, because something inside her, inside the sane her, didn't want to understand. Smells she didn't want to identify because . . . because. Things she didn't want to look at, to see.

Even glimpses were bad enough. Because she thought there was a body lying prone on a big, flat rock, blood dripping, shining in the firelight, and it didn't even look human anymore.

Who had done that? *Why?*

They were all around her, moving, perhaps dancing as they chanted. In the shadows mostly, but occasionally a flicker of the bonfire would catch the gleam of eyes or the wet maw of an open mouth chanting.

Chanting . . . something. Slowly at first, softly. Then louder. Faster. Frenzied.

And then there was her. As if she stood back and watched, she could see herself. Or someone that appeared to be her, which was what she desperately hoped was the truth. Not her. Just someone who looked like her. Dressed in some filmy white dress with layers and bits that fluttered as she danced and whirled. Barefoot, her hair loose and whipping about. Layered or not, the dress was nearly transparent, more obviously so when the layers and bits lifted and shifted with her movements, and it was utterly clear she was naked underneath it.

Naked. Aroused.

It made her want to turn away, to writhe in shame and disgust. Because she, that other *her*, that stranger, was wild, pagan, and dancing with total abandon, out of control, growing more frenzied as the chanting grew more frenzied. A shadowy partner danced with her near the bonfire, a partner who was clearly male and clearly aroused as well, because he was naked.

She couldn't see his face because he was wearing some kind of mask, but the firelight glinted off sweat-slick muscled flesh as he danced with a grace that was riveting.

That was what Nellie *hated*, that she couldn't look away, couldn't turn away and run from this. She stood frozen, somehow apart from what was happening or wanting to be, staring, watching herself—watching that *stranger* that looked like her—behave in a way she never had, never *could*, in some kind of ceremony or ritual or, hell, just insanity, and what she felt even over the disgust and shame and bewilderment was this awful certainty of . . . inevitability.

It wasn't a dream. Wasn't a nightmare. It was something else.

It was something real.

And it terrified her.

The chanting grew louder, the shadows in the background moved with more frenzy, she moved with more frenzy, and then she started taking off the filmy white dress, the sheer layers of it falling away from her, her sweating face twisted in an expression of lust, and the naked man was reaching for her, his hands grasping—

And she woke with a cry, sitting up in bed, Leo whining anxiously beside her.

She wrapped her arms around him and held on to his warmth and strength, his reality, knowing she was shaking and frightened. She could still hear the thunder, softer now as the storm wandered away, its task finished.

It had found her.

OUTSIDE THE ODD little motel, the crows gathered, as they had every night since Nellie had arrived. Oddly silent for birds that weren't usually.

Two. Four. Ten. Finally a dozen in all. A couple perched on the motel's sign. Others perched on tree branches, a few on the old three-rail fence that fronted the motel's property and was supposed to be decorative.

Some of the crows looked up as thunder rumbled in the distance, but their attention never strayed far or for long from the motel room with the curtains drawn.

The one with *her* inside.

They were silent, the crows. Wings flapped occasionally, but no normally raucous *caw* of sound escaped any of them.

They just watched. And waited.

TWO

Geneva forced herself to spend the rest of the day snapping pictures around town and talking pleasantly to people, as she had been doing for the last two weeks. Building solidly on the cover that she was here to photograph the often genuinely stunning views of the landscape, as well as the historical architecture, for a planned book of her wandering photographic "journey" of the Southern Appalachians.

One small town at a time.

She had lunch at one of the cafés, indoors because it was *cold*. She hadn't noticed it so much that morning, but as the day wore on she certainly did.

As she always did, she cautiously opened up her mind now and then, hardly more than sending out a seeking tendril of telepathic energy to probe her surroundings. And, as had so often happened in the last two weeks, what she sensed was . . . unusual. Sometimes there was only static in her head, a faint crackling like between stations on a radio. Other times she was able to pick up a thought or two from the people around her. The sort of normal thoughts most people had, about what was going on in their lives at the moment, large and small worries or frustrations and sometimes contentment or unclouded happiness.

And sometimes—often—nothing; thoughts hidden behind mental or emotional walls the SCU had found more common in small towns, where everybody knowing your business tended in some people to result in protective barriers erected unconsciously. Though usually not quite so . . . solid.

In any case, she sensed virtually nothing that helped her, and she was very conscious of the nagging feeling that the static, while baffling, was also important, and that maybe she should drive her rental a safe distance from town, as she had for her only check-in so far, and find a landline phone to contact Bishop.

But Geneva was stubborn. It was her job to figure this shit out, and she intended to do just that.

The day seemed to crawl by. She had supper out as well as lunch, partly because she was hungry and partly because she wanted to try again to pick up any of the militia chatter—making other cautious telepathic efforts, though so far she hadn't been able to read a single one she'd identified as militia. And they were not, she'd quickly discovered, talkative to strangers. At all. Nor did they seem especially chatty to townsfolk, though always pleasant.

They were a lot more like a solidly disciplined law enforcement or military group than most of the militias she'd encountered, and though it was a bit reassuring to see no outward signs of fanaticism such as shaved heads or ugly tattoos, she had not been able to find out anything about their beliefs and motives. Other than the obvious one of keeping order in Salem.

She had mentally tagged a couple dozen citizens of Salem as belonging to the militia, almost entirely from actions, behavior, and the very few snippets of conversation she'd overheard one way or another. There were a few women but mostly men, and she had a strong feeling she had yet to encounter whoever was in charge of what was in effect local law enforcement.

She *really* needed to find out who was in charge. In two weeks she had overheard only two names that sounded as if they were held in a great deal of respect, and she had neither met nor encountered either man yet. Finn had been one name, Duncan another. Finn seemed to be high up in the day-to-day operations of the militia—she thought, since she'd caught quite a few snippets of conversation that included the phrases "Finn said" or "Finn wants us to" . . . whatever.

But she hadn't been able to find out any real, solid information. She wasn't even sure which of the families they belonged to, though she had a strong hunch they came from the original five families that had settled this valley and founded the town hundreds of years before.

She was more than usually frustrated by the lack of information, which is why she sent out carefully narrowed seeking tendrils to probe those around her whenever she was in a restaurant or even just walking around town, even though she was also worried her own seeking might be picked up by someone else.

Like the wrong person.

So by now, she was extra-cautious when she reached out, increasingly bothered by the static and the walls. The static because she was afraid it originated somehow in a human source and was getting stronger, which indicated increasing power of some kind, and the walls because she became gradually convinced they were the more rare kind that usually hid psychic ability, active or latent.

She hadn't recognized another psychic as she'd wandered around the area snapping pictures, but that wasn't unheard of, even though until now she would have said it was more usual that they tended to recognize each other. She normally did, being a very strong telepath. But in Salem . . . the walls she sensed were . . . really thick. Like from a lifetime of practice.

The sort of practice born psychics grew up with.

So she shored up her own walls and went about what she had carefully established as her normal daily routine, finally returning to the B and B when it was too late and too dark for her camera to be a good excuse to be out and about. And because it was damned cold. She greeted the ever-present Ms. Payton at the desk of the B and B and cheerfully imparted the information that she had two rolls of film to develop.

Normally she wouldn't have been so forthcoming while on a case, but in this instance she had made a point of explaining that since she used professional cameras and developed her own film, she'd be setting up a temporary space in her suite for such work and requested that the area not be disturbed by housekeeping.

She was absolutely certain it had been disturbed, searched, at least twice during her stay, and not by any of the maids.

But Geneva had found a place to conceal any damning evidence that she wasn't what she claimed—even though it had not, until now, been needed. Anything a searcher would have found before today could have done no more than confirm her cover story.

There was a second bathroom in her suite, and it was just large enough for her needs. She borrowed a small table from her sitting room in order to have enough space for her trays, and there was already a pullout line in the shower meant for guests to hang up anything they wished to drip-dry over the bathtub.

Perfect.

She spent the next couple of hours developing the pictures from one roll of film, ignoring the other for the moment. She made two copies of every shot she'd gotten at the dump site. When she was done, she took one set of copies into her sitting room and spread them out on the large coffee table, first turning on several lamps and drawing the drapes across the wide windows and the sliders that led out onto her balcony.

It might have been no more than her usual caution, but Geneva had been disturbed more than once to find herself under observation—by a crow. They were all about the area, so that shouldn't have bothered her. And if she'd had a different job, maybe it wouldn't have.

But she worked for Bishop, for the SCU, and she had learned to be wary of things that bothered her.

The crows bothered her.

So just in case one of them landed on the railing of her balcony and decided to look in at her . . . Well, just in case.

Geneva studied the pictures one by one. All they told her, individually and in total, was that someone had been tortured somewhere else and dumped here, where organs from the trunk of the body had been removed and set aside. She had no clue what had happened to the brain, or at what stage of the process it had been somehow removed, along with a substantial part of the skull.

The photos also told her that whoever had dumped the body had painted a lot of nonsense on some rocks rolled around the remains, presumably to thoroughly scare the shit out of anyone who found the place.

It had certainly terrified and horrified the hunter, although Geneva thought the human remains alone would have done that, mutilated as they had been.

As she saw it, there were two options most likely. Another person had gone missing after heading to Salem, information Bishop had not been able to get to his agent since her one and only report to him very early on. Or an unlucky hunter or hiker had been in the wrong place at the wrong time, a victim of opportunity, and had been sacrificed.

Because she didn't have any doubt about that. This was not the work of a serial killer, or a onetime murderer, or somebody who'd gotten pissed at this poor man and murdered him for the Universe only knew what senseless reason. This was ritual, yes, but not of the serial-killer sort.

It wasn't anything she recognized as Satanism or any of its many offshoots. Not the sort of occult most people would think of as such. This, her training, experience, and instincts told her, was an even darker, thankfully rare type of ritual, an attempt to gain power by causing the maximum amount of agony to a victim. A human victim. Because death released energy, and a death in agony released a *lot* of very powerful, very negative energy.

And now the static Geneva had been aware of and on guard against since arriving became even more troubling. Because if someone *was* sacrificing people in prolonged torture, and if that person or those people were doing so for the purpose of creating and absorbing energy, then it was the darkest energy, and anybody on that deadly path had an agenda. A very bad agenda.

It was a possible answer—at least in part—for why three, possibly four, people had come to Salem to die. If they had died, and had died like this, which she could not, even now, be certain of. So far, all she had were these photos of one victim and a dump site she was almost positive would by this time have been sanitized. She hadn't been able to take any biological samples, both because she'd lacked the necessary equipment and because she hadn't dared leave any signs of her own presence there.

There would be no human remains now, she was sure. No signs of rocks painted with nonsense symbols in blood. No sign of a young man tortured to death. No sign anything bad had happened. And no news of it down in Salem. The militia would see to that.

But who were they protecting? That's what Geneva didn't know, what her best efforts had failed to uncover. Common sense said they could have been involved in the torture or murder at worst, or covering up what was happening under orders, willingly or not. *But whose orders?*

They looked like ordinary citizens, dressed casually without uniforms, and sported no badges or insignia she'd been able to see. But she *had* spotted handguns in shoulder holsters and clipped to belts under thick winter jackets or coats. It was an open-carry state, but as far as she could tell, only the militia felt the need to go armed. Or, perhaps, had made certain they were the only ones who were, no matter what state law was.

Otherwise . . . ordinary. Not, of course, that monsters boasted horns and a tail so they could be easily identified. Not human monsters, at any rate.

And there was, clearly, at least one monster in Salem.

She picked up one of the photos and forced herself to study it, seriously disturbed by one thing more than any other. As far as she'd been able to determine, only one organ had been completely missing from the remains.

His brain. And she wasn't even certain it was missing. It could, given the condition of the skull, have simply . . . exploded somehow, leaving nothing except microscopic bits only a forensic pathologist could see.

And Geneva didn't have a clue how that was even possible.

BETHANY HICKS KNEW she'd made a bad mistake when the first crow landed silently on a low branch of the tree she'd been hiding behind.

She looked up cautiously, not a whit reassured by the bird's bright-eyed but seemingly benevolent gaze. Nervously pulling her coat tighter around her because it was really, *really* cold, she yanked her attention away from the crow and stared once more at the church. Not that it looked like a church, really. Just somebody's old house tucked back in the woods where you couldn't see it from the road. Or, really, from anywhere except close. An old farmhouse made more than a little creepy because the only light she could see through windows dressed with nothing except sheer, gauzy material was candlelight. Moving around all through the house as though people with candles were following some pattern she couldn't recognize.

She could see the lights. But not the people.

But she could hear them.

They started chanting in a language Bethany didn't understand. And it struck her as extra-creepy that she could hear the chanting even though every single window she could see was closed against the cold January night.

She felt a prickling sensation on the back of her neck, and at first thought it was the eerie chanting that was spooking her. But then something made her look up slowly to find that the lone crow had been silently joined by two friends, all three regarding her with bright crow eyes.

There were a lot of crows around Salem, so she was familiar with them. Crows were big birds and made a lot of noise when they flew close, Bethany knew.

These hadn't made a sound.

And all of a sudden, Bethany didn't really care what was going on in the spooky old house back here in the woods at the edge of Salem. She didn't care if it was a church or not. She didn't care what they were doing in there, not a bit.

All of a sudden, she didn't want to break off one of the geraniums in the pot on the front porch, the ones Jason swore were real even though it was *January* and they shouldn't be real, shouldn't be blooming. She didn't want to steal a flower and run and show it to Jason and the other boys to prove she was brave.

Bethany didn't feel very brave.

She didn't feel brave at all.

Holding her breath so there was no mist at all in front of her face, she backed away from the tree, her gaze flicking back and forth from the strange house with its increasingly creepy chanting sounds that seemed to grow louder as she backed away to the three watching crows that turned their heads in perfect sync to watch every movement she made.

She backed away slowly, her heartbeat thundering in her ears, until she couldn't see the house or the crows, until the silent, dark woods closed around her, and then Bethany Hicks ran as fast as her long ten-year-old legs could carry her.

And she almost made it.

WEDNESDAY

Geneva followed her established habits when she went out just before lunchtime on Wednesday. She carried her camera; she smiled at people; she took a few pictures of stunning scenery. And all the time, behind her pleasant facade, she was mulling possibilities, questions, speculation.

She wouldn't have been the first agent to complain that the job was too often like putting together a jigsaw puzzle without knowing what the finished picture was supposed to look like. Trying this piece, then that, rotating, flipping, trying to see the pattern.

The fact that there always *was* a pattern was the saving grace. It was just usually difficult as hell to find it.

And the extra senses that were tools in her investigator's toolbox hadn't been a lot of help on this one so far. She had picked up little telepathically. Practically falling over the frantic hunter had been sheer happenstance.

Worse, after her speculations and tentative conclusions of the night before, she was even more wary of using her telepathic senses. Especially once she was roaming about today and was uneasily aware that the static she sensed was indeed growing stronger and seemed to hang over the town now like an invisible cloud that made her skin crawl just a bit.

It hadn't been like that yesterday. Or else it had, and she hadn't sensed it as strongly, for whatever reason. It wasn't, after all, that unusual that her extra senses might wax and wane in strength; very often they seemed to have a mind of their own. And they could be affected by external energy sources, so there was also that troubling thought.

But maybe it was only her growing uneasiness over the victim she had found, solid evidence of evil lurking, that made it seem to her today that there were even more walls around her now, walls blocking the minds of people who smiled pleasantly and casually at her as she passed.

Maybe. Or maybe that building static was changing things somehow. Changing those around her. Changing her. Walls could strengthen and weaken even as paranormal senses could and did, but they were built for a reason, shored up for a reason, and whether it was to keep something in or something out, it roused the caution in Geneva's nature as nothing else could have. So she went carefully and used only her usual senses as much as possible.

She had worked her way to the end of Main Street, to the playground, almost a part of downtown, and because she was preoccupied, she very nearly missed it. A young and quavery voice expressing worry and concern.

"You didn't do nuthin' wrong," a still-young but tougher voice was saying as Geneva found herself a bench on the other side of the hedges where she could hear but not see. She fiddled with her camera, head bent over the seeming task, listening intently.

"I never should have dared Bethany to do it, and you know I shouldn't of. It's too far, up in them woods, and I told her"—the young voice quavered even more—"I told her she had to sneak out after bedtime, or it wouldn't be a real dare."

"Jase—"

"I told her she had to grab one of them flowers off the pot on the porch, *beside the front door.*"

"Jase, she prob'ly just got scared and ran home. You know she prob'ly did."

"She wasn't at the bus stop this mornin'!"

"Listen—"

"She wasn't at lunch neither, so that's why I snuck out and went over to her house. It's empty, Trev, nobody's home."

"*That's* why I had to come sneaking out myself to find you? Jeez, Jase, her dad works out at the paper mill, and—"

"No, they *left*, that's what old Mrs. Carney said. She was out walkin' her dog and I asked, and she said they packed up their car even before the school bus came this morning and left."

"Well, then Bethany—"

"She wasn't with 'em, Trev, that's what Mrs. Carney said. And she looked for her special, 'cause she's the only other person that old dog of hers likes. Growls at me, like he did when I asked her. But . . . but Bethany didn't leave with her family, Trev, I know she didn't. An' it's all my fault!"

Geneva shut out the voices, concentrating instead on sending a very narrow seeking tendril toward the boys on the other side of the bushes. The minds of children were always difficult and often chaotic, thoughts darting here and there, sometimes only fragments. And she hated invading someone else's mind without so much as a by-your-leave anyway, so that made it harder.

But she guarded herself as best she could and probed, carefully, looking for a memory of that place young Jason had sent Bethany Hicks, and looking for the address of the Hicks home because it would save her time.

She got both, more or less, hazy and incomplete, but enough of a trail for her to follow. And just in time, because she heard a scolding adult voice, and both boys were rushing away with lame excuses and pleas for mercy . . .

Geneva sat there on the bench for a few moments, still fiddling with her camera, head bent as she apparently focused on whatever she was doing, while inside her trained and experienced mind she was carefully building up her shields. Because even though it had happened in the flash of an instant, she had a new and very uneasy sense that a second person had touched young Jason's mind just as she had in that moment. And that maybe, just maybe, whoever it was had known she was there too.

It was extremely unsettling.

She was alone here, and undercover, with no authority. With the sharp-eyed militia about, she hadn't dared carry her own weapon, leaving it well hidden in her room at the B and B. Not that she was defenseless without her gun, but still.

With an effort, she shook off the growing uneasiness. She would be even more cautious, that was all. Just take care and do her job, same as always. But as she rose from the bench and set off on a seemingly rambling walk, camera in hand, she could feel that slightly crawly sensation on her skin that experience told her was energy of a negative kind, and wondered if Bishop knew the static in this town, whatever its source or the agenda behind it, was getting stronger. She probably needed to let him know that.

But, in the meantime, she had a house to break into. And another one up on the mountain to find.

THREE

Bethany had no idea where she was when she woke up, her head aching, memories fuzzy. And she felt sick, like when she'd had the flu and hadn't been able to keep anything down.

She started to move, then stopped, eyes still closed, when her stomach protested and she had to choke back what was rising in her throat. It was a long time, she thought, before she was able to slowly open her eyes.

She was . . . where was she? It was dark, but not so dark that she feared she'd gone blind. Dim light coming from just around the bend of . . . of what looked and felt to her like a cave. Maybe close to the entrance since there was some light, but she was afraid to hope. There were a few caves and old mine shafts in the area, she'd heard, though her daddy had forbidden her to go exploring for them.

She wished now she had. Not that it would have helped her, probably. She was at the back of a cave or a mine shaft, just tall enough for a man as tall as her daddy to stand upright, and maybe wide enough for two of them to stand with outreached hands touching the walls and each other.

She wanted to cry out, to scream for help, but a primitive sense deep within warned her to make no noise until she was certain where she was. And because of something else.

Because the really scary thing, the thing that made her shiver even though it wasn't too awfully cold in the cave, was that within that small, hacked-from-rock space, she was in a cage.

It was just large enough for the small cot she lay on—she could see that as soon as she sat up—and again just tall enough for a tall man to stand up in. She didn't get up, but judged it would only take her two or three steps from the cot to reach what looked like the door of the cage.

Closed by a shiny chain and padlock that looked a lot newer than the crisscrossed, rusting metal of the cage itself.

She didn't know what time it was. How long since she had been taken. Where she was. Or who had her—and why.

That last unknown scared her even more than she'd been before, because she knew nice people didn't put little girls in cages and hide them away in caves. And because . . . because there had been whispers she'd heard about stuff the grown-ups hadn't intended for her to hear, about bad things that had happened to people up in the mountains.

Up in the mountains.

Where the caves were.

Quantico

Noah Bishop, chief of the Special Crimes Unit, was an impressive man even when seated and seemingly at ease. It might have been the obvious strength of his broad shoulders that was hardly disguised by the formal suit he wore; it might have been the way his powerful hands rested almost negligently on the closed file on the table before him. It might even have been the lean face that was handsome and somewhat enigmatic, marked by the level gaze of striking tarnished-silver eyes beneath winging brows, and by a dramatic, exotic widow's peak of raven black hair on his high, curiously unlined forehead.

It might also have been the odd, stark streak of white no wider than two fingers winging back from his left temple, or the very faint but visible scar that twisted down that left cheek, lending him an air of danger that was not at all deceptive.

It might have been all that, Grayson Sheridan thought as he joined his unit chief in the conference room that was seldom used except for briefings, or unless a case was local. But he thought privately—he hoped, being pretty much surrounded by telepaths most of the time—that

Bishop was impressive simply because he was one of those innately powerful men, natural leaders, who came along maybe once in a generation but usually even less often than that. A man who commanded others seemingly without effort, winning the absolute loyalty of those who worked with and for him.

A man who was, in simple reality, changing the world.

And how many humans could say they had done that?

"You'll be taken to your drop point just west of the Trail tomorrow morning," Bishop was saying in his low, calm voice, seemingly oblivious to the other man's thoughts. (Which might or might not be true, given his truly formidable telepathic abilities.)

"It's in the Southern Appalachians, isn't it?" Grayson said with more resignation than anything else. "Salem. One of those little towns all but forgotten by time." It was entirely possible, after all, to more or less hide an entire town in the old, forest-dense Appalachian Mountains. Or more than one town, if it came to that.

"Afraid so. Relatively close to the North Carolina–Tennessee border, very remote, and the topography alone makes it unusually isolated even for that area."

Which was saying a lot.

Grayson made a mental note to study a topographical map of the area tonight, for all the good it was likely to do him. And to unearth his good hiking boots as well as some basic but unobtrusive survival gear that had come in handy in past situations; he believed in being prepared for anything. He focused and considered a few potentially important questions.

"Psychics?"

"Our undercover operative doesn't know for certain."

That was a surprise. "Nobody's been able to scan the place?" That had become a step Bishop virtually always took preliminary to sending in any of his agents, partly due to unpleasant surprises in the past—and partly due to the number of psychics they had discovered over the years, far more than they had expected to back in the beginning. Some, unfortunately, playing for the other side.

So now they had quite a few members of the unit who were virtually always able to determine the presence of other psychics in a given area without themselves getting too close. And that had come in handy more than once.

"I've sent three different people close to the area, and all they got was static," Bishop said. "It's something we've encountered before, and it's never been a good thing; it usually means energy being used or contained, either by natural geography or by a psychic or psychics. The issue is that contained energy tends to interfere with our energies as well, even alter our abilities in a worst-case scenario, which has been known to cause problems for us—and with us."

"Great," Grayson muttered. He paused, then added, "Just how remote is this place, anyway?"

"You've walked the Trail, haven't you?" The Appalachian Trail was a bit over two thousand rugged miles long and attracted both day hikers enjoying a day in the wilderness and thru hikers geared up and determined to walk the entire Trail.

Grayson nodded. "North to south when I took a year off from college; that took me seven months. South to north the year before I joined the SCU; that took six months. About average." It had been a test of endurance and survival knowledge he had enjoyed, but even more, the second trip along the Trail had given him the solitary time he had needed to consider all his options and think about his future before taking a job in which the psychic abilities he'd spent a lifetime hiding would be incorporated into the toolbox of an investigator and cop.

"Then you know what a wilderness those mountains are, even with scattered towns and major highways crisscrossing them."

"I know fugitives have vanished for lifetimes in those dense forests. I know I encountered some . . . strange people, and at least a few pretty strange small towns not far off the Trail during my hikes."

"Then you're probably more prepared than most to find your way to Salem, and explore the surrounding area if necessary."

Grayson eyed his boss. "Uh-huh. So it's that remote."

Bishop went on as if he had not heard the question. "You've read the brief. A loosely organized group of militia members seems to be what passes for law and order there, at least for all intents and purposes, and word has it they have a low tolerance for lawbreakers. Which may be one reason the general crime rate is reportedly low. There is a sheriff over the county who apparently deputized at least some members of the militia in order to grant them law enforcement authority, but no sheriff's office in Salem, apparently no regular visits to the town by the sheriff, and he was . . . less than forthcoming with information. We were warned to stay away. And not with any degree of subtlety."

"Don't we have to be invited in?"

"Normally. Officially. But two of the missings are from other states, so if any crime *is* involved, it crossed state lines; that would make it federal. And there are other . . . factors. We have more than enough reason to believe this situation is anything but normal."

What the hell am I getting into?

"Don't carry your weapon openly unless and until you're certain that's best; the laws in the state allow open carry, and you'll be known to be hiking in rough territory, so your rifle will be expected. As for your handgun, we both know it's best to figure out who else is openly armed and why before you decide to be. Don't volunteer that you're with the FBI or, indeed, any law enforcement agency, especially a federal one; conceal your credentials where they aren't likely to be found unless you need them. Don't lie unless the occasion calls for it, but if it calls for it . . . be creative. And don't volunteer information. As I said, you'll be taken to an appropriate spot just west of the Trail early tomorrow morning and dropped off there to hike the rest of the way, so you won't be driving into town, but expect your room to be searched, possibly even bugged."

"Bugged. In a small town in western North Carolina."

"Best not to be caught by surprise by any . . . possibility."

Salem

It wasn't all that easy to sneak into a house in a nice little neighborhood in broad daylight on a Wednesday morning, but Geneva managed. She slipped around back unnoticed, automatically noting the yard clutter that indicated a home with children, like the big swing set and netted trampoline.

She also saw the water bowl meant for a sizable dog on the back deck, but since she'd already reached out telepathically, she knew they had either boarded him somewhere or else taken the family dog along on the very sudden "vacation."

Last night, one of the three little Hicks girls had vanished, and today the rest of the family had left abruptly, all signs except the haste pointing to a vacation out of town.

No Amber Alert had been issued. In fact, as far as Geneva had been able to cautiously determine, there had been no police report at all, and if the militia knew or cared, there was no sign.

It was the same with Bethany's school. If they had any doubts that Bethany was safely with her family, no one betrayed anything unusual. Geneva had gotten close enough to know that.

Yet now, when she managed to slip into the Hicks house, bypassing a really good alarm system, she found a home that bore the usual cheerful clutter of a family—and signs that packing had been done in haste. There was a neat bedroom for Bethany—her name was on the door, as her two sisters' names were on their bedroom doors, in cheerful Disney plaques with stardust and favored characters—and inside were schoolbooks for the current year, and clothing, toys. Everything neat, perhaps unusually so. Even that little suitcase with her name on it one would think she would have packed if visiting family away from Salem was neatly in the closet.

In her sisters' rooms, clothing was a bit messy, and small suitcases with their names on them were not in the closets.

Every sign told Geneva that little girl had not left with her family. And yet not a single sign pointed to her having disappeared mysteriously. Other than one guilty little boy, nobody at all seemed worried about Bethany Hicks.

Except Geneva.

She stood in the approximate center of the house and opened her senses, trying to pick up *something* even though she knew she was alone in the house. A few times doing this job—a very few times—she had managed to pick up what Bishop called "residual thoughts" at a location. The more emotionally disturbed the person or people had been, the more likely they were to leave that sort of trace energy behind them, though even then it seldom lasted more than a few hours.

Geneva had the ghostly sense of bustle and hurry, of muted voices and anxious thoughts, even an initial panic that had climbed rapidly before being damped down by . . . something. And then . . . hurried but cheerful packing, bright talk of visiting family . . . down in Florida. In Florida, where it wouldn't be cold. Just a short break, a little trip . . .

In the middle of the school year.

The ghostly sense faded, then vanished. Geneva was standing in a very empty house.

With a very baffling puzzle piece to add to all the rest.

Quantico

Grayson frowned slightly at his boss. "Okay, we all know by now that you hold back information, for reasons we all have various theories about but seldom understand—at least until all the shouting is over. Would it do any good for me to ask you for hints of some kind of shit like that?" His tone was wry.

Deadpan, Bishop said, "No." Then he smiled faintly. "All I can tell you is what I already have. Be careful. One thing concerns me most. We have three missing people. And if our information is correct, there have been three deaths of supposed hikers within the same window our missings were in Salem. Officially accidental deaths, as per the militia and the sheriff. The militia apparently discovered the bodies, and those were dealt with quickly and with no fuss. According to the sheriff, the bodies were cremated. He refused to identify them but insisted their remains had been returned to their families."

"You don't believe him."

"I have a suspicious mind."

"You think it was our missings."

"Since it isn't our jurisdiction, there was no way the sheriff was going to confirm or deny that, even if he could, which I doubt. He simply insisted the remains had been returned to family."

"You believe he was lying."

"I believe the official record is that careless hikers on or near the Trail at the worst time of year back in December, when there were at least two snowstorms, were killed in accidents that are hardly uncommon. As to what really happened . . . we've found no evidence or witnesses to say anything different."

"You believe they may have been murdered." It wasn't a question.

"I believe it's more than possible. And if our missings were lured there for some reason they refused to explain to friends, only to meet their deaths . . . People have always tried to summon power of one kind or another, and the commission of dark or evil acts quite definitely creates dark energy."

"That static around Salem?"

"Possibly. If so, a definite warning flag."

"So I should be prepared for anything—and everything."

"That would probably be wise. Our motto if not our mantra." Bishop's voice became brisk again. "Salem is a very small town where strangers are bound to be noticed—and not especially welcomed, even for welcome tourist dollars. Though tourists do visit throughout the year, and the townsfolk accept them. They even grudgingly accept the occasional visitor who comes down off the Trail for a break of a few days or even a few weeks.

"That's your cover, and it's believable, especially this time of year and given the equipment you'll have. There's a B and B that actually caters to that sort of visitor. Use your real name, but remain as low-key as possible, at least until we know what we're dealing with; if either the militia or the sheriff gets curious enough to check you out, they'll find only information on an ordinary citizen who inherited a small company here in Virginia and is known to take time off every year to hike various trails and mountains.

"We do not want to make a law enforcement presence obvious. Or even detectable, if possible. For that reason, we sent in the undercover operative a couple of weeks ago; her orders are to scout the town and area, observe and gather information, but not take any action until you're on the scene."

"So I'm the primary?" Grayson wasn't certain how he felt about a partner, however deeply undercover. He was a bit of a loner and hadn't worked with a partner in . . . a long time.

"You are. But keep in mind she's one of our experts in the occult and may notice signs you wouldn't if that turns out to be a factor. She can also handle herself in any sort of situation I've known her to encounter, she can live off the land as well as you, she's more than qualified with any handgun or rifle, and some of her early years were rough enough that she had to learn some down-and-dirty street fighting that taught her to use whatever weapon is near to hand when necessary to defend herself." Bishop paused, then added almost musingly, "I once saw her take out a man with a high-heeled shoe."

"A shoe?"

"Yes. And he had an Uzi."

There was a warning, very uncomfortable bell going off in Grayson's head. Because there were few agents in the SCU who specialized in the occult as most people understood that term. Fewer of those with extensive experience in either rough hiking and living off the land or fighting in deadly situations without standard weapons.

And there were even fewer SCU agents with those traits who were *also* experienced in undercover work, able to work alone, and comfortable operating without either backup or supervision, sometimes for months or even longer; that talent was a very specific one, and seldom needed on SCU cases.

Seldom. But not never.

"Bishop? Who's the undercover agent?"

"Geneva Raynor."

Trust Bishop to totally bury the lede.

"Shit," Grayson muttered.

Outside Salem, Wednesday Night

Nellie had gone to bed early, hoping to sleep without dreaming, a forlorn hope. The nightmare had come swiftly, but this time, as she had once or twice before, she'd been able to wrench herself free of it before the worst of the fear gripped her. She had a feeling her odd abilities had helped her do that but didn't want to think about it very much.

Now she was wide-awake and it was barely midnight. Dawn was still hours away, and Nellie knew she would not be able to go back to sleep. She finally let go of her dog and reached to turn on the bedside lamp, then leaned down to haul her big leather shoulder bag from the floor up onto the bed.

In a zippered pocket that wasn't all that obvious unless you knew it was there, she found and withdrew an envelope, its edges yellowed with time. On the front of it was simply her name, in an unfamiliar printed handwriting.

Nellie

She opened the envelope slowly and pulled out a single folded piece of stationery, its crease showing signs it had been opened and closed many times before.

She had memorized the message nearly a year before, when her father's attorney had shown up to deliver the note—ten years after Thomas Cavendish's death in a somewhat inexplicable accident. She hadn't been able to match the handwriting to any of the few examples of her father's writing she'd had in her possession, especially since virtually everything she did have bore only his scrawled signature. That, at least, was the same, signed at the bottom, witnessed and notarized.

The message, according to the absolute certainty of his longtime attorney, who had been the witness, had come from Thomas Cavendish, had been written by him and delivered to said attorney formally and with specific instructions. Which he had obeyed scrupulously.

He hadn't waited around to see what the letter said, and Nellie didn't know whether to be glad or regretful about that. Perhaps he could have shed some light. Then again . . .

Nellie,

We've never been close, you and I, and I regret that. But there are reasons, good ones, which, unfortunately, you will have to discover for yourself. Reasons for which I cannot atone, because if you are reading this, then I am dead, by whatever means, and was not able to stop what threatens you now. Not able to save you. This letter has been delivered to you on your 29th birthday. Before your 30th birthday, you **must** *go to Salem, where our family's roots were deeply planted long ago, where my line and yours originated, and quietly seek out a man named Finn. He will know you. He may even seek you out. He can help you. He is, perhaps, the only*

man who can. Please, Nellie, go to Salem. And be
careful. Trust your intelligence and your abilities,
but hide your abilities as long as you can, for they
will mark you to some as an enemy and to others as
a tool. Use your mother's maiden name, and avoid
telling anyone you are a Cavendish. You will learn
why soon enough. There are people who will try to
stop you from doing what you have to do, and you
must not allow them to, no matter what. It would
mean your life. Trust no one but Finn.

I have always loved you.

Dad

FOUR

There had been many things in Nellie's life that had baffled her, some she had either figured out for herself or else simply learned to live with. Like the crows that had been around her since childhood, their numbers increasing as she'd entered her twenties. And other baffling things that had remained unnerving mysteries.

Her father had remained one of the mysteries.

She studied the strange letter from him, absently smoothing the paper.

It was a weird letter.

Weird? Jesus Christ.

Nellie's first impulse had been to tear it into tiny pieces and flush the whole thing, at least in part because her father had not been involved in her life for a long time, even before he had died. In fact, he had barely been a part of her childhood.

Still, she hadn't destroyed this letter that came seemingly from beyond the grave. She had instead thrust it into the very back of a drawer in her bedroom desk and done her best to ignore it, forget it. Only to find herself, night after night, pulling it out and reading the message again, frowning, disturbed on a level so deep she couldn't even explain it to herself.

She didn't even know what it was *about*, for Christ's sake!

Weeks, then months. But the closer she came to her thirtieth birthday, the stronger had been her uneasy certainty that she had to go to Salem. A town she had never heard of, far less been aware she had any personal connection to.

A specific town with a not-uncommon name that had been very difficult to find when all she had to go on was that her father's family had its roots there.

Even in this age of information overload, there were some things so very specific or so old that they were simply difficult to find using anything handy like a search engine. She'd had to dip reluctantly into genealogy, and it had been time-consuming to find her father's branch of the family tree and from there trace it back to a small town named Salem three hundred years in the past.

But she'd done it, her own determination catching her off guard and bothering her, because against all logic it . . . felt important. Imperative. It felt like something she had to do, letter or no letter.

And that was disconcerting as hell.

Still, she had pushed aside the second and even third

thoughts, especially once she had located Salem. Because once she had, the pull to go there had grown steadier by the day.

She had no idea how long this . . . thing she was supposed to do would take, so she tentatively planned for a couple of weeks. It had actually been simple to take an indeterminate leave of absence from work, largely because Thomas Cavendish had set things up carefully to impose the least burden on his daughter, allowing her to choose how involved she wished to be in his business.

The one truly considerate thing she could ever remember him doing for her.

Leo whined softly, and she automatically reached out her free hand to rub his broad head and pull absently at the silky black ears. "I don't know what this is all about," she confided softly to her dog. "If I had any sense at all, I'd just ignore it. But . . . all Dad left me, really, was stuff. Material things. And questions. Nothing of him. Nothing to help me understand him, understand the way he was. And this . . . this might be my last chance to do that. To understand him. To understand why there are things I can't remember no matter how hard I try. Blank spaces in my life."

Too many blank spaces.

Too many missing memories.

Like virtually anything about her mother. She had vanished when Nellie was a toddler, just . . . run away, abandoning her husband and child. That was what Nellie had been told.

All she had been told.

And then there was the other thing. The thing she and her father had never spoken of.

She had never been sure that he'd even known his daughter was . . . different. But it seemed he had known, had even accepted the strange abilities she'd learned in her earliest childhood to hide.

And he'd never said a word to her. Until the letter.

Nellie drew a breath and released it slowly. "I don't think we have a choice, Leo. I don't think we ever did. And I think that scares me more than anything else."

GENEVA SLIPPED THROUGH the woods, silent, her passage not noticed or at least not announced by the dogs of Salem as she passed by some of the outlying houses. Not that she expected them to give her away. She liked dogs, they liked her, and by now they'd most certainly grown accustomed to her almost nightly rambles all around town. She'd made sure of it.

Most usually greeted her from the backs or sides of fenced yards, more curious and hopeful than suspicious, especially since she'd made it a habit to carry a generous pocketful of doggie snacks for those she encountered, until even the most wary of them had been pretty well won over.

Tonight, though, there weren't many dogs out at all, or pets of any kind, and no doubt most livestock was shut up warm and snug for the night in the very tidy barns the community boasted.

It was dark and it was cold, bone-chilling cold, the

coldest night by far she'd experienced here yet. Even though she had dressed for cold, and from the skin out, she was still shivering, and already looking forward to a hot, hot shower later tonight. Damn cold. Even if never before this bad, it was nearly this cold every night, or at least had been since her arrival a couple of weeks previously. No matter what the weather reports said, it was always ten to twenty degrees colder in Salem than in the general area outside the valley—including the higher elevations.

Which was one of the oddities.

She had wondered more than once if it was all the granite around this valley and underneath it, hard stone God only knew how deep that had frozen miles below the surface and down to its very atoms and never thawed from the last ice age, which had ended more than ten thousand years ago, continuing to radiate an unusual chill even today.

An unnatural chill.

If she had dared, she would have sent a message that he should pack for the Arctic, or at least bring along his thermal underwear. But as much as she would have enjoyed doing that, and imagining his expression when he received the message, once on the job she was all business.

Well, except for that one time.

Which would not be repeated.

Frowning, she focused on the here and now, her job. Because even though the dogs of Salem would give her a pass, she was a lot less certain of what else she might encounter in these dark, eerily silent woods. She had, after all, more than once on previous outings observed sentries of a kind, and had too narrowly avoided solitary men she was almost certain had been armed also moving silently about in the forest for reasons she had yet to discover.

The militia on patrol? Maybe. But against what? Or who? The faint, seeking telepathic tendril she'd cast about her on those occasions had been yanked back behind her shield, a precaution against the possibility that one of those men might have caught her probe. After that, she'd used all the woodcraft she knew well to move silently and cautiously.

That had been fairly close to town, making her a bit wary of exploring the higher mountain slopes. At least until yesterday morning, when she had found the remains of a man tortured to death. She was venturing again higher up the mountain tonight; she had no idea whether that meant she was less or more likely to encounter the militia. But seeing Bethany's home had left her grimly determined to do whatever she could to find that child.

Alive.

And even if she set Bethany apart, there was still just too little information she'd been able to discover about Salem, and too much of that came second- or even third-hand.

She really, really hated it. Born to solve puzzles, that's what Bishop had said once about her. That she was one of those people who simply couldn't bear things that didn't make sense and had to endlessly examine and toss and turn puzzle pieces until every piece clicked into its proper place and she understood the picture.

All she had after two weeks here was a box of puzzle pieces and no idea what the picture was supposed to look like.

The closest thing to real, hard evidence she had so far was the photographs of the mutilated victim—and since she had snuck back up there after visiting the Hicks home earlier in the day, she knew only too well that the entire area had indeed been sanitized.

So—no body. Photographic evidence that wasn't enough. She hadn't dared get close enough to take a biological sample the first time she'd been up there in the hopes of possibly identifying the victim. And by the time she got back up there, finding anything viable was simply impossible.

The militia was very, very thorough.

So just more puzzle pieces for her frustrating puzzle.

It *looked* like a normal little town on the surface, and most of the people appeared normal, sounded normal, acted normal—but her spider senses were tingling like mad, and other than a single sense, hers weren't especially well honed.

Behind the smiling faces and pleasant greetings was . . . something else.

The whole place . . . *felt* wrong.

Which was why she was searching these woods rather

than going directly to what she believed was her destination: that house out in the middle of nowhere that Bethany had been dared to approach alone.

Geneva paused next to a huge oak, her gaze roaming all around, trying to see beyond the closest trees and able to see quite well despite the lack of moonlight. Her spider senses really weren't any good when it came to vision, but Bishop had told her to *believe* they were, and that actually seemed to help make her normal vision at least a bit more acute, but . . .

It was another odd thing. Sometimes these woods were really, *really* dark, and sometimes they weren't. And it didn't have a damned thing to do with moonlight or the lack of it.

It was almost like the trees, evergreen and hardwood, sometimes decided to huddle close way up high, lace their branches soundlessly to form a sort of roof and shut out the light. For whatever reason. As if there could be a reason.

It was an eerie thought, but not the first time she'd thought it.

I'm missing something. Even with extra senses I'm missing something important. I have to be. There's too much weird and . . . off . . . in this place, this town, without there being a . . . center. A nexus. Someone or something pulling all the strings. Because it isn't just one weird thing; it's a hell of a lot of them. People. Animals. Things. Places. Actions. Habits. Even the air itself sometimes holds a whiff of something that makes my skin crawl, and I don't think it's

just all the static. No matter what it looks like on the sur-
face, no matter how normal, underneath is something bad.
And every once in a while one of them gives it away. Veiled
glances and guarded conversations. Smiles that never touch
their eyes. The flicker of a thought that doesn't make sense.
That weird militia that really doesn't act like any I've ever
heard about, especially the guy giving most of the orders but
not, apparently, the one really in charge. And in a town
this small where so much else is connected, where so many of
the people are connected, there has to be a center point . . .
or overlapping . . . or something . . .

So why hadn't she been able to find it?

She heard a faint fluttering sound and turned her head
to see, without much surprise, a huge crow not twelve
feet away, perched on the lower branch of another tree,
regarding her with bright black eyes and eerily sentient
curiosity. It wasn't the first time one of her night rambles
had drawn an escort.

Another of the weird, unsettling things about Salem.

They were everywhere, both day and night, and
watched everything, the crows, saw everything. Usually
singly or in small groups, in town as well as in the woods.

There was something very weird about the way they
hung around. And watched. What she had yet to discover
was who—or what—they reported back to. Because that
was something else of which she was positive, even if only
pure instinct made her so certain of it. The birds were
sentries, spies, escorts; every sense she could command
told her that much. The watchmen on the walls of . . .

whatever was being hidden and guarded in this town. Whatever was being done secretly. Perhaps they were even weapons, though she had never yet seen them attack anyone.

And the townspeople seemed fairly oblivious to them. From all appearances, they didn't consider the presence of one or more on this or that tree, this or that street sign, this or that railing, at all odd.

But it was odd. It was even eerie.

The Birds.

Yeah, while you're sneaking through dark, dark woods on a dark, dark night, think of a creepy movie that scared the shit out of you as a kid. That'll help.

A second crow joined the first, this one soundless. And then a third, also making no sound.

Neat trick, that.

Uncanny.

Unnatural.

She wasn't especially afraid, because it had happened before and had ended well, with her safely back in bed. Possibly because she had each time gone no farther, retreating at once, choosing not to, on those occasions, test the sentries, not to keep pushing on toward . . . whatever. It was what her instincts were telling her to do now.

She should stop. Go back to her room, maybe continue the search tomorrow, in daylight.

Except that she couldn't do that.

Because unlike all the other nights, tonight she had a

definite purpose. Tonight she had to find that house out here in the middle of the woods and look for a little girl no one else seemed to realize was lost.

But the crows . . .

Turn around and leave. Go back to the B and B. These are . . . a line. A red line. Go no farther.

That was . . . eerie. Almost like an alien voice in her head.

Surely not. Her shields were up, even though it actually made her head hurt to *not* use them in a situation where she should have. She was depending on woodcraft and her usual senses, because . . . because she wasn't sure why. Except that it seemed to her the right way to do this.

As for the crows, the odd thoughts in her head were just because their presence made her wary, as it always did, but especially here and tonight, at a level deeper than the cold chill of this place. She had the feeling the crows were only sent—or only made sure she became *this* aware of them—when she got too close to things they guarded.

Guarded for their masters.

Them. The men behind this.

She didn't know who they were, though she doubted it was the militia, or at least not entirely. Not that a lack of certainty had stopped her from speculating. An educated guess—based on the fact that five families had formed an alliance of sorts and had pretty much carved this town out of wilderness hundreds of years ago using muscle, determination, intelligence, and not much else—marked their descendants, or at least some of them, as being the ones behind whatever this was.

So maybe they, or one or more of them, with the militia as their soldiers—some of whom she was fairly certain belonged to those families—formed to keep order just the way the families liked it. That was how it looked.

On the surface. But Geneva had developed, over the years, a nose for the rot that lay beneath far too many pleasant surfaces. And all her senses had been warning her to be cautious, be wary, even without the crows. The surface might seem unthreatening, creepy crows notwithstanding. But beneath—

She was yanked from her thoughts by the realization that she had been too still for too long, too lost in thought and speculation, that she should have moved the instant her instincts or that alien voice told her to go no farther, retreated as usual, and by the fact that the three crows were suddenly looking beyond her rather than at her.

Oh, shit.

"Good evening, Miss Raynor. Taking the night air?" The voice was deep, calm, male, and not in the least threatening.

Which did not in the least reassure her. Because there was something in that voice, something that made the hairs on the nape of her neck quiver even as every instinct she could claim shrieked a warning that she was in trouble. Bad trouble.

All of a sudden, it was even colder than it had been.

———

DUNCAN CAVENDISH STOOD at the window of his large house, with its view down to Main Street, only the streetlights and various security lights shining now, so late, and he felt powerful. He had always *been* powerful, of course, in many ways. The head of his family, the most powerful of the original Five, he was listened to by the other heads, their offspring and soldiers. He was respected.

He was also feared.

Duncan knew that. He liked it. But he was cautious about it, because no man is invincible, and because he knew very well that even fear would not stop the other four families from moving against him if they knew exactly what he'd been doing and why. In fact, fear might spur them to act before he was ready.

He had to be even stronger to keep them at bay. Even more powerful.

And he had to eliminate the threat Nellie Cavendish posed. She would be here soon, he knew. He lacked the Talent of precognition, but he'd had her watched for a long time, and he knew where she was, knew she was hesitating miles outside Salem.

Knew she would come because she had to.

He had not been able to find out for certain how powerful or even how many Talents she possessed, not now, but . . . As an infant, her Talents had already begun to manifest, and what manifested so early promised great Talents to come. Great power. A simple, ordinary bout of colic had brought down on Salem one of the worst storms Duncan could remember. Oh, Thomas had denied his small daughter had caused that, had even tried to laugh it off, but Duncan knew. He'd seen the child's face.

When baby Nellie cried, storm clouds began to gather. And when she gurgled happily, the skies were clear and trouble-free.

Duncan knew. He knew because he knew the family history better than Thomas ever had, and he knew more than one Cavendish ancestor had possessed that particular Talent. And that, in every case, it had gotten stronger as they had grown into adults, at times becoming uncontrollable.

Dangerous.

It was, after all, one of the Talents that had caused their family and the others to create the Barrier generations before, a wall placed by those of another Talent in a young mind to protect both the child and the families—and the town. It had become a normal thing to do, and yet Thomas had refused to place a barrier in his infant daughter's mind. His resistance had surprised Duncan, angered him, in part because he was certain that Sarah, with her own inborn Talents, had strongly influenced his brother. Thomas's refusal had led to their final confrontation and Thomas's decision to take his small family and leave Salem.

Duncan pushed aside the vague, nagging question of whether Thomas had ever truly been certain that his beloved wife had not left him by choice. Duncan hadn't been willing to risk her further influence over her husband—and their daughter. She'd possessed too much of the Talent herself to be allowed that.

He wondered, as he always did, just how much of that she had passed along to Nellie.

It was part of what he feared, that what there was in her untaught mind might rage forth—and destroy. He couldn't be sure. All he *could* be sure of was that whatever Talents Nellie possessed would reach their full strength by the time she turned thirty. It seemed an arbitrary number, but their family had proven it to be accurate to within a few months.

The Barrier, when placed correctly, contained those energies, and it did so quite well as a rule.

Sometimes the Barrier began to fail on its own by the time the child grew into his or her twenties, the Talent refusing to be denied. Other times the wall seemed to smother the Talent so that it went latent, often for that lifetime. Fear of Talent could create its own Barrier, which is what Duncan suspected had happened with Nellie. Any of the Talent raised outside Salem virtually always feared the Talent and tried to be normal.

But where it existed, no matter how it was created, the Barrier could be destroyed, Duncan had discovered. And when it was destroyed, if the Talent lying behind it was great enough, that destruction released enormous power.

He had discovered that, experimenting deliberately on a cousin whose branch of the family had left Salem long ago. That was when he had seen and understood that he could become even more powerful himself. If he did it correctly, that Talent released was something Duncan could claim for his own.

He wanted it.

He wanted it all.

FIVE

When he was set down at his drop point very early Thursday morning—by an eerily silent green chopper, the sort of which he knew Bishop used in these parts—Grayson was only a couple of miles, as the crow flew, from the Trail, and from there he'd be hardly more than two or three miles from Salem. As the crow flew.

Adjusting the heavy pack he carried with ease, he set off in a direct path for the Trail. He had no reason to suspect that watchers lurked this far from Salem, nor did he believe Bishop would have picked the drop point unless it had been thoroughly scouted ahead of time, likely by SCU members or Haven investigators. Nevertheless, once he was into the trees, he immediately changed direction.

He took a meandering path to the Trail, looking all around him with the experienced scouting gaze of one

whose life had more than once depended on his awareness of his surroundings. He saw no one, though he
crossed several faint trails made by wildlife, and at least
one that appeared to be used on a fairly regular basis by
humans.

But he also found two old campsites in the general
area, rings of rock placed roughly, cinders and traces of
old ashes within, so drew the conclusion that this was
one of those places passed by word of mouth from hiker
to hiker about various locations where it was relatively
safe to camp.

He left the area untouched and moved a bit more
swiftly until he reached the Trail itself and crossed over
it to the east. He encountered no one, which didn't surprise him; even this far south, it was a hardy and experienced hiker who braved the Trail in January.

Or a fool.

He was well down off the Trail and beginning to angle toward the northeast, and Salem, when he crossed
another trail. This one gave him pause, and for a moment
he hunkered down to get a closer look.

It was actually two trails, or two parallel narrow
tracks. Made not by any wheeled vehicle, but by feet.
Human feet. His trained gaze could see shoe and boot
marks and even, faintly, the marks of bare feet.

Bare feet. In January? Or, for that matter, anytime
during the last two or three months?

The trail was well-worn enough to tell him it was used
on a regular basis—but not every day.

Grayson hesitated, then followed the parallel tracks,

staying well to the side of both. He was heading in the general direction of Salem, but since he was well off the Trail, he doubted that many, if any, hikers would have stumbled across these tracks. Especially since the forest grew more dense, with the tracks he followed barely visible in the absence of light.

He used his spider senses, enhancing his vision, even though he knew the price he'd pay for that later. He also shifted his pack a bit, so he could more easily get to the rifle strapped across the top. Just in case.

Grayson always expected trouble.

The parallel tracks came abruptly out into a clearing, and Grayson stopped, going only as far as he needed to in order to see what there was to see.

It was a flat area, probably no more than sixty feet across before the mountain began to both climb and descend again. In that clearing was a single standing stone wall that rose to a point at the far end, with the other walls that had once risen to join it now only a tumble of stones that had fallen or been placed mostly inside the structure. The original building had probably been no more than twenty-five feet from the entrance to that still-standing wall.

And it was old. It was very, very old.

Grayson's guess was that it had once been a church, typically one of the first buildings settlers erected when they chose their new home, especially in this part of the world, though he would have said this one was in an odd place in relation to Salem.

Then again . . .

In the semicleared space of the interior, someone had constructed a rough altar stone. Obviously hacked from a single larger slab of rock, the oblong was about two feet wide and at least six feet long, and laid across two big boulders beneath that brought the altar, Grayson estimated, as high as his thighs.

He wasn't about to move closer; he could clearly see that the ground all around the structure was of the sort of loosely powdered dust that left tracks. He could see many, with the two trails he had followed continuing to the gaping doorway of the structure, and a number of tracks in between and around.

But what disturbed him, what kept him within the woods and back away from the structure, was the fact that he could see the rusty brown of dried bloodstains on that stone altar. A lot of bloodstains.

Grayson studied as much as he could see from his position, then worked his way carefully around the structure, always staying well back and counting on his enhanced vision to show him what there was to be seen.

There were a few streaks and splashes of dried blood on the two partial walls, and some on the stones that had been moved to clear space for the altar, but he couldn't tell how old they were.

No signs at all of human remains.

He knew it was a lot more likely that some poor animal had been slaughtered here in a ritual sacrifice than it was that a human being had been a victim. In a normal world, at least.

The world he lived in was rarely normal.

After a thoughtful while, Grayson studied his surroundings carefully for landmarks, fixing this spot in his mind. He shrugged off his pack long enough to remove and use his camera to take a number of pictures of the building, the clearing, and the parallel tracks leading to the spot from as many angles as he could manage. Then he put the camera away, shrugged on the pack again, and continued down the mountain, following no path now but heading for Salem.

It was still early, not yet noon; if he had not detoured to follow the tracks, he probably would have been in Salem by now. Still, Grayson didn't hurry, and he frowned as he picked his way down the mountainside. He was not an expert in the occult, but that didn't mean he hadn't picked up knowledge of it here and there as most of Bishop's people had. And what he'd seen back there in that . . . church . . . pointed to the occult. Or at least to something very like it.

Geneva had been here two weeks; she may well have found what he had found, or she may have been concentrating on the town itself. Until they met up and compared notes, there was no way to be sure.

No way to be sure of anything.

Especially with Geneva in the picture.

BETHANY HAD NO idea how much time had passed, because the faint glow of light just beyond the curve of the cave never seemed to change. She had cried quietly at first, for a long time, until her eyes were swollen and her nose ran and her throat felt raw. Shudders of fear had racked her slender body as she sobbed, and even though her thick jacket and other clothing kept the faint chill at bay, she felt so cold, so cold and alone.

At some point she had cried herself out, at least for the moment, and curled up on the cot without blankets or a pillow or anything except the thin, musty-smelling mattress, and somehow she had fallen asleep.

When she woke, the momentary confusion of where she was and what had happened returned, but before she could begin to cry again, she saw that a little tray had been slid through a slot near the floor she hadn't even seen before. It held only a shallow bowl and cup, small enough to slide easily through the cramped opening.

Bethany sat up and leaned forward, able to reach the tray easily from the cot. The cup held only water, and only a few sips of that. The small bowl held a thin liquid that, when she cautiously tasted it, proved to be luke-warm chicken broth.

At least that's what it tasted like.

Bethany wanted to cry again. Because there was so little. Because someone had delivered the tray and she hadn't awakened to ask the desperate questions and plead as she wanted to plead to go home. Because she was afraid. So afraid.

The pinched feeling in her stomach told her that supper had been a long, long time ago. So Bethany fought back the tears and placed the tray beside her on the cot, lifting the bowl and cup to drink the broth and the water. The broth was salty, and too late she realized it made her more thirsty; her vague plan to try to save some of the water in case nobody came again vanished as she drained the cup.

She told herself she should be brave, like the heroic kids she saw on TV shows and in the movies, brave and smart enough to get herself out of this cage.

With that prodding her, she managed to get to shaky feet and step out to touch the cold, rusty metal that formed her cage. She tried pulling and pushing only to find no give at all in the metal. She hooked her fingers and tried to pull upward. Again, the cage didn't budge. Then she looked for an opening other than the pad-locked door and the shallow slot that had admitted the tray and its contents.

She thought she must have checked every inch of the four sides of the cage, even stood on the cot to try to reach the top, only to find her stretching fingers inches short of their goal.

Not that it mattered, she thought wearily as she sat down on the cot again, scrunching back and lifting her legs so she could hug them against her body. She was still cold. And despite the broth and water, the pinched feeling in her middle remained.

Rocking back and forth a little, Bethany Hicks began to cry again, silently.

THE FACT THAT it took Grayson most of the morning Thursday to cover the scant few miles from his drop point to Salem was hardly something he could blame on the pause to study the ruins he'd found. He told himself he was simply out of shape. It had been a few years since he'd done any serious hiking, after all. And the Trail was serious, especially the section he'd been called upon to traverse just coming from west to east across it.

Never mind that he was a daily runner *and* worked out with a few of his fellow SCU agents in mixed martial arts at least two or three times a week. Never mind that.

Ass. You know what it is. You know the truth. You're just not sure what mood you'll find Geneva in. She could be utterly professional and pleasant.

Or she could shoot you.

The truth was, he figured he had a fifty-fifty chance either way. He decided to ignore the truth, at least for now.

He was, after all, on a job, and hardly had the time for the nonsense in his head. Later. Later for all that.

Or maybe never. Never would be best.

Pausing on the faint trail leading down the mountain to the valley, he pushed everything else from his mind and absently adjusted his heavy pack as he studied as much of Salem as he could see.

Peaceful little mountain town, to all appearances. Spread out over most of a pretty valley, the far third of it, or roughly that, farmland. Dairy, from the looks of the cattle he could see when he focused his spider senses intently enough to get a good look at the far end of the valley.

He blinked and rubbed his eyes with one hand, reminding himself not to keep doing that. He'd already strained his eyes following those tracks; why add to the problem for no good reason? He'd have a headache later, dammit, if not a migraine, and for what? So he could see the dairy cows he'd already known made up part of Salem's local economy?

He knew the basics, from the initial brief and what information he'd studied on the trip to his drop point. Five families who had been among those who had originally settled the town more than three hundred years before still controlled the major businesses or industries that provided most of the jobs for the townspeople.

Five families. The Blackwoods, the Cavendishes, the Deverells, the Ainsworths, and the Haleses.

Their descendants were still *the* families of Salem, the town leaders, elected or not. The ones who owned most of the land and controlled the major industries that kept the economy of Salem healthy and, really, more than adequate, if not flourishing, especially for such a small, isolated place.

The Deverells owned a huge paper mill miles outside town on one of the cold mountain rivers, its facility designed to be divided between the mostly automated mass production of the sort of paper most people used in their daily lives and a smaller, far more labor-intensive section where beautiful, expensive, specialized paper was still made the old-fashioned way, with vintage tools and machinery the Deverells might well have brought along with them in their wagons hundreds of years ago.

Grayson was vaguely surprised there was still a demand for that sort of thing. Did people even write elegant letters on elegant stationery in these days of texts and e-mails?

In any case, the mill provided quite a few skilled jobs for true craftsmen and craftswomen living in Salem, as well as a number of machinists, maintenance people, and other specialists to keep the equipment of the mass-production side of the company running and in good order. There were also the usual necessary office staff and administrative positions providing jobs, even careers, for townspeople. And as far as Grayson had been able to find out, all positions in the company, all jobs, paid very well indeed, with benefits like very good insurance and generous yearly bonuses.

Way to earn dependable loyalty from your workers.

And it was the same with the other four families and their businesses as well. Good working conditions, generous pay and bonuses, safety standards above what was required by law.

An interesting variation on a company town. Only Salem was a Five Company Town. Something the town itself benefited from, at least financially.

The Ainsworths ran the huge dairy farm Grayson had spotted earlier that occupied most of the relatively flat land at the far end of the valley some distance outside Salem.

There had been a company upriver from the paper mill that for decades had produced electricity for the area; owned by the Blackwood family, it had begun years before to transition to solar, which provided more

company-trained skilled jobs and, as of only a couple of
years before, provided all the power for the town via solar
alone, a rare monopoly for a power company, especially
for one in a mountainous region.

Clean energy. A necessary product in high demand
supplied at reasonable prices, and still more company-
trained jobs for the townsfolk. As were also provided
by the Cavendish bank and the Haleses' small-town real
estate empire.

Salem was as close to being a completely self-sufficient
town as any he had ever seen or heard about. It was certainly protected geographically from most any man-made
disaster, though forest fires and the rare flash flood from
one of the mountain streams were always possible. And
winter storms could be fierce.

Still, a very self-contained town way, way off the
beaten path and yet with the resources to support its
population comfortably. A population surrounded by
wilderness.

It was probably one reason why the unnamed militia
group, likely made up of at least some current or onetime
survivalists, had chosen to settle here.

Which was reasonable. But . . . oddly weird when you
added in the fact that they were the accepted agents of
law and order in Salem, this calm little town where, according to their website, hunting was forbidden for sport
and strongly discouraged for food. An open-carry state,
but hunting was discouraged here. Definitely weird. And
he had a hunch he wouldn't see anyone openly carrying
guns while walking the streets of Salem no matter what

the state law said. That was unusual. That was unusual as hell.

And the main question uppermost in Grayson's mind about *that* particular issue was whether the militia maintained law and order in Salem because that's the way the townsfolk liked it—or if they'd been given little or no choice in the matter.

"I SHOULD HAVE been able to stop it," Finn said into the phone.

"You can't be everywhere. You can't control everything. And you know that." The voice on the other end of the connection was deep and calm and held an authority that was curiously without force and yet one to command easily.

"I can damned well try." He drew a breath and fought for control, something usually his without effort. "If you're right about the others, your missings, they at least made it to town."

"They grabbed him before he ever reached town. There was nothing you could have done." That other voice was matter-of-fact rather than consoling.

"Maybe, but that makes four. Four young people dead in only a few short weeks. Tortured in ways I don't even want to think about. Duncan's feeling pushed, or he never would have ordered that. Never would have moved so fast."

"Yes. I know. Because Nellie's coming, the virtual unknown who could upset all his plans. And then there's you. Your loyalists are nearly half the militia. You're a threat, and one Duncan can't deal with directly without upsetting the balance of the families in a way that would turn them all against him. They're on your side, even if they haven't said so openly. But they'd rather avoid any confrontation. They're afraid of Duncan."

"I know. And Nellie is his last chance to shift the balance in his favor. She's . . . special. Not just with the Talent virtually from birth, but she's a Cavendish."

"He hasn't found others?"

"No, not even from other families. Not like Nellie. She's the last of the direct descendants outside Salem. The last with the Talent, at least."

"He's certain she has it?"

"He's certain. Just like you were."

"So he'll try to control her, at least initially."

"Yeah, long enough to put into action plans I'm sure he's already made to get her into his hands. In fact, I'm betting he's already been trying to influence her, test her resolve, maybe her Talent."

"How?"

"He has . . . a Dreamer under his control. The Dreamer can't force someone, but once they're asleep he can lead them into a dream. A created dream, down to the last minute detail."

"Building an illusion in someone else's mind? Even a sleeping mind? That isn't an ability I've ever heard of, much less encountered." There was interest in the deep voice, but with an underlying tone of wariness that said he was well aware of both the positives and the negatives of any Talent.

"And you've heard of most, I know. Maybe this one is . . . peculiar to Salem. To us. So much is." He paused after the wry comment, then returned to his point. "If I know Duncan, which I do, what the Dreamer will create in Nellie's mind will be a terrifying nightmare."

"To scare her off?"

"Maybe, for a while. To buy himself more time. I really think . . . he believes he can gain more power by the things he's doing. I mean actual power. The Talent is strong in him to begin with, because he's a Cavendish and a firstborn. The fact that Thomas was unable to stop him in any sense is, to him, only more proof he's meant to be the leader of all five families and in complete control of Salem. He believes that."

"And Nellie?"

"I know he's had her watched the last few years. Maybe he saw enough to convince him she's even weaker than Thomas was, but not quite safe enough to just let her be. And I'm sure he wonders what she might have inherited from Sarah, because she had amazing strength of will as well as Talent. So, first, he'd try to control Nellie. Scare her, panic her, look for a way to . . . lure her to come to him, confide in him. He is, after all, her uncle. If he can control her, she's a weapon he can use, maybe even power he can draw on to increase his own. If he can't control her . . ."

"There'll be another body."

"He has to be sure Nellie will never be a threat. And unless she comes to him willingly, which neither you nor I believe she will, then he'll have to destroy her, destroy the threat she poses. Maybe the way he destroyed Thomas's Talent. Maybe something . . . more permanent. Maybe another body. If he can get his hands on her, destroy her that way, it means more power for him. He needs more power, and we both know where the strongest, darkest power comes from. So, yeah, he'll . . . sacrifice again. He can't take the chance Nellie will just leave here and never come back. She's a Cavendish. A very large part of her birthright is here—Thomas's half of what their father divided between them; all the paperwork is being held by an attorney down in Atlanta, an attorney who sends in an independent auditor to go over the books once a year, as per that original will. The attorney holds everything Nellie needs to claim her inheritance, and he's spent years waiting for Nellie to contact him."

"Once she finds out about the material side of her birthright."

"Yeah. I'm not at all sure Thomas was wise to keep that from her, but he'd built another successful business in Charlotte and knew that would be hers with no ties to any other Cavendish."

"And yet she's going to Salem."

"And we both know why." Finn sighed. "Duncan wants it all. And I doubt he believes even he can persuade Nellie to sign everything over to him. Which I'm betting is his plan, if he can lure her to him."

"She can't sign under duress."

"In Salem? The law bends to Duncan's will."

"I hadn't realized it was that bad."

"Not something I'm proud of, but it is. The way things have been here for a long, long time. As for Nellie, as long as she's alive and not under his control, she's a potential threat. Because he knows, or at least suspects, what she might be able to do if the Talent is strong in her. What she's capable of."

"She doesn't know. Not all of it."

"Then she has to be told. Or she has to learn. Before he can get his hands on her. And she'd better be strong. According to my father, Thomas Cavendish literally burned out the Talent trying to stop him. And when he failed, all he could do to save his family was grab them and run. And even then . . ."

"I managed to trace Sarah Cavendish."

"And?"

"You were right. She didn't get far."

"So." He stared out the window of his office at downtown Salem, not seeing what was so familiar. "Thomas lost his wife. His own life. And now his daughter is on her way here. His only child, the last of his line. The last of the direct line of Cavendishes stretching all the way back to the beginning. And the only one capable of stopping this insanity."

"If she can."

"Yeah. If she can."

SIX

The question on Grayson's mind as he looked out on the town of Salem was whether he should shrug out of his pack and reposition his rifle so that it didn't lie obviously crossways just beneath the top edge of his pack. Within easy reach. Not, at least, while he made his way into town.

"Hey."

Grayson had realized minutes before that a couple of college-age men carrying bulky backpacks had been climbing the path up from town toward him, but he hadn't focused his attention on them until one of them greeted him in a friendly manner.

"Hey," he responded, equally friendly. "Just getting started?" He was somewhat relieved to see that both young men carried rifles as he did, strapped across their backpacks.

They paused a few steps below him, and the one who had not spoken until then grimaced and said, "It took longer than we expected to get all our gear together, even though we started early."

Grayson noted the gear, much of which was suspiciously new, and silently debated a warning. "Going up to the Trail?" he asked.

"That's the plan," the first said. "Far as we can get today, anyway."

"Day hikers or thru?" Grayson asked, still pleasantly.

"Definitely not thru," the second said. "Not this time of year. A day or two *maybe*. And south. I bet it's sheer hell heading north."

"It is," Grayson said. "Lot of snow this year. Treacherous hiking. Camping isn't much fun either, even this far south."

"Did you come down from the north?" the first asked incredulously. "In January?"

Grayson smiled easily. "No, I've only hiked thru north to south from spring to early fall. The best time, really. This time just a week or two starting down in Georgia. But it's getting too cold for my taste even this far south. A real bed and decent food have been haunting my dreams. Thought I'd come down and spend some time in a pretty little town. That's Salem, right?"

Both men nodded.

"Home?" Grayson asked them.

For the first time, he caught a fleeting uneasiness in both faces, needing no extra senses, but the young men continued to smile, and the one who had spoken first said, "Well, family home. We're college roommates, taking the winter semester off. Salem isn't big on bars or pool halls, with or without live music, and after all the holiday fuss nobody's in the mood for parties. Our one cinema isn't much to shout about when it comes to variety. Not many other choices for activity unless you like pickup basketball on the park court or touch football if you can find enough other players. Most our age have gone back to school. So . . . we're mostly stuck with riding the trails or hiking. Today it's hiking. Though if it's really cold up there, we may be back down before dark."

"Probably," Grayson agreed, still pleasant. "I've been wishing for that real bed in a nice heated room for the last few days."

"Hales B and B is your best bet," the second one said. "It's at the north end of Main Street, can't miss it. This time of the year, they almost always have rooms. With comfortable beds." He grinned.

Grayson returned the grin, though fainter. "And hot water for a nice shower?"

"All the modern conveniences, and a damned good breakfast to boot. And it's fairly central to what recreation we do have. Our little cinema is just off Main Street, and there's a good gym offering day passes. Martial arts studio with an award-winning instructor, if you're into that, also offering classes or just workouts for visitors. Restaurants and cafés in town are handy, within walking distance."

"He's biased," the first one said. "His family owns the place."

As if suddenly recalling his manners, the biased one held out his hand. "Connor Hales."

Grayson shook it firmly. "Gray Sheridan," he responded.

"And I'm Robert Deverell," the other said as he shook hands. "Welcome to Salem."

Grayson thought there was a faint note of something not quite welcoming in that pleasant voice, but he ignored it. "Thanks. And good luck hiking. It actually gets a bit warmer as you climb, for some reason."

Neither offered to explain that reason. Still smiling, they began to move past him, with Connor Hales adding a cheerful, "Hope you enjoy your stay in Salem."

"I'm sure I will." Grayson half turned to watch them for only a moment, then resumed his contemplation of the town below for another moment before beginning to move down the faint trail. He had no idea if Hales or Deverell might have looked back at him, or if someone else might be watching and had seen him coming down off the mountain, but he knew that standing too still for too long would draw attention. Unwelcome attention.

Hales B and B. It was where he was staying, though he didn't have a reservation. He was, after all, just coming down off the Appalachian Trail for a break in the cold winter, unplanned, so a reservation would have looked odd. It was one reason he had more or less hinted for recommendations from Hales and Deverell.

He continued down the trail, keeping his footing easily even with the heavy backpack, skilled enough that he was able to keep at least half his mind on the puzzle that was Salem.

Besides the companies of the major five families, there were of course other businesses in town. The usual ones. Couple of car dealerships. A bustling coffee shop that offered wine and beer as well—after five o'clock. A pet store that offered everything a pet owner could possibly need, including day care.

There was a large bookstore offering plenty of books as well as a nice selection of crafts and artworks made in Salem, a bakery locally famous for its bread and desserts, and several hair salons (at least two of them day spas), as well as an honest-to-God barbershop. There was a video store right beside a store specializing in electronics.

There were at least three good restaurants with varying cuisine, a couple of more casual cafés, and several clothing boutiques whose prices didn't actually make a hopeful shopper wince. And that was just on or immediately off Main Street, in the downtown area.

A Main Street that boasted a grassy, beautifully landscaped town square kept meticulously, with benches from which to enjoy the flowers and burbling fountain from spring to fall, and the seasonal decorations and plants during winter. Christmas decorations had been mostly taken down with the holidays not long past, but it appeared that Salem enjoyed decorative lighting woven attractively among the bare branches of several trees in the town square and lining both sides of Main Street.

It was, on the surface, absolutely perfect Small-Town America.

On the surface.

But setting aside that apparent site of some kind of possible occult activity, the oddities of the town itself bothered Grayson, and one of those was simply the population of Salem.

Excluding transients who were just visiting, mostly during tourist season, the population of townsfolk hadn't varied by more than fifty people in as many years.

There weren't *only* five families, of course, a fact he'd considered briefly before. There were others who had come here over the centuries, and some had put down roots, remaining for generations. Even some "new" families had moved here in recent years, both retirees and young families, the latter perhaps partly drawn by a public school system rated the best in the state. But there were not as many newcomers as one might expect in a pretty little town like Salem with much to offer as a home.

Not nearly as many as one might expect.

Which was odd, definitely odd. A nice little pretty town with a healthy economy and room to expand—but that didn't, really. Not in terms of population, as in a reasonable number of total strangers moving in fairly regularly to live, and not in terms of businesses; the "newest" business of any kind in Salem had been established nearly a decade ago.

It struck Grayson, whom even his closest friends would have called a suspicious bastard, as almost . . . deliberate population control. As if someone, at some point, had decided that Salem would be so big—and no bigger.

And that was damned odd just as an idea, a concept, never mind the practicalities of just how to maintain a finite number of citizens without some pretty damned hands-on management most Americans would surely have resisted. There was no law limiting the size of families, but Grayson supposed, thinking about it, that other . . . measures . . . could be taken.

The food supply was mostly controlled, and the town's central water system came from the same cold river where the paper mill had existed for generations.

Population control . . . Something in the water?

And that wasn't just an odd thought; it was absolutely chilling.

FRIDAY

Nellie packed Leo's toys, one pried from his stubborn mouth after some discussion of the matter. Put on his harness and hooked the leash.

With the big suitcase packed and waiting on the floor at the foot of the bed, its handle sticking up, and Leo sitting with wholly visible patience beside it, she paused and sat down on the bed. She drew her big purse/satchel close and opened it again, this time studying the contents absently as if she expected to find something unusual there. But everything looked as it should.

Well. Almost.

The letter was tucked away in its discreet side pocket. Her gun in another, not visible to a casual glance. Her cell phone was in its outer pocket; she'd charged it all night but fully expected to have it go dead within a few hours whether or not she used it. There was the usual purse clutter of a small pack of tissues, a tube of lip balm, a compact she used more for the mirror than anything else because she wasn't really a makeup girl, a couple of scrunchy-type hair ties and a pocket comb and brush, and a few pens, one clipped to a small notebook.

There was also a small pocket address book of the type people seldom carried these days because all their information was kept on their cells and other devices. She could never trust her devices; any of them might be drained of power and therefore useless when she might badly need them, a lesson bitterly learned. Nellie had always considered it ironic that there were old-fashioned ways such as this one that she had to cling to because of her abilities.

And there was the billfold. It looked as if she'd had it for a while, its leather just scuffed and creased enough to look as if it had been carried and used for at least a couple of years. Inside was the usual cash—not too much to seem suspicious—plastic debit and credit cards from a bank she had never used, and her driver's license.

All in the name of Nellie Reed. Reed. Her mother's maiden name. All the IDs she carried, including the current license and registration for her gun, were in that name.

Another surprise from her father's Charlotte attorney, sent to her only a week or so before she had finished her arrangements and begun packing for Salem.

Your father asked that I send this to you before you left.

She would have found that more unnerving if it hadn't been for the fact that she had called him on impulse to tell him she was going back to her father's hometown for a visit. For some reason she hadn't even explained to herself, she had wanted *someone* to know where she was going.

He hadn't asked any questions, for which she was glad. Just seeing the very professionally faked ID and a very healthy checking account balance in that bank she'd never used before had unnerved her enough. There had even been paperwork to put in her car, inspection slips and proof of insurance and registration, all in the name of Nellie Reed.

It occurred to her sometime later that she would need her actual ID, or at least enough of it to prove she was Nellie Cavendish—if she needed to. So her real driver's license was secreted away in one of her shoes, between the insole and outsole.

James Bond stuff.

Except that was fiction. It was fiction, and besides, he always had lots of helpful gadgets and stuff to assist him on his mission. She didn't even know what the hell her mission was supposed to be.

Dammit.

Again pushing aside doubts, Nellie reached into her bag and pulled out her gloves. They were custom-made, black, whisper-thin leather much stronger than it looked, skintight, and covered only her hands, buttoning at the wrist.

She put them on with the ease of long practice, smoothing the leather almost compulsively, wondering, not for the first time, if the gloves would give her away. Could they? Not that she could risk *not* wearing them. And it was January, after all.

Gloves would be . . . expected.

Wouldn't they?

Nellie hesitated again, staring at her gloves, and then closed the bag with a smothered curse. Nothing to do but push forward and find out what the whole thing was all about.

And he'd known she would, her father.

He'd known.

Bastard.

BETHANY KNEW MORE time had passed, but she still didn't know how much. She had worn herself out a second time and had fallen into a deep sleep in which nightmare creatures chased her, claws stretched out to catch her as she ran and ran through a twisting cave filled with rusting cages and crying little girls.

She woke suddenly with a whimper, the terror still raw in her throat, shaking her body. She forced herself to take several deep breaths, suddenly aware of two things. She was really thirsty.

And she really had to pee.

She cringed away from the idea of pushing her jeans and panties down and squatting in a corner of her very small cell, feeling shame and guilt. But if she didn't do that . . .

Bethany pushed the thought away and tried hard not to think of her painfully full bladder. She concentrated again, as she did every time she was awake, on how she could escape.

She didn't have any of the Talent, so she couldn't call on that. Her family wasn't gifted that way. She wasn't even supposed to know about the Talent, really; she knew that much from listening to grown-ups when they hadn't realized she was there.

The five families had almost all the Talent; she knew that. Oh, there were a few others scattered about, or she was pretty sure there were. Only they weren't helped like the Five helped their own people learn to use the Talent.

So sometimes things happened.

Sometimes the people who didn't belong to the Five but had the Talent messed up and did things they weren't supposed to because they couldn't control the Talent.

That's what Bethany had heard. And she'd heard that sometimes . . . not often, but sometimes . . . people outside the Five who had Talent just went away.

She tried to concentrate on that, on anything that helped her forget where she was. But it only worked for a little while, and then she found herself whimpering again.

She wasn't strong or tough, no matter how much she'd like to be. So all she could do, really, was sit in this cold cell inside the damp cave that was beginning to feel very, very small, and try as hard as she could to wish herself elsewhere.

But not even the vivid imagination she used to pretend was her own special Talent could magically take her somewhere else. Instead, she opened her eyes to find she was still here, in this awful cage in the awful cave.

She had put the little tray with its little cup and bowl right at the narrow slot where someone had pushed it through. She had even pushed it partway through that slot, hoping that someone would hear or peer around that curve she couldn't see around and understand that she was really hungry and awfully thirsty.

That had been before she had fallen asleep the last time. But the tray was still there, with its cup and bowl still as empty as she had left them. And she thought it had been a long time since she had drunk the little bit of water and thin chicken broth.

A very long time.

Bethany tried not to let that scare her even more.

She really tried.

NELLIE WASN'T SURE what she had expected Salem to look like, but it surprised her. Maybe because it looked so . . . normal. The road into town brought her in at one end of what must have been the downtown area, sort of on a rise, so she could rest her foot on the brake—there was no traffic near—and look down and see both the town and most of the valley spread out.

She counted three shining white church steeples, which was typical for this part of the country; there would probably be smaller, less obvious churches, most not mainstream Baptist but close enough that they were acceptable or at least tolerable to the people of Salem.

She could see a car dealership, strands of multicolored triangular flags fluttering in the breeze and one of those tall, tubular, air-driven figures that bowed and leaned and looked altogether weird but had become a normal part of advertising some sale or other.

Nellie could see only one bank from where she paused on the rise, but it was a large one, one of the biggest buildings in town. A range of other businesses, including dozens of small stores or boutiques, restaurants and ca-fés, a drugstore (not called a pharmacy), and at the far end of Main Street, some distance from the "end" of downtown, what looked like a large grocery store.

Normal.

It was a Friday afternoon, though still early, so there were people about, far more foot traffic than cars. Most walked with a purpose likely due at least in part to the chill in the air, though a few seemed to stroll or window-shop, and there was fairly brisk traffic going in and out of the various stores and businesses. Nellie counted four people walking dogs, which made her feel a little better about having Leo with her; clearly, walking dogs down-town was allowed, as long as they were leashed.

It was what the somewhat remote but efficient innkeeper of the Hales Bed and Breakfast had told her when Nellie had called ahead to make her reservation. "Well-behaved" dogs were welcome in the B and B and in the town itself. Though not, of course, in restaurants, unless it was one of the cafés with outdoor tables.

Nellie hadn't exactly been left with a warm and fuzzy feeling of welcome after that conversation, but she had reserved what Ms. Payton had referred to as a mini-suite: bedroom, bathroom, small sitting area, and even a compact kitchenette.

Unusual for a B and B, Nellie thought, but she hadn't stayed in enough of them to know how unusual. She did, however, like having the option of stocking her little kitchen and eating in at least some of the time, especially since she not only was accustomed to living alone but was also traveling alone and disliked eating alone in restaurants—in small towns, at least. In large cities, no one noticed or cared.

At least all the space of the suite gave her options. Especially since she had no idea what she was supposed to do here and had no idea what the doing would involve even when—if—she figured it all out. Maybe there would be paperwork.

She heard a half-stifled giggle escape her throat and told herself to get a grip. That was when she looked off to the left and saw three crows perched on the back of a sidewalk bench, regarding her steadily.

She should have expected it, but Nellie nevertheless felt a little chill of . . . not fear, precisely, but anxiety. And she was feeling something else, not from the crows (because she refused to feel anything from crows, anything at all) but from the town itself. There was a . . . a queer energy in the air, she thought.

Even more oddly, she felt almost as if it gathered around her, invisibly but as ever present as the crows had always been in her life, somehow . . . protecting her? Sustaining her?

Odd thoughts. Odd feelings.

More baffling things she could not explain.

Leo nudged her arm just then, and Nellie realized she had all but stopped her car on the rise looking down at the town. She was lucky it was a nudge from her dog and not the blaring of a horn behind her, she thought, quickly easing off the brake.

"Thanks, pal," she murmured.

Leo rumbled a response—she thought—as he, too, looked around at the scenery of Salem. Rather more warily than usual for him.

She located the B and B easily enough since it was on Main Street just a couple of blocks this side of downtown. Convenient; most everything except the large grocery store at the opposite end of town looked to be within easy walking distance.

Hales was, as most B and Bs tended to be, what had once been a family home, though a very large one. It had to be more than twelve thousand square feet, she thought, possessing a very large footprint on a very generous lot, especially in a fringe-downtown area. And if it had been added to over the years, as it likely had been, nobody had been allowed to ruin the Queen Anne architecture, of which it was a very fine example indeed.

Three floors, as far as Nellie could see. The ground floor had the traditional wraparound porch; there were numerous balconies on the second floor and plenty of big dormer windows on the third floor promising the likelihood of at least half a dozen rooms up there. It might have been freshly painted and was obviously scrupulously maintained. Everything was very, very clean and in excellent repair. Even the windows gleamed in the weak winter light, as though freshly polished inside and out.

She parked in the obvious small lot on one side of the building, not quite hidden from the road by low shrubs, and got out. There were only a couple of other vehicles, which she assumed meant either that Hales wasn't very busy right now or that other guests were out and about in their cars.

She left her luggage in the unlocked car but took Leo along after a quick detour to a grassy area at one corner of the lot clearly meant for dogs; it boasted a red fire hydrant and an attractive dispenser of plastic poop bags over a lidded trash can.

They really had thought of everything.

When Leo had thoroughly sniffed and then marked his territory, they went back across the lot and followed one of several brick-paved paths, this one to the wide front steps leading up onto the porch. There were numerous seating areas, including several rocking chairs and small tables, but they were deserted of people. Not that Nellie was surprised. It really was cold; she was very glad of her thick sweater, her long, soft scarf, and the thick jeans that were for use rather than fashion.

But she had a very odd feeling of burning her bridges as she trod up the steps toward the door.

SEVEN

Moments later, Nellie was signing a register at a neat desk in a very nice, very large foyer/lobby. There were clearly numerous antiques fitting the period of the house, but additionally, more modern furniture blended seamlessly to provide both beauty and comfort. There was what looked like a library off to one side of the huge foyer, along with a second large room, what was probably a parlor with ample relaxing seating for guests, and double doors opened into a spacious dining room with numerous tables of varying sizes on the other side. There were a couple of closed doors toward the back that clearly led to storage or office space, and two wide hallways that Nellie guessed housed more than one ground-floor suite disappeared past either side of the stairs.

The stairs themselves, carpeted by a deep red runner that looked brand-new, swept up from the rear of this central space, very nice and wide, with beautifully ornate newel-posts.

"Hales was completely updated a year ago," Ms. Carol Payton told Nellie in a voice that seemed only a bit less remote than it had over the phone, though pleasant enough, like her pleasant smile. "All the bathrooms were redone, the heating and central air, and of course the electronics. Satellite TV. And we offer Wi-Fi, as I told you; the passcode is printed in your keycard folder." She pushed that across the gleaming desk to Nellie.

"Thank you."

"I'll send Jim out for your luggage. He's our handyman and usual night porter, as well as whatever else we need him for. I'll take you up to your suite. I'm sure you'd like to get settled in. I've put you on the second floor. There's a large balcony, though you may not find it comfortable this time of year. But the rooms on the second floor are more spacious, and since you weren't sure how long you'd be with us, I thought you might appreciate the extra space."

Nellie murmured something approving, adding that her bags were in the backseat and her car unlocked.

"We usually don't need to lock our cars in Salem," Carol Payton said, coming around the desk and making a gesture with one hand that summoned a lean, middle-aged man seemingly out of thin air.

He nodded to Nellie, then headed for the front door without asking which car it was—though she supposed he didn't have to, at least not today.

Nellie followed Ms. Payton toward the stairs, not calling Leo to heel because he always stuck beside her while leashed.

"Beautiful dog," Ms. Payton said, surprising Nellie.

"Thank you. Too many people I run into tend to be wary of Pit bulls or any of the bully breeds."

"I grew up with them." Without giving Nellie a chance to respond to that, she led the way to a front suite on the second floor. And it was indeed spacious. It was also beautiful, with the same mixture of antiques and more modern pieces, including a huge bed with a fluffy white duvet that made Nellie want to fall onto it and take a nap. The big bathroom boasted a claw-foot tub that looked equally enticing, and the sitting room was large, bright, and furnished for comfort.

"Flat-screens here in the sitting room as well as the bedroom," Ms. Payton was saying briskly. "The kitchenette is right over there; you can have it fully or partially stocked if you wish. There's a brochure in the drawer beside the stove from the big grocery store in town; you can call in or go online and place an order, and it's delivered here, or you can shop for yourself. Hales is, however, known for outstanding breakfasts, so we always recommend you try those before deciding about that meal.

"We're also happy to provide bedding for your dog. There's a storage room at the end of this hall, labeled, with pet supplies, including a wide selection of beds and bowls as well as toys. Feel free to choose whatever you like and keep it here."

"Thank you," Nellie said rather blankly. She could recall staying in about three extremely upscale hotels in large cities that provided something comparable, but to find this sort of specialized service in such a small, isolated town was . . . unusual.

"He's also allowed on the furniture," Ms. Payton added calmly. "We believe in making certain our guests are comfortable."

Before Nellie could offer another thank-you, Jim returned with her luggage, which he carried into her bedroom and placed on the bench at the foot of the bed, leaving as swiftly and silently as he had arrived, without giving Nellie a chance to tip him.

She made a mental note to leave gratuities in envelopes addressed to anyone who provided a service for her without lingering for a tip; it struck her as that sort of place, which, again, was rare in her experience.

"Feel free to come and go as you please," Ms. Payton said. "You have the keycard that unlocks the door to this suite; the exterior house doors are locked at midnight, but Jim or our other night porter will be happy to let you in if you happen to come in later.

"Now I'll leave you to settle in. If there's anything you require, anything at all, please don't hesitate to call down to the desk. You'll find the breakfast menu on the coffee table in here, along with the list of amenities and services we provide. I trust your stay will be pleasant, Miss Reed."

"Thank you," Nellie said, watching the older woman briskly leave the suite, closing the door firmly behind her.

She unfastened Leo's leash and explored the suite more thoroughly, still surprised by the comfort and space. French doors opened out onto her balcony from the sitting room, but after a brief visit and despite a lovely view of downtown Salem, Nellie and her dog both returned to the warmth inside.

Unless the weather warmed up considerably, she didn't anticipate spending much time out there. And since it was January, she doubted the weather would be warming up anytime soon.

She looked down at Leo, who had already found all the corners and returned to her and was looking at her expectantly.

"I know you want a walk," she told him. "But I want to unpack first. And we need to visit that pet room she talked about and see if there's a bed or two you like."

He made the soft huffing sound that tended to be indicative of scorn. Or so she had decided.

"Yes, I know you'll sleep on my bed when I do, but let's see what they have before you pass judgment."

Leo made another of his odd sounds but accompanied her amiably into the bedroom to help her unpack. His toys were still stowed away in one of her bags, after all.

GRAYSON, WHO HAD checked in late morning the previous day, saw from his unobtrusive chair in the front parlor the attractive young woman with the black, impressively muscled Pit bull arrive and check in. He didn't realize he'd been tense until he saw that not only was she petite rather than tall and athletic, but her hair was a soft brown, not bright red, and felt himself relax.

Dammit.

She didn't even have a dog. Or never had, anyway, as far as he knew. Besides which, she was already *here*.

Okay, so he hadn't seen a sign of Geneva yet, even though he'd managed to sneak a glance at the old-fashioned register at the front desk and found that she'd checked in as scheduled more than two weeks before. Since he'd been given the spiel about coming and going as he pleased, with a keycard to his second-floor room and the information about the night porter being on duty, he knew it was entirely possible that Geneva had come and gone more than once since he'd checked in, eluding him easily, whether on purpose or just because she was Geneva. And if she'd slipped in and out late last night, she probably hadn't needed to trouble the night porter.

She could be very slippery when she wanted to be, and since she knew he was here by now she probably wanted to be.

So he shouldn't necessarily expect to make contact with her right away.

Except that he was uneasy, and past experience told him that kind of uneasiness was the sort he should pay attention to. Even with all his shields up and as strong as he could make them, he caught flickers of emotions from, he assumed, those nearest him, and they were . . . wary. Especially when he had strolled to the downtown area earlier, ostensibly to check out the bookstore—he had bought two paperback novels—but really to make sure that the weekend edition of the town newspaper delivered to his room early was the only one available.

Everybody he'd encountered had smiled and been friendly. On the surface. What he'd felt underneath had been wary.

From quite a few people.

It was an oddity in his experience, and it worried him, especially since he'd felt the same thing the day before. He was also aware, especially when he'd been outside, of the energy that appeared to be centered on the town. The few emotions that had slipped in past his walls had been . . . odd. Like actual static on a radio, almost crackling, and that was not how he'd ever sensed emotions.

And either that or something else made him physically uncomfortable, just enough for him to be aware of it. Like a live current occasionally brushing past him. Or a tendril of energy. He grimly shored up his walls, wondering if there were a lot of psychics in Salem—or only a handful of them. Either way, assuming they existed, they were either untaught or badly taught, since they were apparently unable to contain their own energies, or else were using those energies in ways they had never been meant to be used.

Dangerous ways.

It could be either, and until Grayson knew, there wasn't a thing he could do except guard his own abilities and keep all his normal senses on alert.

He'd killed a couple of hours or so after he'd checked in Thursday morning and unpacked in his room by wandering downstairs and settling in with the air of a tired man, seemingly relaxed in front of a brisk fire in the parlor. He saw few other people, but some he assumed were guests, coming and going. Saw the woman at the front desk seldom leave it, never getting far away for long. He'd remained in the parlor for a while, establishing what he intended to be a habit the people around him would cease to even notice.

Then he'd walked to town, choosing the first restaurant he'd come to in surface idleness to have a late lunch, assuming a pose of just-on-the-edge-of-drowsy weariness. The place had been busy but not crowded, with most patrons, he guessed, townsfolk. He'd done the same thing that evening, choosing a different restaurant and finding it Thursday-night busy.

Both times, the food was good.

Both times, people had seemed casually friendly but left him to himself.

And both times, the undercurrent he'd felt had been wariness.

He hadn't seen a sign of Geneva. Not in town and not here at the B and B. He hadn't dared start a search for her.

He had not slept well.

So here he was again, settled in the parlor, the weekend edition of the paper that was published on Friday before him and his entire attitude one of taking things easy and looking at the paper with only idle interest. Without even having to turn his head, he noted the attractive woman with the gleaming black Pit leave with the casual air of someone going out to walk her dog and explore.

By the time he gave in to worry and slipped upstairs

and to Geneva's door, he hadn't seen another guest that day, even though at least a dozen were registered.

He used his special keycard gadget to get into her room, all the while mentally rehearsing what he would say if she happened to catch him at it.

But not only did Geneva not catch him, a quick look around convinced him she had not, in fact, returned to her room the previous night—assuming that was when she'd last left the place. She had hung out her DO NOT DISTURB sign, which might have meant she'd known she wouldn't be back last night and didn't want the maid service to notice. Or it might simply have meant she still disliked strangers cleaning her room when she wasn't present; when it was time for housekeeping, Geneva's habit was to make sure she was there while the maid was.

He remembered that about her.

NELLIE DECIDED TO give Leo his walk after she unpacked, so they set out from the B and B while it was still only a bit past early afternoon. She had nothing in mind beyond a little exploring—and possibly a late lunch at one of the restaurants with outdoor seating, because she'd never gotten around to having breakfast that day.

She had dressed for extra warmth before starting out but still felt the chill of the air on her cheeks and, occasionally, the cold bite of a gust of wind even though it wasn't a particularly windy day.

Leo, being a shorthaired dog, was wearing a blue, fleece-lined hoodie sweatshirt; he hated clothing as a rule and could shred an outfit in less than five minutes if left alone while wearing one, but he condescended in very cold weather. He walked obediently at Nellie's side on a loose leash, looking around him with a curious and benign gaze.

The few people they encountered on the sidewalk nodded politely to Nellie and took note of her dog without comment, except for one small boy who asked if he could pet the doggie. His mother, rather to Nellie's surprise, nodded to Nellie and waited with a smile for her to give permission, then laughed when her son kissed Leo between his eyes and then hugged him exuberantly.

"His name is Leo," Nellie told the boy.

"Leo! I love you, Leo!"

As Leo reciprocated by licking the giggling boy's face with the usual Pittie enthusiasm, the child's mother merely said, "He loves animals, and they always love him."

"Then he has a gift," Nellie offered with a smile.

"I think so. Come on, Joey, you've been outside long enough. It's too cold for our usual ramble. Say good-bye to Leo. I'm sure you'll see him again."

Joey planted two more kisses on Leo's broad head, then said happily, "Bye, Leo!" and accepted his mother's hand to continue on their way.

Nellie and Leo continued walking, and it was several minutes later that Nellie wondered why the woman had not introduced herself or asked Nellie's name. That was more usual in small, friendly towns, she had discovered. She hadn't been in Salem *quite* long enough for the local gossip mill to have spread her name around, and people were always curious about strangers, especially when the traditional tourist season hadn't yet begun.

It bothered Nellie, though only in a vague, nebulous way she couldn't really put a name to, just like that odd tingling on her skin bothered her.

But she was probably just being paranoid. This was a tourist town, after all, and it was true of tourist towns that lots of people passed through in all seasons to visit without offering their names or learning the names of any of the townsfolk. And her research had told her that there were hardy souls who hiked the Appalachian Trail all year long, hikers who were known to come down off the Trail from time to time to rest or wait out especially bad weather in small towns like Salem.

Probably welcome to have "tourist" dollars off-season.

So why was it bugging her?

And anyway, none of that explained the faint tingling she was aware of, not so strong that she wanted to rub her skin but just strong enough for her to feel it. She felt it—and then the sensation dimmed a bit, as it had before, and she had the curious image in her mind of something being pushed away, held away.

She passed a sidewalk bench and was not at all surprised to see a crow watching her intently. Oddly, this time, she didn't feel unnerved by the scrutiny so much as thoughtful.

It was weird. Like something on the tip of her mind she needed to remember.

She pushed the thought away for the moment since

they had reached one of the restaurants with a small out-door seating section. Even on such a cold day, one man was seated with coffee and a newspaper, his back to the occasional gusts of wind, and a young couple sat huddled in coats and enclosed in a visible aura of intense romance, gloved hands locked together on top of the table and blissful faces close.

Nellie chose a table roughly between the other pa-trons and sat down, relieved when a waitress in jeans and what looked like a parka came out to take her order.

"Excuse the outfit," she said with a laugh, "but I'd rather look weird than freeze." She eyed Leo and added, "The manager would probably let you bring him just inside if you want to. I mean, it's *really* cold out here today."

"Thanks, but we'll be fine." Nellie studied the single laminated menu for lunchtime and, mindful of the cold, ordered a bowl of chicken vegetable soup and a sand-wich, with coffee. "And could I get a bowl of chicken broth or something like that for my dog?"

"Sure, no problem." The waitress whisked the menu away. "I'll be right back."

Nellie absently stroked Leo as he sat beside her and looked around at as much as she could see of the town from where she was. Very clean, very neat. And no de-serted buildings or obviously failing businesses that were visible, at least here on Main. Reasonably busy for a Fri-day afternoon, with cars passing and people on foot walking briskly.

It wasn't until her gaze turned in that direction that

she realized the bank was no more than half a block away, and that from this angle she could read the rather discreet sign above the discreetly impressive entranceway.

CAVENDISH SAVINGS AND LOAN

It startled her for only a moment, but then she realized it made sense that her father would have continued in some form of the family business after he left Salem. Gone on working in the field he'd known best, finance. Though the company he had founded not long after Nellie was born had a slightly different name—and purpose.

Cavendish Investments Limited.

She was mulling that over, frowning a little, when a brief growl from Leo gave her just a moment's warning before a man sat down in the chair on the other side of her table.

"Hey, Nellie," he said pleasantly. "Welcome back to Salem. My name is Finn."

DUNCAN CAVENDISH COULDN'T remember a time when he hadn't both hated and feared his younger brother. Others might have called it jealousy, but he had known he was the superior of the two: taller, stronger, faster—and better able to use the Talent.

He had, after all, fought his way through the Barrier far younger than Thomas had, younger than was the custom, and had spent those years in learning to control what he could do.

And adding power.

In the early years he had felt a twinge or two of guilt at the means he used to gain more power, but as time went by he grew far less squeamish. They were only animals, after all.

And the power . . . the *power*.

It hadn't helped him father a son by the three wives he had married and divorced in quick succession as each proved barren. Because it wasn't, of course, *his* fault that no children were produced, sons or daughters.

Yet Thomas had gotten his young wife pregnant almost as soon as the wedding cake was cut, and even though Duncan had been relieved when the child had proved to be a girl, he'd received a blow only a few months later. One of the Blackwood elders, her Talent the farseeing, had sought him out and told him that Thomas or his daughter would destroy Duncan.

She had been very sure, and she was never wrong.

That was why Duncan had crossed the line in his seeking for more power, committing an act even he had known would damn his soul for all eternity. But that act had granted him the power to face Thomas and literally drag from his younger brother, his blood kin, the Talent Thomas had possessed.

He was not sure, even now, how Thomas had survived that, but he had managed. And he had spirited away his wife and child so quickly that Duncan had, for some time, lost track of them.

By then his own power had grown yet stronger, and he was able to find Sarah Cavendish, who had fled her husband and young daughter for whatever reasons of her own, and his agents had dealt with her.

Thomas and his daughter had been more difficult. Thomas might have lost his Talent, but he was smart and he was careful. He somehow found a way to protect his child as she grew, and managed himself to elude Duncan's agents until the girl was in college.

Since then . . . Duncan had tried more than once to get at her, without success. He wasn't sure what protected her, whether Thomas had defied custom and taught his daughter as she grew, at least enough so she was able to protect herself, or whether Sarah had left her daughter some gift meant to be triggered as she grew older.

It infuriated Duncan to not know why all his efforts failed.

Still, he had known she would, at the proper time, return to Salem. All of the blood with Talent returned here, compelled by a calling buried so deeply in their minds they rarely even guessed it might be something placed inside them by powerful other minds, even as the Barrier was placed.

Most came on their own, but Duncan had realized he would have to gain as much power as possible before his niece returned here, and so he had triggered four others of the blood to return early to Salem, using the careful, mysterious lures he had learned worked best.

And they had come.

But . . . none had survived the breaking of the Barrier. He refused to accept the idea that his methods had been too harsh, too hurried; he had needed, and they should have provided him what he needed, what he craved. Greater power. Greater control over his Talents.

He had gained . . . some. He could feel it. Some.

But not enough.

To gain enough, he would have to cross a final line.

To face Nellie and to defeat her, to tear from her all that raw Talent she had been born to possess, he would have to command the ultimate power.

And that came only by the sacrifice of the innocent.

EIGHT

Nellie stared across the table at the blond, blue-eyed man who was probably a couple of years older than she was, and said merely, "Finn who?"

"Deverell."

Finn Deverell was about six feet tall, she judged, and had the look of an athlete, or at least a man who kept in shape. He had blond hair a little longer than was currently fashionable, and mild blue eyes that Nellie was certain were deceptive.

Despite her father's letter—or perhaps because of it— Nellie wasn't about to blindly trust this man or any other. So all she said was, "I don't believe I invited you to sit down. I'm about to have lunch. I'd rather have it alone."

Beside her, Leo growled again, undoubtedly alerted by the tension she was trying hard to keep out of her voice.

Finn Deverell glanced at Leo, still smiling faintly.

"You can reassure Leo I'm not going to hurt you," he said.

He must have been near enough to hear me tell the little boy, was all Nellie could think.

"I don't think I'm going to tell him that," was what she said. "I don't, after all, know you."

He didn't respond immediately because the waitress returned just then, with a tray holding Nellie's lunch and a generous bowl of gently steaming chicken broth for Leo. Plus a large cup of coffee for Finn Deverell.

"Hey, Finn," she said casually as she began unloading the tray.

"Sally. Would you mind reassuring Miss Reed that I'm not an axe murderer?"

She laughed, clearly amused. "He's okay, Miss Reed. Sort of the unofficial town greeter for tourists."

Before Nellie could respond to that, wondering in the few seconds allowed to her how he had managed to find out her name, Finn took the large bowl of chicken broth and bent to set it in front of the obviously alert, intently watching Leo.

"Here you go, Leo."

Nellie waited until Sally had unloaded her tray, grinned at them both impartially, and returned to the warmth of the restaurant, then glanced aside at her dog and said quietly, "It's okay, Leo."

He immediately began drinking the warm chicken broth. For many reasons, such as the fact that she traveled with Leo and couldn't always control her or his surroundings, and so as to avoid danger, Nellie had carefully trained Leo to accept food from no one but her unless she gave him the okay.

Nellie fixed her coffee the way she liked it, then began eating her own soup and sandwich, ignoring Finn Deverell.

If anything, it seemed to amuse him. He drank his coffee and gazed around idly, his appearance and manner those of someone who had just stopped by to chat.

He made a few innocuous comments about the weather (unusually cold), the scenery (gorgeous as always, and he'd be happy to show her some of the most gorgeous), and the amenities to be found in Salem (and he'd be delighted to play tour guide). His voice remained pleasant and calm, his smile unruffled. And it wasn't until Nellie finished her lunch that his casual friendliness dropped away to reveal something a lot more quietly intense.

She'd been right about those deceptively mild eyes. They could and did turn sharp in the space of a heartbeat. Sharp enough to cut somebody.

"I know what your father told you, Nellie. I know he told you that I could help you. That you could trust me."

If he knows that . . . he knows who I really am.

"All I know," she said after a long moment and a deliberate sip of her cooling coffee, "is that a man who trusted most of my upbringing to a paid nanny and various schools, and never showed any interest in my life otherwise, *told* me I could trust you."

"You trusted him," Finn said.

"Did I? He might have been a sperm donor for my

mother, but he was never a father to me. So you'll have to forgive me if I decide to make up my own mind about whether I can or should trust anything he had to say about anyone. Including you."

"You trusted him," Finn repeated. "You're here."

"I was curious." Driven. Compelled.

"With your upbringing and the kind of message I'm certain he left for you, it would take a lot more than simple curiosity to bring you to Salem. Especially using an alias."

And that makes me sound like a criminal.

Message? Did he know about the letter, or merely guess that would be how Thomas Cavendish would have left information when he had died years before it had to be delivered? Or did he know that her father had died?

Nellie said, "I don't know what you're talking about."

"Of course you do."

She was silent.

"He died more than ten years ago, didn't he?"

It wasn't really a question.

"Yes." Okay, so he knew that. But the fact that he was aware of that information didn't particularly impress Nellie; her father had been a wealthy, powerful man, and such men made news when they lived. And when they died. Though it struck her as definitely odd that the message had even named Finn—if this was, indeed, him— since he would have been barely out of his teens when Thomas Cavendish had written the letter.

"And the message he left for you, a written message he had notarized and held by a trusted lawyer, was to be delivered into your hands well before your thirtieth birthday."

"He told you," Nellie said mechanically. "Long before I knew, he told you."

Finn didn't deny that. Instead, blue eyes still intense, he said, "You wrestled with coming here. You waited for months. Your thirtieth birthday is coming up. January 15. Not long now. Why did you struggle against coming here? Because he wanted you to come here? Because he told you that you had to? Or because you *felt* you had to and didn't trust your own instincts?"

Nellie hoped she didn't betray the surprise she felt at that. She was certain her father had been in touch with this man before he died, even shared the idea of the message, what was in the message. That made sense, even if she didn't understand the why of any of this. And it would certainly be easy enough to share her birthday, or for Finn to find it on some public record. But the rest?

How could he have known her reaction to that letter?

How could he have known how she'd *felt* about it?

"Nellie—"

"Admit it. He was in touch with you before he died."

"Of course he was. That's hardly the point."

Nellie thought it was a large part of the point. And so *like* her father to put her fate, apparently, into the hands of a stranger—a relatively young stranger at that time—and to tell that stranger personal things long before he bothered to tell them to his daughter.

"You need my help," Finn said.

"Your help with what? With some mysterious errand

my father chose to insist I figure out for myself? An errand he insisted was dangerous?" She kept her voice low even though there was no one close enough to overhear them. "I don't see any danger looming over me. This seems like a perfectly pleasant little town, and certainly no threat to me."

"Appearances can be deceptive."

With an effort she hoped didn't show, Nellie ignored that. She wanted to get up and leave, just walk away. And return to the B and B and pack and get the hell out of here.

But she was bitterly aware that there was enough of her father's stubbornness in her to prevent that.

Dammit.

She forced herself to smile casually. "I don't have anything in particular in mind to *do* here, other than be a tourist and take a break from a hectic life. Sleep late, maybe do some hiking and riding, shop. Enjoy the scenery. So just what is it you propose to *help* me with, Mr. Deverell?"

As if what he was saying was perfectly normal and even conversational, he said, "I propose to help you survive this visit to Salem, Nellie Cavendish. I propose to save your life."

GENEVA RAYNOR, AS just about all who knew her could attest, was a woman who could take care of herself. She got herself into trouble from time to time, sure, but she also got herself out.

Usually.

Right now, however, she was experiencing some highly uncharacteristic doubts. Because she had searched every single inch of her prison, every *fraction* of an inch, and could find no way to get herself out of here.

Even where *here* was, was an open question. She had been in the woods north of town, watched by the sentinels, the crows, and then she had heard his voice asking a seemingly casual question . . . and then everything had gone black.

She didn't think he had hit her because her headache was not of the caused-by-a-blunt-instrument variety. She'd had enough of those to know. And she also thought she would remember a Taser for the same reason. So her bet was an injection of some kind.

However he'd done it, he had knocked her out in seconds, leaving not so much as a bruise she'd been able to find. When she woke up, she had been totally alone in this place. And still was. She knew she was alone because she'd taken a chance and dropped her shields, in the beginning as soon as her head had cleared and several times since, reaching out in every direction, trying to touch another mind. Any other mind. And . . . nothing.

She was alone, all right.

Maybe in a cellar. Not a cave, she thought, because the beams in the ceiling high above her looked like floor joists to her. So probably a cellar. Or some other underground place, because the walls were mostly hard-packed dirt with the consistency of cement, walls that had been there a long, long time, like the floor, and there were no windows, no stairs.

There was no exterior door, she was reasonably certain. What there was, was a single door in one relatively small section of the wall that was brick, a large, heavy door, dark, rough wood with big, thick iron hinges—of the kind one couldn't just knock a pin out to loosen—bolted in place, and no doorknob or handle of any kind on her side. And even though there were no stairs or steps, the bottom of the door was a good two feet or a bit more above the hard dirt floor, which was another indication that it led into whatever building housed this cellar.

Geneva habitually carried hidden on her person several small but useful tools; they had obviously searched her and had found all but one of them. The remaining tool, though narrow and slender, was exceptionally strong—but so far she hadn't figured out a way to use it to escape her prison. It wasn't a digging tool, and hard as she'd looked along the walls and floor, she had not been able to find a single crack or seam. Even the mortar of the ancient red bricks on that one section of wall refused to flake off under her careful touch, let alone chip. As for the door, she had cautiously sounded it with a series of careful knocks and was convinced it was both unusually thick and unusually solid.

Still, she tore four of her nails painfully in trying to find something, anything, on her side of the door to grip, wedging them into the seam where the door should open only to find nothing to grip and the door unmoving.

She might have thrown the single lidded bucket in the prison at the door in her rising frustration, but since its use was obvious and definitely necessary, she had not done that.

Since she couldn't wear a watch or carry a cell phone, and since her prison had no windows, Geneva had no idea how long she had been here, or what time it was. Unlike some other SCU members, she had never learned to compensate by developing a reliable clock in her head. And even if she had, there was no sunlight or moonlight to offer any aid.

Her best guess was that she'd awakened here no more than two or three hours after she'd been knocked out, and after that . . . The rest of Wednesday night. Thursday at least, and maybe Friday. Was it Saturday yet?

Maybe.

The two large plastic bottles of water they had left for her were half-gone despite her sparing use, and the two large plastic lidded containers of a kind commonly found in grocery stores for food storage, one holding weirdly normal individually packaged sandwiches like those that usually came out of vending machines and the other holding a generous number of individually wrapped protein bars, were also depleted by at least a couple of days of hunger, she thought—again, despite her careful, sparing consumption.

She had the healthy appetite of an active, athletic person, and aside from being a tall woman, her psychic abilities tended to require at least a normal amount of food as sheer fuel. She hadn't reached the point where she felt drained, but she felt weaker than normal now because she'd restricted her rations, ignoring appetite, and that only added to her problems.

She was hungry, she was frustrated, and she was chilled.

Time was passing.

The half dozen thick, tall pillar candles they had left, along with two boxes of matches in a plastic baggie, still had a reassuring amount of burning time left in them, because she'd been cautious enough to light only one at a time and sparingly; five nearly whole candles were left. Though the light of a single candle didn't exactly brighten up her prison and further hampered her efforts to find a way out.

And the dark corners were getting to her; her imagination was beginning to conjure things crouching in them, just glimpses from the corners of her eyes. And, of course, they were nothing but innocently empty corners when she took her candle and looked more closely.

There was nothing in here with her.

She was sure of that.

Almost sure.

She was also getting pretty damned tired of sleeping—when she wasn't pacing and could at least nap—on the bare, lumpy, single twin-sized mattress on the dirt floor.

They might at least have left her a pillow and blanket.

It wasn't exactly cold in her prison, certainly not as cold as the outside temperature; she judged this room to be almost entirely belowground, and it seemed to maintain a fairly consistent temperature in the low sixties. And she'd been dressed for the cold, so there was that. But to say she was comfortable would have been a gross misrepresentation of the truth. There might not be frostbite in the offing, but feeling constantly chilled was both uncomfortable and a considerable drain on her energy.

Plus, there were the bugs. She hadn't *seen* any bugs yet, but she had to be surrounded by them. Burrowed into the hard, hard walls, or lurking in the dark corners only to scurry away when she approached with her candle. She tried not to think about it, but she didn't like bugs. Especially spiders, spinning their sticky webs and creeping across people's faces in the night—

Geneva drew a deep breath and let it out slowly, reaching for control even if it was only an illusion.

She didn't want to admit even to herself that she was scared, but she was. She was also mad as hell, baffled because she had even more questions than she'd had before, and since her fate was clearly in the hands of others, she had no idea if she would even leave this prison alive.

The food might have reassured someone without an educated and experienced imagination, but that wasn't Geneva. Just because they were feeding her *now* didn't mean they intended to keep on feeding her.

She could think of a dozen reasons why a captor would feed a prisoner for just a while and then stop—and none of them were good.

To muddle up estimates like time of death and how long she'd been missing before she finally turned up, for instance. To starve her at their leisure, for whatever awful reason. Or maybe they'd put something in the food, the water, that was working on her even now, nibbling at her determination, her will, her strength, some kind of slow-acting poison or, perhaps worse, something that would alter her thinking, make her paranoid, even nuts . . .

It was bad enough to have a vivid imagination; it was hell to have an educated and experienced imagination.

And too many war stories that would have scared the living shit out of average people.

Because even if she wasn't as good as some others claimed to be at measuring the passage of time just by instinct or her very underdeveloped internal clock, the water and food and candles told her time had passed. Two days at least, was her guess. And not a sight or sound of another living soul.

She thought about those now four bodies almost all the locals pretended hadn't turned up deep in the woods, the bodies so mutilated there'd been no way to tell by looking who they had been or how long they had been out there, never mind how they'd been killed. That was what they'd briefly thought, the locals, a passing pity for careless hikers who'd gotten themselves killed slipping on winter-slick rocks or something like that.

The militia had taken care of such *accidents* so quickly, quietly, and smoothly, Geneva had almost missed picking up anything about the first three dead during her first week here. If it hadn't been for her brief telepathic encounter with the shaken hunter, she'd likely never have found that fourth body. Or what was left of it.

As for what the locals believed, there had been only bare mentions of the unfortunate first three "hikers" noted in the December newspaper editions Geneva had one night quietly broken into the local library to check out.

As for the remains she herself had found, no mention of him had appeared in the next day's newspaper at all—though Geneva *had* picked up a few stray uneasy thoughts from townspeople since she had found that fourth victim. Not even the militia, it appeared, was able to keep the deaths absolutely quiet. And some unnerving details were getting out.

Still, in those vague musings Geneva had picked up, it seemed either carelessness or wolves were always the culprits. It was what they believed, what they'd . . . been told? Sad, but those hikers had been warned not to hike way up there along the Trail unless they knew what they were doing, because all hikers were warned.

And it was *winter*. Even the most experienced hiker had no business walking the Trail this time of year.

Hikers. As far as Geneva could tell, that was totally accepted, that the dead had been hikers just passing by and, really, no concern of the people of Salem. It was one of the eerie things about this town. People who really did seem unusually, even unnaturally, undisturbed by horrible deaths in their general area and uninterested even in whom the bodies belonged to. In her experience it was just the sort of thing that made locals jumpy as hell even if the dead *had* been careless hikers.

But not in Salem. Nobody seemed to be much interested in, far less affected by, the deaths.

And no official actions had been visible. No statement or announcement. Nothing at all. The bodies just . . . vanished. And not a soul whose mind Geneva had touched seemed the least bit curious about that, never mind not being horrified. And that was just weird.

Unnatural.

Geneva shivered.

She had felt a slight current of air coming from a finely meshed screen in the ceiling surprisingly high above her, a regular occurrence, but so far she had found no way of getting up there; it was well out of her reach. Not that reaching it was likely to help, since she judged it to be no more than ten or twelve inches square. And whatever lay beyond it was a mystery, since she never saw a light or any movement, or heard any sound.

It was quiet. Too quiet. Silent.

Silent as a grave.

Dammit.

And where the hell was Gray, anyway? Surely he'd come looking for her despite her message? She knew him well enough to be fairly certain of that. And he must have arrived in Salem by now; she knew where his drop point had been scheduled to be and it was only a few short hours of hiking from there. He should *be* here by now, and settled in, and following the planned routine of settling in, a tired hiker, and idly looking through the local newspaper because he always did that.

So where the hell was he?

For the first time in her life, Geneva, though she considered herself something of a loner, understood how solitary confinement could drive someone out of their mind.

NINE

After so carefully checking Geneva's room, Grayson returned to the parlor and again occupied himself with his newspaper, a half-empty coffee cup on the table beside his chair. He heard Ms. Payton return to the desk from whatever errand had taken her away from it, even though she walked with a catfooted lightness that was rarely natural. Grayson decided absently that he had a nasty, suspicious mind.

"*Does she know when I'm arriving?*" he had asked Bishop about Geneva.

"*Approximately. The day you should reach Salem if you encounter no trouble, but not the specific time, obviously. You could be delayed on the Trail for some reason.*"

"*Makes sense. And she knows it's me?*" He'd immediately felt like an idiot asking that, but Bishop had replied as though the question were perfectly reasonable.

"*Yes, you were always the logical person to send. Aside from the physicality and experience required to hike in rugged terrain and make certain no one doubted you could have hiked the Trail, your spider senses are extremely well developed, and your empathic senses are near the top of our scale.*"

"*And you're so sure an empath and a telepath are going to find whatever's going on in or around Salem?*"

"*I'm sure you're the right team to go looking for whatever's going on in or around Salem.*"

A typical Bishop nonanswer. He would, of course, have his reasons for teaming Grayson and Geneva, but neither of them would likely ever know what those reasons were.

Their last teaming had been a professional success, but as far as the personal went . . . Grayson was pretty sure he still had the scars. He thought that perhaps Bishop might be wrong about their pairing—even though he very rarely erred in those instincts—because he and Geneva were just too much alike.

Most of the successful teams within the SCU, many long-term, worked so well because they complemented each other. A strength or weakness in one was countered by the other. Balanced. In abilities and skills, definitely—though not always in temperament. Lucas and Samantha Jordan, for instance, both had fiery tempers and had been known to "disagree" about something with a force that should have stripped the paint from the walls, and yet they were a deeply bonded, totally devoted couple and an excellent investigative team.

But he and Geneva . . . He might have been able to best her at MMA, he thought ruefully, but he would have hesitated to bet against her even in that. Otherwise, they possessed many of the same skills and abilities. Their psychic abilities differed, but they both had hair-trigger tempers, generally under their control.

Generally.

But he still thought they made an odd team, and he was dubious of Bishop's clear faith in them.

At the moment, however, Grayson was simply wishing he was the telepath of the pair. He'd always been lucky to catch a fleeting sense of her emotions even with his walls down, and then only when—he suspected—she allowed it. But she had reached out and touched his mind more than once when his walls had been up, and all too easily, from his point of view.

So maybe she wasn't in trouble. Surely, he thought, she'd reach out if she was in trouble. Even to him.

Except . . . she was stubborn as hell. And inclined to believe she could get herself out of a jam. No matter what that jam might be.

The problem—one of the problems—was that she'd been here two weeks longer than he had, and except for one very brief report early on to Bishop from a landline phone thirty miles outside Salem basically saying she didn't trust any kind of communication from inside the valley and to therefore not expect regular reports from her, Grayson didn't have a clue what she'd found or whether she'd discovered something dangerous.

Worse, Bishop didn't have a clue, or at least said as much. He tended to have a sense of where at least some of his agents were and whether they were in trouble or danger, and Geneva was one of those. But here, in Salem, that connection had been . . . interrupted.

The "static" Bishop had referred to might be acting as a psychic barrier, at least between him and his agents. Grayson knew without even trying that the sense he himself usually had of Bishop—not thoughts but a sense of contact—was absent here and now, lost about the time he had started down off the Trail toward Salem.

What he didn't know, what Bishop didn't know, and maybe Geneva didn't know even after two weeks here, was exactly what the static was, where it originated, and why it could block the usually easy contact with their unit chief without also interfering with their individual psychic abilities.

So far, at least.

Something natural to the area itself? Wouldn't be the first time. Something unnatural, paranormal, perhaps the psychic spillover of energies? Also wouldn't be the first time. But either way, it was, as Bishop had noted, not a good thing.

Not trusting normal routes of communication . . . that was just Geneva, or at least had been in the past, so not really a clue that something might be wrong. She was, if possible, more suspicious than Grayson was by nature. And, though he wasn't at all sure if Bishop knew it, she was perfectly capable of using any handy excuse to avoid making regular reports.

They also had that in common.

Grayson pretended to read the paper and considered the situation uneasily. His first instinct was to go out looking for Geneva, but he knew better than to just start walking around town and asking questions. Or even just walking around town trying to act like he wasn't looking for someone. For one thing, they weren't connected in any way as far as Salem was concerned, and Geneva might well have discovered it would be best to leave it that way. So blundering into a situation without knowing much, far less anything she might have discovered in the past two weeks, was an invitation to disaster, especially since three missing people who had disappeared here had been the reason both Geneva and he had been sent in.

He was busy silently cursing Geneva's mania for secrecy when his absently wandering gaze landed suddenly on a classified ad on the newspaper's page. He was surprised, first, that hard copies of newspapers still bothered with "personals" columns, what with all the myriad ways people could sell or trade items so much faster via various platforms on the Internet now.

But in a small town with what he'd already discovered was an uncertain Wi-Fi connection, he supposed sticking to at least some of the old ways was probably smart. There were two pages of ads, a few large and most smaller, some of them from local businesses but quite a few from people looking to buy or sell some item. There was also one marriage proposal, a request for a date to a high school dance, someone looking for a lost cat, two ads from persons looking to sell used cars—and a message from Geneva.

GS, if you're looking for me so you can apologize,
you must know I'm still mad at you. I'm not a little

*girl gone missing, you are not the boss of me, and you
don't tell me what to do or where to go. Or who to see. I
can take care of myself and I don't need you. I'm
careful. Stay away from me. Red*

HE KNOWS WHO *I really am. But what does that mean?
Something? Nothing? And what did he mean, welcome
back to Salem? I've never been here before.*

To give herself a moment to think, Nellie fed her half-eaten turkey sandwich to Leo, who was pleased to take it, and then brushed her gloved hands off, tossed her napkin on the table, and pushed her bowl and plate to one side.

Practice, which she'd had a lot of one way or another, kept her expression calm.

Finally, after a sip of her coffee, she said, "Survive Salem. And what—or who—in Salem is going to try to kill me?"

"So your father didn't tell you." It wasn't a question.

Nellie stared at him. "As you noted, my father's been dead for more than ten years. And I was told he left Salem at least twenty years before that. You can't be much older than I am. Want to tell me just how it is you claim to know him?"

"I never claimed to know him."

"Just to have been in contact with him long enough to learn what he did or didn't tell me."

"Yes. Just that. Some of it, at least. Some other things

through my own father, who knew your father very well. Thomas told you that you could trust me. That I was the only man in Salem you *should* trust."

The only man. Now, why did that part of what he said make something in the back of her mind abruptly sit up and pay even closer attention?

Nellie smiled and knew it was one of her corporate board smiles, the kind she'd been told was a little scary. "I don't trust easily, Mr. Deverell. And I certainly never knew my father well enough to trust anything he told me. I make up my own mind. You're a stranger, and so far you haven't offered me a single concrete reason why I should be afraid of anything or anyone in Salem. When you're ready to do that, let me know. In the meantime, I'm going to pay for my lunch, and then Leo and I are going to continue our walk."

"I don't suppose you'd let me pay for your lunch," he said, and it wasn't a question.

"I don't suppose I would." She pulled the worn billfold from her bag and placed a few bills under her coffee cup, more than enough to cover the meal, Leo's broth, and even her unwelcome companion's coffee. Plus a generous tip.

Then she returned the billfold to her bag and rose, holding the bag on one shoulder and picking up the end of Leo's leash with the other hand. "I would say it was nice meeting you," she said pleasantly, "but that's something else I'll make up my mind about."

He had climbed to his feet when she did, but he didn't follow her as she left the outdoor café and continued down the sidewalk with her dog. And neither one of them said good-bye.

He just stood there looking after her. She could feel it.

Nellie's thoughts were chasing themselves in circles. *He knows who I really am. How? Is it important? Does he really know I should be afraid for my life here? How does he know? And why should I be afraid? Afraid of what? Who? What the hell is going on here?*

And why don't I just pack up and get out now?

Nellie really didn't have an answer for that last question, any more than she had answers for the others. Whatever inexplicable urge had driven her here was now holding her here. Whoever or whatever Finn Deverell was, her father had connected him to . . . the thing she needed to do here in Salem.

Whatever the hell that was.

Logic told her that, sooner or later, she would have to talk to Finn about all of it. Unless she discovered the answers for herself, on her own, which was unlikely when she didn't even know where to start looking because she didn't have a clue what it was all *about*.

In the distance, she heard the faint rumbles of thunder and noticed one or two surprised glances upward from others moving along the sidewalk, probably because the forecast had been for clear skies and no bad weather.

Damn. She was upset, so of *course* it was going to storm. And considering just how upset she was, unless she could calm herself down, it would be a doozy.

Luckily, she had a lot of experience at calming herself down.

Although the several crows sitting on lampposts and watching with bright eyes as she passed didn't help.

Nellie debated her next move as she strolled along, looking at the buildings they passed with the somewhat detached curiosity of a tourist. Ignoring the crows. She didn't pause at the entranceway to Cavendish Savings and Loan, though she noted it was doing brisk business on this Friday afternoon.

Not so surprising, as the only bank in town.

But there was a crow perched on each of the old-fashioned light brackets on either side of the bank's name.

She tried to keep her mind calm and quiet, used every trick she had learned over most of a lifetime and a few tricks learned more recently to not let anxiety and panic get the best of her. It only half worked, but half was enough to quiet the distant rumbles of thunder. For now, at least.

Not for the first time, she wondered with her forced calm what would happen if the "perfect storm" once theorized to her actually happened. A powerful electrical storm right overhead—and her feeling too angry or afraid or just otherwise upset to be able to control herself. Or the storm.

"I could hurt somebody, that's what you're saying."

"What I'm saying is that you could control a great deal of pure energy. Or not control it."

"It would be destructive."

"Very likely. With control, you could at least . . . aim at or away from a target."

"I won't be a weapon. For anyone or anything."

"That's the last thing I want. You must know that by now."

"I don't want to hurt anybody."

"None of us do. Aside from the emotional, moral, and legal consequences, the last thing we need is for the nonpsychic population to get the idea we're something to be afraid of. I mean seriously afraid of. And some would be afraid. Others would try to use what we can do to aid their own agendas."

"As weapons. That's more likely than—than something positive, isn't it?"

"Probably."

"No. I don't want to be a weapon."

"I know that. So wear the gloves. Practice the meditation techniques, the tricks to distract your mind, whenever you can. And try not to bottle up your emotions. Enough internal pressure can destroy even the . . . most durable container."

"That's all I am now? A container?"

"You're a human being with a rare ability. Learn how to live with it or allow it to destroy you."

"You're a comforting bastard, aren't you?"

"I've seen it happen both ways, Nellie. I've seen it destroy, and I've seen it produce remarkably strong people who accomplish many positive things. I'm betting you'll be one of the latter."

Nellie was no more sure he'd been right about that now than she had been then, some years before. But the alternative was something she didn't like to think about. At all.

Except . . . she was here. And if her father had been right, if Finn Deverell was right, then there was a threat to her here. A threat to her very life.

So what if she found herself face-to-face with that threat with no help at all? What if it came right down to survival? How would her "rare" ability manifest itself?

And would she be able to control it?

GRAYSON STARED AT the ad for longer than he wanted to admit, baffled by several things. For one, she had used the nickname he sometimes used with her, Red. Which she hated, she'd said, because it was no part of her name the way Gray was part of his.

It was part of her appearance, he had retorted, eyeing the very red hair that was only one of the attributes that made her so memorable.

Still, she hated the nickname and always called him on it. Usually in blistering terms. So why use it now?

But then he remembered who had left this ad directed, clearly, to him. Geneva. She was slippery and could be twisty as a barrelful of snakes, but she was a pro. She would have avoided using her own initials. She'd known he was coming, knew it was his habit to pick up a local newspaper as soon as he arrived and go through it front to back as part of familiarizing himself with the area and its people, and she'd known he would have arrived with virtually no information she may or may not have uncovered in her two weeks here.

He doubted she had expected trouble when she had last left the B and B—except that Geneva always expected trouble. And she had, obviously, already been focused on something she considered troublesome or worrying. So she'd placed this ad probably only the day before, or whatever day she'd left the B and B, knowing she would go out that night—last night or the night before—and scheduled it to run for several days around his expected arrival date. Just in case. Just in case she wasn't here to fill him in or even to point him in a direction he needed to start exploring.

Just in case.

Trying not to let his unfortunately educated and experienced imagination consider all the reasons why she probably hadn't returned to the B and B last night or today and may have been gone for two or three days for all he knew, he studied the ad more carefully.

This is Geneva. You know how she thinks. Professionally, at least. You know that. If she thought there was a chance she might not be able to tell you anything in person—for whatever reason—she wouldn't leave a note in her room or mail you a letter or any shit like that. But she'd leave a message where she knew you were likely to find it, and in that message she'd at least try to point you in the right direction.

Which meant that within this ad, which read rather like a teenage girl in a snit at her boyfriend, was a very specific message, likely only a few words.

It would have been easier to go to his room and find a pen and paper, and frown over the message in earnest and in private, but a nagging uneasiness kept him in his chair, focused on the ad but trying not to frown.

A message. So. Throw out the extraneous stuff, the stuff he knew or she'd expect him to know, the stuff she knew he wouldn't . . . think of her. Things he'd know she wouldn't have said, at least not in this way.

He stared at the ad, and though he'd never tried to use the spider senses quite like this before, he focused hard, pushed, thinking about a message Geneva would leave just for him.

For a moment, maybe two, the paper got fuzzy and the words blurred. A throb in his head told him he'd pay for this later, but he kept his gaze focused on the newspaper, on the ad.

And pushed. Maybe harder than he'd ever pushed before.

What are you trying to tell me, Red?

Nothing at first, just the message, an ad like all the others—

And then something changed. Words suddenly darkened, went bold, leaping out at him from the rest of the ad.

*GS, if you're looking for me so you can apologize, you must know I'm still mad at you. I'm not **a little girl gone missing**, you are not the boss of me, and you don't tell me what to do or where to go. Or who to see. I can **take care** of myself and I don't need you. I'm careful. **Stay away from me.** Red*

That was it. Her message.

He closed his eyes for a minute, one hand lifting to rub them and then the ache between them, trying to think. Wondering briefly if Bishop had any idea the spider senses could work like that. If not, he'd certainly want to know, to find out if they could work the same way for other agents.

Then Grayson concentrated on the message.

GS, you're looking for a little girl gone missing. Take care. Stay away from me. Red

She didn't want him looking for her—that was what the last part meant. Either because she didn't want the two of them to have any connection in the minds of the folks of Salem, or because . . . because she'd at least considered the possibility or probability that by the time he arrived she could be hip-deep in trouble.

She wanted him to start looking for a missing little girl, not one who had been abducted or otherwise obviously stolen, Amber Alerts issued, but simply one who was not where she was supposed to be—and never mind whatever was going on with Geneva.

Dammit.

"Headache?"

He looked up, startled, to see the innkeeper, Carol Payton, gazing at him with professional sympathy.

With hardly a pause, he said, "Borderline migraines, I'm afraid, that sometimes cross the border. One reason I came down off the Trail to take a break. They seem to be worse in winter. Something about the barometric pressure, I think the doc said."

"Probably the elevation too," she said, brisk but still with that professional note of sympathy in her voice. "Not that I want to lose a paying customer, but maybe you should spend your winters closer to sea level."

He managed a smile. "I hate the beach. Love the mountains. So . . . I suffer. A masochist, I guess. Anyway, I'm about to call my doc and ask him to send a prescription to a pharmacy here in Salem. He's done it before when I've been traveling. That and a few hours' sleep should knock it out."

"At least for today?"

"At least for today," he agreed ruefully. The fact that he really did actually suffer from annoyingly full-blown migraines that were almost always badly timed, never mind the "borderline" spider-sense-induced sort, lent his voice a sincerity he never had to fake.

"Well, good luck," she said. "We only have one pharmacy, by the way. Smith's Drugstore."

"Got it. Thanks, Ms. Payton."

She did not, as many innkeepers would have done, ask him to call her by her Christian name. Instead, she merely smiled with her usual professional courtesy and left the parlor to return to the front desk and whatever work awaited her there.

One of the neatly dressed waitresses came to silently top off his half-empty coffee cup, checked that he had sugar and milk, and then slipped away just as silently.

Grayson looked up to intercept a glance from Ms.

Payton, who smiled mechanically and returned to her paperwork.

So I'm being watched.

And fairly closely, at that.

Because all "outsiders" were watched?

Or was there a far less innocuous reason?

TEN

Grayson had offered Ms. Payton an excuse for returning to his room, so he did just that. He actually did call his doctor—a doctor who was not in the FBI but was a friend of Bishop's and treated quite a few of the psychics in the SCU, especially with their common headaches and occasional migraines and even blackouts—and requested that the prescription that sometimes helped his headaches be called in or faxed to the drugstore in Salem. His request was approved, but only after the doctor got on the phone himself and asked a few brief, familiar questions.

None of them could be sure, after all, if the psychic abilities they used might one day damage their brains. Or already had. So medical as well as psychological questions and frequent examinations were the rule rather than the exception within the SCU.

Grayson thought they might be the healthiest unit in

the entire FBI just due to Bishop's caution and the understandable curiosity of doctors.

Unless their brains shorted out one day, of course. Then being otherwise healthy wouldn't mean a whole hell of a lot.

"It's just the same old thing," he told the doctor. "I strained my eyes, and my head is pounding. It's not too bad now, but I'm in the mountains and I'd rather have the meds if I need them."

The doctor, who knew better than to ask too-specific questions on a line he had not been told was secure, said merely, "I'll fax in both, then. One you can take and still function normally during the day, and the other to help you sleep. We both know the migraines and even mild headaches get worse over time if you don't get enough sleep."

It was a familiar warning, and one Grayson had learned the hard way to listen to. "Yeah, okay, Doc. Thanks."

"Call if anything changes," the doctor ordered rather than requested, and hung up.

Grayson cradled the receiver of the landline phone in his room, wondering for an absent moment if the doctor would report to Bishop. It only took that moment to realize that of course he would. Medical ethics and privacy laws were one thing, but Bishop needed to be aware of the physical and mental condition of his agents, and sometimes direct communication just wasn't possible even if agents always understood what was going on with them physically and mentally. Which they as often as not didn't, especially when on a case and pushing themselves and their abilities to their limits. Bishop would have thought of that and arranged things accordingly.

Shrugging off that realization, Grayson got his almost empty backpack out of the closet in his room. All his clothing except what he'd been wearing had been sent to be cleaned as soon as he'd checked in, and it was already back. What hadn't been left neatly folded on his bed was now hanging neatly in his closet, which amused him briefly since the very casual and even rough clothing of a serious hiker looked odd on hangers.

He got his laptop out of its zippered compartment of the backpack, along with various cords and cables and what was obviously a solar charger—which would have been his only alternate power source on the Trail everywhere except at periodic rest stops set up for hikers. And even then the solar charger could be used only sporadically, given weather and forest cover.

He carried everything to the compact desk in his small sitting room and got the equipment connected, plugged in, and booted up.

He debated silently for some minutes before using the Wi-Fi password for the B and B. His laptop, which appeared innocent and ordinary, had beneath its very deceptive surface enough firewalls and other layers of security to impress someone with top DOJ clearance. And it would take someone with that level of expertise to even realize the security existed.

It would take all the skills of a very, *very* gifted hacker to get through that security.

Grayson was one of the lucky team members of the SCU; he could use electronics, even wear a watch, without either draining them of power or shorting everything out.

Geneva could stop a clock by standing too close to it, and if she even touched a laptop or tablet, it simply died. Smart watches refused to even light up long enough for her to get them buckled around her wrist, and cell phones gave up and died almost as quickly. Within seconds. Hotel keycards were one of the banes of her existence, since she had to have them remagnetized every single time she wanted back in her room (or pick the lock if she was being slippery). She had also been known to blow out lightbulbs in a room if she got really pissed or otherwise upset.

And Grayson had no idea why their abilities created such different reactions in them. Technically, they were both receivers; he picked up emotions and she picked up thoughts. The fact that she had touched his mind more than once . . . well, that was something different, not so much a reaching out as . . .

He decided not to even finish that thought.

The point was that although Geneva had brought a drained cell phone, a tablet, and a very nice laptop with her (the latter two both plugged in, in her room, charging fairly normally if she had stayed the hell away from them), it was because to not have those now-common devices in her possession would have seemed weird indeed to anyone even casually interested in her presence here. But all were useless for communication as far as she was concerned. And she hadn't trusted the landline in her room here, for whatever reason.

Some kind of trouble. Bound to be. So—

Again, he stopped himself from following a path of thought. He couldn't think about Geneva right now.

GS, you're looking for a little girl gone missing. Take care. Stay away from me. Red

He rubbed his eyes with both hands briefly, telling himself he could stand the headache for a bit longer, that he could wait to go collect the prescriptions that would help.

He had to start looking for a missing little girl. And when children were missing, there was no time to waste. The statistics on the life spans of children in unfriendly hands were dark indeed.

Today's weekend edition of the local daily newspaper he'd been reading earlier, the *Salem Chronicle*, had not contained a single article about anybody missing, far less a child, but that didn't stop him from using his laptop to tap into a data bank of state newspapers.

Only to discover that the *Salem Chronicle* did not keep back or even current issues online. Anywhere. And the newspaper did not publish an online edition.

Shit. Microfilm?

There had to be a newspaper "morgue" somewhere, after all. Newspapers kept some kind of electronic copies of their publications because the newspapers themselves were too fragile to trust their continued existence into posterity, and the information they contained was always valuable sooner or later for historical research. So Grayson was willing to bet that the entire historical record of the *Chronicle* was on microfilm either in the town library—or some storage room in the newspaper's own offices.

Either way, whatever information the *Chronicle* might have published was out of Grayson's reach, at least for now. Because he couldn't think of a single damned good reason why a weary hiker just stopping in for a little rest and warmth would be at all interested in back issues of the local newspaper.

"YOU'RE SURE?" DUNCAN asked his lieutenant in the militia. He was sure himself but wanted confirmation.

"It's her, all right. Not a dark Cavendish like most here; looks just like that picture you showed me of her mother. She's using an alias. Reed."

"Her mother's maiden name." Duncan shook off yet another nagging question about what, if anything, Nellie had inherited from her mother. "How long is she booked into Hales?"

"Two weeks, with the possibility of an extended stay." Expressionlessly, Aaron Cavendish, a cousin of Duncan's, added, "She has a dog. A Pit, probably ninety pounds or better. I'm betting he'd go for the throat of anyone threatening her. So far, he hasn't left her side."

Duncan frowned. He hadn't counted on a dog. Not

that it mattered; dogs could be dealt with, if necessary. In the meantime, he had his innocent, and the moon would be full on Sunday. Two days, and he'd have the power he needed to confront his niece and take whatever Talent she possessed, just as he'd taken her father's.

"I want her watched," he said calmly. "Not obviously. She'll have the usual . . . escort . . . but I want you or those you trust to watch her as well. I want to know where she goes, who she talks to—"

"She's already talked to Finn. The sidewalk tables at the café."

Duncan frowned. "A friendly conversation?"

"I'd say not. Whatever he was trying to sell, she wasn't buying. Walked away from him with her dog and didn't look back."

How far would Finn go to interfere? Duncan wasn't sure. He'd never been able to read the boy. All he could be certain of was that his loyalists in the militia outnumbered Finn's. And that the full moon was only two days away.

"All right. Don't worry about Finn for now, but have your man standing ready in case we need Finn distracted from the girl. Easy enough to cause problems at a newspaper office, I should think."

"Yes, sir."

Duncan nodded a dismissal and turned back to the big desk in his study. He pondered the problem of Finn for a few minutes, considering how to best turn Nellie away from any advice or information that young man might offer. When the solution came to him, he could only smile at its simplicity.

He picked up his phone to call the Dreamer.

FACED WITH NO access to back editions of Salem's newspaper without calling far too much attention to himself, Grayson thought briefly, then tapped in a command for his system to check all newspapers in the Southeast, looking for articles about little girls gone missing, last seen within a five-hundred-mile radius of Salem. He would have preferred a narrower search area, but he wanted to get as many decent-sized newspapers as he could, and that meant at least a couple of the nearest cities.

Which were not close.

Even as good as his system was, it took a few minutes, and he spent those minutes staring into space and wondering why the newspaper—or someone else—had decided against making their information available online. It was such a common practice today, even in small towns. In fact, most newspapers these days published an electronic version, often daily, because it was cheaper and because "news" was a constant stream of information rather than specific broadcasts on some kind of predictable cycle as it had been in the old days; so many people got their news, virtually as it happened, via their phones or tablets. So why, at least as far as local news went, was that different in Salem?

There was probably a good explanation, but Grayson couldn't think of one offhand. It wasn't as if this were a town left behind by technology. They had satellite TV, Wi-Fi, cell towers. Maybe the Wi-Fi was a bit unstable, but that was common in mountainous areas. And the whole town was powered by solar, for Christ's sake.

He opened a second window on his laptop while the search program worked busily in the background, and discovered quickly that he could access the usual social media platforms. He found the names of the five families among Facebook pages and connected at least a few to people actually living here in Salem, though it looked to be something only the younger generations used, and for the usual self-centered, overly dramatic, far-too-personal selfies, other photos, and musings or rants about their lives.

As far as he could tell, very few people beyond high school age even had a Facebook page, Instagram, or a Twitter account.

Well. Not so unusual, that. His own mother still didn't trust cell phones.

Not so unusual in his experience that it was mostly the kids who really used Instagram and Twitter, Snapchat, and most of the rest of the social media platforms. Apparently kids, at any rate. It wasn't something he could be absolutely certain of, because so many people used screen names or other pseudonyms, and because too many hid behind alternate identities.

For both good and bad reasons.

He could set his system to begin the slow crawl through social media looking for specific keywords, just as he was searching newspaper archives for those same keywords, but even narrowing those down as far as he was able, what he expected was a boatload of information that would take forever to wade through. Social media was just too damned vast and couldn't really be accurately narrowed as to actual physical areas covered because of all those pseudonyms and false identities, which often included "adopted" hometowns or cities. Everywhere.

Maybe a DOJ analyst or six with a monster mainframe and top clearance to dig into the code of the actual platforms could at least weed out a boatload of extraneous information. Maybe the Bureau could. But those avenues were closed to him, because he was here quietly and because there was no "official" investigation going on in or around Salem.

Yet, at least.

Before he could begin to swear out loud about that, a quiet beep informed him that his search program had finished combing through those newspapers within his search parameters that *were* archived online or in databases to which he had access.

All the major newspapers within five hundred miles, and at least a dozen more from small cities and small towns. He'd had to make more than a few assumptions as to what he was searching *for*, of course, because he had so little to work with. A "little girl" could have been any age below, he was guessing, thirteen, so he had used that as an arbitrary marker. Because Geneva had used the phrase "gone missing," he was assuming she knew or believed she knew it hadn't been a parental abduction or runaway, that it hadn't been traffickers—and that whether it had even been reported was a large question mark. A little girl had disappeared, reasons unknown. Means unknown. He was assuming it had happened recently, perhaps even since Geneva herself had arrived in Salem, but he was uncertain enough of that to add a couple of weeks and set an arbitrary time limit of a month. Geneva also, clearly, had seen or picked up nothing to lead her to believe the little girl was dead.

Just missing.

He was reasonably sure she had picked up most of what information she had telepathically; her cover was as a professional photographer putting together shots mostly of the gorgeous scenery for a coffee table "travel" book on the Southern Appalachians. And that cover gave Geneva every reason to wander around pretty much to her heart's content as long as she had that very professional camera—or two—hanging around her neck. Two cameras, in their cases, were in her room, which told him she had very likely slipped out late at night, which was a habit of hers on a case.

That was not a cheerful thought.

He was certain she'd taken one or both with her while out during the day, snapping more shots of pretty scenery to add to those already on rolls of exposed film and printed out, neatly stacked in case anybody snooped. And while she was wandering around, she could pick up whatever she was able to telepathically. Hence her knowledge of a missing girl.

Grayson stared at the grim number his search had revealed, drew a deep breath, and let it out slowly.

Twenty-eight.

Twenty-eight girls thirteen or younger had gone missing during the last thirty days, last seen somewhere within a five-hundred-mile radius of Salem.

GRAYSON DIDN'T TRUST a video transmission even from his very secure laptop, but Bishop had long ago set up a very, very secure means of receiving from agents in tricky situations transmissions that were almost like cell texts or e-mails but were encoded and protected at both ends. Though even that was limited to those of his agents who could use electronics—or had someone with them they could trust to do so.

With no idea of where the unit chief might be or what sort of situation he might be involved in, Grayson merely sent through a request for a real-time discussion and asked when Bishop would be available.

And wasn't really surprised when an affirmative response came through in less than five minutes. He barely had time to consider what he most needed to communicate before, in the dark window on his laptop's screen, white letters appeared. Bishop was a fast and easy typist. So was Grayson. And neither of them was prone to substitute letters for words or otherwise use text or Internet "shorthand."

What's up, Gray?

Trouble. Geneva's missing, possibly for as long as two or three days. Nobody here seems concerned, maybe because I'm pretty sure she left at night, slipped out late to avoid being seen leaving.

Because?

Her cameras are still in her room, and since they're part of her cover, she'd have them with her during the day.

Okay, makes sense. And?

Left me a coded note in the local newspaper; I worked out it meant I was to look for a little girl gone missing, but NOT to look for Gen. I don't like it, Bishop. I need to find Gen. And since the newspaper does not archive or publish online, and there was nothing in today's paper about a missing kid, I had to search the databases for five hundred miles around Salem. 28 girls under the age of 13 currently reported as missing, or at least were when I checked earlier.

There was a brief pause, and then Bishop responded with a question.

With all the static in the area we both know you should be cautious, but . . . have you reached out?

I let my walls down a little in case Gen reached out. Got a pounding headache and a lot of emotional baggage from the general area, but nothing from Geneva.

What kind of emotional baggage? The usual?

Yeah. Job troubles, money troubles, relationship troubles, resentments. A happy bride-to-be, a worried father-to-be, a preacher concerned he's losing his flock.

Wait. That last. Did you focus on the preacher?

No. I was concentrating on Gen, so only got the gist from everybody else. Why?

A hunch.

Grayson knew very well that Bishop's "hunches" were always more than that, but he was in no mood to probe. He just wanted to find Geneva, and then find a missing little girl who no one in Salem seemed to be missing.

You think focusing on the preacher could lead me to Gen?

I think it could lead you in the right direction. But wait until after dark.

Why?

You know why. With your cover, openly searching any part of the area in or around Salem will draw the wrong kind of attention. It could also connect the two of you. And if Geneva warned you not to look for her, that's probably what she was worried about.

Grayson didn't want to agree with that, but he did, because that's what he believed would have been uppermost in her mind. There was no obvious connection between the two of them, and until he found out what she knew, that's the way it needed to stay.

Okay, okay. It'll be dark in a few hours, maybe sooner. I'll go out at least an hour after that, a bit longer if people here haven't settled in for the night. And do my best to focus on the preacher. What about the missing girls?

I'll get some of our people looking deeper into the records. Geneva found enough to convince her the child was missing. We have to find the same information. Though if she discovered it telepathically, there may not have been an official report. Which means you're still her best bet—to find her and information about the missing girl.

He didn't have to add that there was always the chance Geneva would be in no shape to tell them anything. He didn't have to add that nugget because Grayson's imagination was busy working overtime all by itself.

He thought again that it was a curse to have a vivid

and active imagination. A bitter curse to have an educated and experienced imagination.

Don't count her out just yet.

Bishop might have been reading his agent's mind
from a considerable distance, something relatively new
according to the agents who had been with him longest.
But with the static sensed by their psychics outside the
area, and his own virtually-always-faint empathic sense
of his boss that was normal no longer present, Grayson
doubted it was anything so cut-and-dried as an actual
telepathic connection. Maybe it was simply that Bishop
knew his agents very, very well. In any case, Grayson
didn't question that. He just grasped for reassurance.

We both know she's stubborn as hell. If somebody's been
trying to get information out of her—

I doubt that's why she was taken.

Grayson counted to ten silently.

Which means you know why she was taken. And that she's
alive?

Mad as hell, probably, Bishop answered laconically.

Grayson gave up counting. But for that moment, he
really, *really*, really wanted to know whether the unit
chief's formidable telepathic abilities had mined that
nugget of information somehow, static or no static, or if
he'd gained it in some other way.

Bishop—

Follow your instincts, Gray. The first thing you have to do
is find her. And you need to be cautious. If she's being held
incommunicado it's because they suspect she might find—or

already has found—something they want to keep hidden, or else they're afraid she may get in their way. Or both.

He didn't, Grayson noted, define *them*.

You need to get her out of their hands before she poses a greater threat to them. Find out what she knows. After that, it might be best if you two . . . rediscover an old relationship.

Grayson had been afraid his boss was going to say that.

Why didn't you just send us in as a team, dammit?

This way is better. Follow your instincts, Gray. Find Geneva, whatever it takes. We'll look for the missing girl.

Copy. I'll be back in touch when I know something.

In the meantime, go get the meds for your migraines. And take them.

Grayson didn't even ask.

Copy. I'll do that before it gets dark.

Watch your back. Bishop out.

No more white words appeared on the screen. But Grayson stared at the ones he was fairly certain his boss had meant quite literally. He was to find Geneva.

Whatever it took.

ELEVEN

"Does she know anything?"

"No more than the others did."

"Sure about that? She's using fake ID. None of the others did that."

"The others were descended through the female lines and didn't have the family names. She was born a Cavendish."

"So maybe she was warned being a Cavendish might not be such a good thing to be here."

"Maybe she was. Maybe she's just cautious. Her father's been gone more than ten years, and there's nobody else. Who would have warned her? Who could have?"

"I don't know, and that's what's making me nervous."

"Look, she's acting like a normal tourist. She had lunch at the café and now she's walking her dog around town; that's all."

"And that's another thing I don't like. That dog. One look, and you know he'd throw himself between her and any threat. If she's the one he's been searching for, you know what he'll say. And if she isn't the one, well, same thing. He isn't big on pets, never mind threats. So we'll have to take care of the dog too."

"Don't borrow trouble. We don't know anything yet. We have time to find out what we do need to know."

"It's barely a week until her birthday. That's how much time we have."

"It's enough."

"Is it? What about the woman out at the house? You planning to keep her alive and well another week?"

"She's an innocent."

"Oh, hell, one look and you know she's hardly that."

"You know what I mean. She's innocent in this. Not a part of Salem, far less of the Five."

"We don't know what she is. That's the problem."

"She's a professional photographer here on a job. You saw the e-mails on her laptop just like I did; you saw the darkroom she's rigged in her suite, and all the supplies and pictures. She has an editor and an agent in New York, both of them check out as legit, and both of them know where she is and what she's doing here. She makes money for both of them. You really want to get rid of her and then deal with all the questions *somebody* is going to start asking when their meal ticket vanishes into thin air?"

"Well, I sure as hell don't want to just turn her loose in a week like nothing happened. We found her out in the woods, for one thing, near the house. In the middle of the night. And she's been kept prisoner. How're we gonna explain that?"

"There are things we can do; you know that. So she won't remember anything we don't want her to."

"Forbidden things."

"For some. Not for all. And in . . . extreme circumstances, extreme measures can be justified."

"You think he'll agree with that?"

"He doesn't have to know about it. The last thing he needs is too much attention of the wrong sort, especially now. When it's all said and done, he'll agree with that."

"Yeah, but it's not something he can do—and he won't trust either one of us to do it. He'll have to be sure."

"He will be."

"If you say so."

"I do. Don't worry about the woman. We'll take care of it so she isn't a problem."

"*You'll* take care of it, Finn. Her. Because she's your mess. You're the one who decided to keep her alive."

"Yes," Finn said. "I did."

GENEVA DECIDED SHE was being an idiot. And weak, like some stupid fairy-tale princess bemoaning her fate and longing in her tower for a prince to come and rescue her.

Screw that.

Geneva had lived long enough and seen enough to know that even the best of men weren't princes, and any woman with a grain of sense learned to take care of herself and not count on anyone else—even the best of men—to come rushing to her rescue.

No matter what kind of trouble she was in.

So. Here she was. And she would damned well get herself out of this prison, this *mess*, somehow.

Common sense told her that if anything was going to change here, she'd have to change it. And soon, because *if* they intended to keep feeding her—and that was a big, big *if*—then when the food ran out somebody was bound to come with more supplies. Someone she was reasonably sure would want her unconscious—by some means, possibly that vent in the ceiling—before entering her prison.

And even though she had recognized that first voice when they'd grabbed her, so he wouldn't be concerned she knew who he was, she doubted he'd pop in for conversation while bringing more food and water, even if he did intend to keep her alive.

She hadn't been able to read him, either, so she had no idea at all *why* he was keeping her alive. She had no doubt it had been his decision, because she was reasonably sure he was high up in all this—whatever this was. High up, at least, among the men chosen to keep law and order in Salem.

Their idea of it, at any rate.

Any way she looked at it, if she was going to get herself out of this mess, time was running out.

"My kingdom to be telekinetic for just five minutes," she muttered, startling herself when she heard her own voice and realized she hadn't said anything out loud in quite a while.

The creative cursing had run its course that first day.

Geneva stood there for a moment, then lit four of the big pillar candles and placed one about a foot in from each of the four corners of her prison. The remaining fifth one was lit as well, and went on the floor in the center of the room. Then she faced each wall for a slow, thorough study, moving slightly to make sure the candle nearest her wasn't casting her shadow. She slowly studied—really for the first time—her prison in its entirety.

And that was when she saw a possible way out.

IT WAS NEVER the same dream—and yet it was. The same terror and shame and confusion. The same overwhelming sense that this wasn't *her*, that she was watching in horror someone else do these inexplicable, sickening, unspeakable things while somehow wearing her body.

It was always in the woods, dense woods like those that surrounded this odd little town. There was always a big fire, a bonfire, with shadowy, hooded figures she could never quite make out throwing more branches and handfuls of other things she couldn't identify onto the fire to keep it burning high and hot.

She could never tell if it was a mist or smoke that made

it difficult for her to see clearly, but she never could. The brightness of the bonfire, the shifting human shapes of shadows. Smoke or mist swirling, distorting everything.

There was always chanting. Words she could never make out, or maybe a language she didn't know. Or maybe she just didn't want to understand what they were saying, because something inside her, inside the sane her, didn't want to understand.

They were all around her, moving, perhaps dancing in some kind of primitive rhythm as they chanted. In the shadows mostly but occasionally a flicker of the bonfire would catch the gleam of eyes or the maw of an open mouth chanting, or a hand raised briefly. Men and women, she knew that much.

Chanting . . . something. Slowly at first, softly. Then louder. Faster. Frenzied.

And then there was her. As if she stood back and watched, she could see herself. Or someone that appeared to be her, which was what she desperately hoped was the truth. Not her. Just someone who looked like her. Dressed in some filmy white dress with layers and bits that fluttered as she danced and whirled. Barefoot, her hair loose and whipping about. Layered or not, the dress was nearly transparent, more obviously so when the layers and bits lifted and shifted with her movements, and it was utterly clear she was naked underneath it.

Naked. Aroused.

It made her want to turn away, to writhe in shame and disgust. Because she, that other *her*, that stranger, was

wild, pagan, and dancing with total abandon growing
more frenzied as the chanting grew more frenzied.

Out of control.

A shadowy partner danced with her near the bonfire,
a partner who was clearly male and clearly aroused as
well, because he was naked.

She couldn't see his face because he was wearing some
kind of mask, but the firelight glinted off sweat-slick
muscled flesh as he danced with a grace that was riveting.

That was what Nellie *hated*, that she couldn't look
away, couldn't turn away and run from this. She stood
frozen, staring, watching herself—watching that *stranger*
that looked like her—behave in a way she never had,
never *could*, in some kind of ceremony or ritual or, hell,
just insanity, and what she felt even over the disgust and
shame and bewilderment was this awful certainty of . . .
inevitability.

It wasn't a dream. Wasn't a nightmare. It was something else.

It was something real.

And it terrified her.

The chanting grew louder, the shadows in the background moved with more frenzy, she moved with more
frenzy, and then she started taking off the filmy white
dress, the sheer layers of it falling away from her, her
sweating face twisted in an expression of lust, and the
naked man pulled off his mask, was reaching for her, his
hands grasping—

That was when Nellie wrenched herself from the

nightmare and woke with a cry, sitting up in bed, Leo whining anxiously beside her.

THE DREAMER STIRRED, then sat up slowly. His face was a little pale, and he looked drained.

"Well?" Duncan demanded.

"She pulled herself out of it before the end. Jesus, that hurt like hell. I feel like I have a concussion."

Duncan waved the complaint aside. "When did she pull free? Did she see him? Know him?"

The Dreamer grinned wearily. "Oh, yeah. She saw him. And she knew it was Finn."

NELLIE TOUCHED HER dog reassuringly and wasted no time in leaning over to turn on the lamp on her nightstand. The big bed was as comfortable as she'd imagined it would be, but it had not been able to ward off the nightmare.

And it had come swiftly this time. She'd gone to bed early, and the clock on the nightstand told her it wasn't yet midnight.

She plumped her pillows behind her and leaned back, absently petting Leo as he lay back down near her hip. She wasn't nearly ready to go back to sleep, especially when she heard the faint rumble of thunder in the distance.

Meditation. Right.

She tried some of that, concentrating on remaining

calm, on distracting her thoughts, directing them to memorized lines of poetry, choosing the fun nonsense of Lewis Carroll over anything more serious or darker she had also memorized for occasions like this. Just reciting the verses in her head in no particular order, refusing to allow the nightmare to upset her again. Even though . . .

Calm. She had to be calm before anything else.

It took about ten minutes according to the clock, but when she finally opened her eyes again, she couldn't hear thunder.

"Maybe it works after all," she said to her dog, still working to keep her voice steady. "After a fashion, at least." She hadn't really had to put it to a serious test until all . . . this . . . had started.

Especially the nightmare. But as bad as it had been before, tonight had been especially awful. More than shame and humiliation and the feeling of not being in control of herself, tonight . . .

A rumble of thunder made her start, and she closed her eyes again, trying not to remember Finn's sweating, lusting face as he'd reached out for her, unmasked for the first time.

But what did it all *mean*? Everything in her rebelled at the very idea of being involved in anything portrayed in her dream. No matter what kind of ritual she had witnessed, it was nothing that roused in her anything except revulsion.

Which was a relief that cut deeply into her, though she wasn't exactly sure why.

Pushing that question aside, she replayed, as calmly as

she could, the meeting and conversation with Finn. She'd already done that numerous times, and never reached any conclusion about whether she could or should trust him.

Tonight, after the nightmare, she felt a revulsion not only toward her own behavior but toward *him*. But even as that memory fought its way back to the surface of her thoughts, even as thunder rumbled again, she was conscious of the strangest sensation inside her mind.

Like a door . . . opening. She couldn't see anything, but that's how it felt. An open door . . . and a quiet, reassuring whisper.

They've put this nightmare into your mind, my daughter. It isn't real. They mean to frighten you, to drive you away before you do what you came here to do.

It wasn't her father's voice, Nellie realized dimly.

Then . . . her mother?

Warmth. Love.

I've always been nearby, waiting. Knowing that one day you would come back here. I'm with you now. And when the time comes, I will help you.

"Help me?" she heard herself murmur.

To do what you must. To claim what was always yours. To use that within you to stop the evil here.

"But I don't know—"

You will. Listen to your heart, your instincts. They will tell you who to trust. And those you trust will help you when the time comes, just as I will.

"Mother—"

No more nightmares, my daughter. Amusement like

quicksilver in her mind. *But the meditation techniques . . . those you must use to hold off the storm. Until you need it.*

Nellie opened her mouth to ask something else but felt that door in her mind softly close. She knew somehow that it wasn't locked, and that the promised help would come.

She still felt confusion, but it was less now, fainter. An odd new sensation welled up inside her as she wondered if she had come back to Salem, really, for that. To know her mother.

Thunder rumbled.

Nellie heard it, understanding somehow that this time the storm was coming not because she was upset but because something in her called to it.

Strange thought.

Without thinking about that again, she slipped into the meditation techniques she'd been taught, heard her breathing slow, her heartbeat steady, concentrating on holding steadily inside her what wanted, waited, to escape.

GENEVA HAD TO stand on the lidded bucket, left obviously for sanitary purposes since there had been a roll of toilet tissue sitting on its lid, and it was not exactly a steady place to stand. But she moved it several times to get it in just the right place, where it seemed as stable as possible, then climbed up and concentrated on balance. She used one hand to steady herself as much as possible while the other held the single tool they had not found when they had searched her.

It was a very thin, very flexible strip of metal, easily and comfortably hidden between the insole and outsole of her shoes—and she had one for every pair of shoes and boots she owned, hiking boots included. Easily hidden and very easily overlooked—even during a thorough search.

But its uses were limited. It was stronger than it had any right to be, but it was small, slender. The sharpest end was too flexible to use as a sturdy digging tool— though Geneva knew from experience it could offer a nasty cut to an enemy, not fatal except at the carotid artery in the throat, but a deterrent for certain. It could be a lockpick—but there was no lock visible on this side of the door. Nor was there a handle, which made her balancing act on the bucket even trickier.

Still, Geneva gritted her teeth, balanced herself as best she could on the bucket, and carefully studied what all of the candles burning together had shown her.

That the door was so well fitted there was barely a seam showing its outline, she knew. But with her prison lit as much as possible by five candles placed carefully, she could now see, on the left-hand side opposite the hinges where normally there would have been a handle of some kind, a faint—very faint—glint of metal in the seam.

It was the latch mechanism: The piece of metal that originated in the door was embedded there but moved in and out of the doorframe when a handle or knob was turned. Normally there was at least a plate of metal on both sides of the door to hold the handle or knob and provide a secure seating for the latch, but on this door there was no sign of a metal plate.

But doors worked a certain way, and Geneva had to believe this one was no exception. There had to be some sort of metal anchor on the other side of the door, perhaps a plate bolted securely into only one side. That had to hold the latch in place, and it was what was holding the door securely closed, clearly designed to open only from one side. No sign of an additional dead bolt, but the worry she didn't want to think about was that they might have barred the other side in a much simpler way—by using a stout wooden or metal bar, its brackets also seated into the door itself, since by the way the hinges were placed, this door opened inwardly.

If there was a bar, seated in such a way . . . that was something not even someone as expert a lock picker as herself could force with her little tool. But if it was only a normal locking mechanism . . .

She wouldn't know until she tried.

She held her breath as she slowly forced the thin edge of her slender little tool into the seam where she could—barely—see the latch. She moved the tool carefully, sliding it up and down the approximately three-inch latch, close to the doorframe, hoping with everything inside her that on her side was a curved edge of the latch that might be maneuvered out of the frame and into the door. It was basically the way some people were able to use credit cards to unlock a door without a key.

Using a delicate, skilled touch mastered over years of

practice in and out of the field, Geneva eased her tool between the frame and the latch halfway up its length, then carefully maneuvered the sharp edge until it slipped between metal and wood.

She paused, drew a breath, eased in another fraction of an inch, and then began to exert careful pressure to force the latch back into the thick wood of the door.

She wasn't really afraid of the tool snapping off, but it had occurred to her that she had no real way of grasping the wooden door and pulling it toward her even if she managed to ease the latch free.

But . . . the latch was moving, slowly easing back into the door.

Still fighting to keep her balance on the bucket, Geneva managed somehow to get her free hand against the seam of the door and, still holding the tool carefully against the latch, struggled with as little movement as possible to wedge her short nails into that murderously narrow crack. For the first time in her life, she wished she had long, elegant nails as sharp and strong as claws.

But at least her short nails were strong, and she did her best to force them to dig into the wood just inside the seam—and pulled.

Several things happened then. The door came toward her with astonishing ease, she lost her balance on the treacherous bucket, and she found herself lying on her back, the breath knocked out of her, on the cold, hard floor of her prison, having barely missed the candle burning in the center of the room, staring dazedly up at the door holding steadily half-open.

Trying to catch her breath and not start coughing in case there was a silent guard somewhere near enough to hear, Geneva managed to scramble up, right the over-turned bucket before it could lose its unpleasant contents, and replace it so she could use it as a step. She kept hold of her wonderful little tool with one hand, held the door with the other, and climbed back onto the bucket so she could see out of her prison.

Despite the utter silence and her conviction that she was alone in this place, she half expected to see a guard outside, eerily silent, one she simply hadn't been able to read telepathically, or another locked door, or some kind of alarm, or—or *something* designed to dash her hopes of escape.

But what she looked out onto was a short hallway, and beyond it, dimly lit, was what she thought was a kitchen. Straining to listen, she didn't hear a sound.

Without a backward look at her prison, leaving the pillar candles burning in all four corners and one in the middle, she hoisted herself up and through the doorway, being as quiet as possible. There *was* a doorknob on this side, and she closed the door, turning the knob so that the latch eased back into its place without even a click.

It struck her as a weird sort of prison door, not exactly barred or even locked, merely closed in such a way that anyone inside would—at least in theory—find it impossible to open.

Still, Geneva had the wary feeling that her escape had been too easy. She called on every extra sense she possessed to reach out beyond herself, guardedly exploring in every mental way she could even as her eyes searched for indications of alarms or surveillance. Still holding the precious tool that could also, in trained and skilled hands, be a lethal weapon, she moved forward silently and cautiously to physically explore the house.

TWELVE

Grayson didn't notice the crows until he was, perhaps, a mile from the B and B—and already out in the middle of nowhere. It had taken him nearly an hour to get this far because, just on the possibility he was being observed, even at night—maybe especially at night—he'd been careful not to walk with the purpose of someone searching but rather like an experienced hiker too restless to be still for long simply exploring his surroundings, pausing now and then as if to note landmarks even in the dark. Which he was doing, since this was unfamiliar territory.

Besides which, he was basically heading straight up a mountain, so the hike wasn't an easy one despite the zigzag of his path, especially in the dark, and the changes in direction and pauses to rest as he gazed around with apparent idleness were welcome.

As soon as he'd gone some little distance from the

B and B, he had done as Bishop suggested—or ordered, in so many words—and had dropped his shields completely. Even though his skin had been tingling almost beneath the level of his awareness the whole time he'd been in Salem, what he felt now was stronger. And for the first time he could remember, there was a faint interference—static was as good a word as any other, he thought—between his seeking and those individuals he could read. There were more of them than he'd expected, but the static was something that forced him to concentrate harder than was normal for him in order to get the emotions clearly.

That bothered him, not least because experience had taught them all to be cautious in touching the minds and emotions of others, especially during an investigation.

So he kept up what guards he could while still using his empathic sense, something that was difficult but not impossible. It was both lucky and unlucky that he'd waited until fairly late, when most people tended to be quietly settling in for the evening, especially on another cold, cold night.

So what he had mostly gotten was the sense of a few sleepy discussions, one rather fierce marital argument he had hastily shied away from when it became obvious makeup sex was on the menu, and most people relaxed and watching TV, reading, or otherwise getting ready for bed and sleep.

He had concentrated on the preacher first, trying to narrow his focus and find, sense, that worry and frustration. But it was gone, beyond his reach. At least for now.

But he had felt Geneva almost the instant he stopped focusing on the preacher. Mad as hell, just as Bishop had predicted. Frustrated, baffled—and more than a little scared.

He was fairly sure he had never before felt fear in Geneva, which had quickened his steps once he'd settled on the right general direction. North—she was north of where he stood. Away from town, which he was glad of. The farther he hiked, the fainter grew the emotional baggage he'd picked up from the B and B and surrounding homes.

But Geneva was clear in his mind, her frustration the strongest. The fear came and went, along with spurts of temper, with which he was familiar, and with those emotions a sense of . . . being alone. Being very, very alone. And she did not like it.

Then he felt something else from her, first a sense of urgency, then utter concentration, which very quickly severed any clear connection he had to her emotions. She had drawn them inward and held them under an iron grip because she needed . . . her senses. Because she couldn't allow her emotions to color what she sensed.

For the first time, he wondered if that was why he had so seldom been able to sense her emotions when they had been partners. Not because she kept them deliberately shielded from him—him in particular, which is what he'd often believed—but because strictly controlling her emotions inwardly was part of the process she used to tap her telepathy and other senses.

He was pondering that very surprising new information when he became aware of the crows. Three of them, silent, on the low winter-bare branch of a tree about twenty feet to his right.

Grayson knew one rather extraordinary telepath who could communicate easily with her canine partner, and he knew of at least one empath who picked up on the emotions of animals as well as people, though those emotions were so alien to the way humans felt that the experiences had been described to him as "damned disconcerting" rather than helpful.

Until this moment, Grayson had never picked up any sense of emotions from an animal. But those crows . . . He realized he had stopped dead and was staring at them, clearly visible even though the woods and their own coal black color should have made seeing them difficult.

But he saw them.

And they were . . . guarding?

With his shields down, that's what he felt in them, a sense of . . . responsibility. Duty. They were guarding. No . . . keeping watch.

For a moment he had the urge to look around him frantically, because what he felt from the crows underneath the duty was something very deep and very dark, something threatening. It was their fearful knowledge of . . . master. One who commanded them. And that was a very eerie thought, especially since he didn't think they were commanded because someone had trained them.

This was something else, something very different and, even in this cold, cold place, chilling. But even as he felt that, he also felt that tonight, for whatever reason, they were alone out here.

Just keeping watch.

He wondered, then, what they would do if whatever they watched presented some kind of threat. Would they attack? Crows were carrion birds, he thought, but that wasn't to say they wouldn't be willing to tackle living prey for the right reason.

Sly amusement.

Okay, now, that *was* disconcerting.

He hesitated for only a moment, then turned his head, having to concentrate to break that very much damned disconcerting experience of too much knowledge in bird heads, never mind the sly amusement, and focus once again on Geneva. He was inordinately relieved when he picked up her emotions quickly and easily.

Ah. She no longer kept an iron control on her emotions because it wasn't necessary. Because . . . because her senses had told her there was no threat. She wasn't angry or frustrated anymore—though she was still very aware of being alone. She was . . .

What was she doing?

Searching?

He thought she had somehow gotten free of that place that had made her angry and frustrated, that had made her afraid. And, being Geneva, instead of getting her ass away from there and as far from trouble as possible, she was stealing the time and risking more danger so she could take a really good look at her surroundings.

Dammit.

He didn't look back at the crows as he pushed on, aware that they remained where they were, silently watching him continue on without them.

He really didn't want to find out if they were still amused by him for their own unknowable bird reasons.

Still, he went cautiously, calling on all the woodcraft he'd learned over an adventurous lifetime to move silently over long-fallen leaves that the winter cold had made crisp again. It was slow going even when he called on his spider senses to see and hear far beyond his normal range, and he didn't even think, this time, that the migraine undoubtedly lurking once he was done was going to be a real wall banger.

He held on to the slender thread that was his empathic awareness of Geneva, of where she was still searching—and with a growing puzzlement. He couldn't tell what she had expected to find, but whatever she did find baffled her.

Something else he'd really never felt in her.

His sense of distance, well honed, told him that even though he kept moving, his seeming rambling meant he had changed directions so many times that he was still little more than a mile from the B and B, which meant he wasn't very far from town, and yet the woods were dense and silent.

So dense, in fact, that even with all his spider senses at

full wattage, he didn't see the house until he rounded one very large tree and found himself in a clearing that wasn't really a yard.

But there was a house, looking absurdly normal, even to a pot of geraniums beside the front door. And inside, a single light was moving.

Geneva was inside—he knew that; he was also virtually certain there was no one else in the house or nearby.

Still, Grayson was cautious enough to make a slow circle of the house before approaching it, more than a little baffled to find neither driveway nor sidewalk but simply this old, country-type farmhouse in the center of a clearing, ringed by the forest, as if it had just been set down there, intended for isolation.

He did find one end of what appeared to be a very narrow footpath leading to the house through the woods from the general direction of Salem, but otherwise the house might as well have never been meant for occupants or visitors.

Except . . . there was that footpath. And there were filmy curtains at the windows he could see, and no visible weeds grew in the winter-short grass of the clearing. And there was that pot of geraniums on the front porch.

Silk geraniums, he discovered when he finally went catfooted onto the front porch and crossed to the front door. The moonlight, absent in the woods, was bright enough in this clearing to allow him to see clearly, especially with the aid of his spider senses, which were still on full.

He would definitely need the med from the doc to knock him out at some point tonight, or he'd be useless tomorrow.

Grayson's sense of danger was hovering, ever present, but it was more a matter of his suspicious nature and caution born of experience than anything more tangible; all his senses told him he and Geneva were the only people in the area for a considerable distance around this house, probably as far away as the town.

He was somewhat irritably deciding whether to just knock on the front door when it was pulled suddenly open.

Geneva stood there holding a lit candle in an old-fashioned, tarnished brass holder.

"Took you long enough," she said.

He eyed her, considering and rejecting various responses that would undoubtedly have started an argument. But he'd been genuinely worried about her, and even in the added glow of the candlelight, he could see that she wore the finely honed look of the weariness that came of too little sleep and too much stress labored under for too long, so his voice was milder than it might otherwise have been when he replied to her softly snapped statement.

"You obviously didn't need my help. Is there anything in the house worth seeing?" He kept his voice as low as hers had been.

"Nothing that makes any sense. There's no electricity, and water comes from a well with the aid of one of those *really* old-fashioned hand pumps, but the place is furnished and has been recently cleaned; you can smell the lemon cleaner. No dust on anything. Old quilts on thin mattresses on old iron bedframes, plain old furniture, empty closets and cabinets and drawers. Just a stock of candles on the kitchen counter, and a few like this one placed around the house, all with a holder and matches or a lighter nearby."

Obviously, she had conducted her usual thorough search.

Grayson frowned, absently listening to a faint rumble of thunder that sounded far away, but made no move to enter. "I don't get this place," he said. "Do you have any sense of your missing kid?" Another rumble; he wondered if the forecast he'd seen earlier had missed bad weather in the offing.

"That's not the way my abilities work, and you know it. I can tell you she wasn't kept in the cellar where I've spent the past couple of days or so, and there's no sign she was kept here in the house. As for any psychic help in finding her, I never touched her mind, so there's no connection I can reach for."

"But you picked up she was missing telepathically?"

"Yeah. From a little boy down in town. He'd dared her to come here at night—the local haunted house, I gather, where nerves and courage are tested by the kids— and pick one of these geraniums to prove she'd been here." Geneva glanced out at the pot of silk geraniums and frowned briefly, but added, "He was guilty as hell and worried sick, poor kid. But not *quite* worried enough to tell an adult what happened; he was talking to a friend, who basically told him it was no big deal. Nobody else seems to even be aware she's missing. She came out here Tuesday night; her family left abruptly on a vacation on Wednesday."

"Missing a kid."

"One of three daughters. Their names were on their bedroom doors, written on those decorated plaques with stardust and Disney characters. I got inside the house before I came up here to find this place, and there was nothing to indicate the parents were the least bit concerned. They just . . . left."

"Planned vacation?"

"No way for me to know. Nothing was marked on the calendar on their fridge, and it looked like every school event or meeting, doctor appointment, or planned attendance at local events was. Besides, in January? I tried something new for me, something Bishop said I could do, and picked up some really faint residual thoughts. And there was some panic there, worry—and then cheerful packing for a happy trip out of Salem. It stinks, Gray."

"And you believe she's been missing since—?"

"I think she was grabbed when she came up here, so sometime Tuesday night."

"That's more than forty-eight hours, Red."

"I know that," she snapped. But, again, softly. "But I don't believe there's a pedophile trolling in Salem, which means she was taken by someone for reasons other than the usual obvious ones. I believe she's still alive."

"Being hurt?" He asked the question evenly.

"No. I can't tell you why I believe that, but I do. She's alive. Probably scared out of her mind, but alive."

"Being held like you were."

"Maybe. Probably. I just don't know why."

His frown deepened, but he was thinking of the crows back in the woods, maybe nearer by now since they appeared to get about with eerie silence, watching and waiting. He had plenty of questions, and he knew Geneva would stand here talking about what she'd found or failed to find and about a missing little girl as long as she didn't feel threatened, but his more primitive senses were warning him to get away from this house, out of this forest, and back to town. And those were senses he'd learned to trust.

"Okay, let's get back to the B and B and compare notes," he suggested.

"You don't want to look around in here?"

"I wouldn't see anything you missed." His matter-of-fact tone robbed it of any compliment. "But I don't like these woods *or* where this house is, and I passed a few crows back there just . . . watching. You know about them?"

Geneva blew out her candle and set it on a table or some other bit of furniture near the door Grayson couldn't see from where he stood, then came out onto the porch and pulled the door shut softly behind her.

"This door wasn't locked, by the way. Yeah, I know about the crows, always around, watching. No matter where you go, there they are. Creepy, aren't they?"

"That would be one word. Guardians? Spies?"

"Both, I think. And maybe more than that. Is it supposed to storm tonight?"

"Not according to the forecast." He listened to another rumble of thunder but could see or hear no other sign of an approaching storm. "And they usually don't pop up out of nowhere in winter."

"One more weird thing to add to the list," Geneva muttered, almost to herself.

She fell in beside him as they left the porch and put the house behind them, neither heading for the faint footpath at the edge of the woods but a few yards away from it, still moving generally south, toward the town. And as soon as they left the clearing, Geneva let Grayson take the lead, saying merely, "I'm not sure how close I was to the house when they grabbed me, so you'll know the way back better than I will."

Grayson bit back more than one question and nodded, but said, "I wandered all over on the way up here, just in case, but I think straight back to the B and B is our best bet tonight. I don't feel anybody else anywhere close. You getting anything?"

Geneva paused briefly, then shook her head. "No. I've nearly fallen over militia members out in the woods this late before, but I'm not picking up any thoughts—or any walls hiding them."

Grayson swallowed another question, this one about the walls. "Then straight back to Hales."

"You won't get an argument."

And she didn't say another word as she followed him

down the mountain, agile as always, her movements silent as always—but Grayson could feel that she was tired, drained, and, as always, angry with herself for that. Her very weariness allowed him to sense her emotions a lot easier than usual, and he knew she wouldn't like that. At all. He knew better than to comment, at least here and now, but chose the quickest, easiest path back to the B and B.

When they were almost within sight of the B and B, they separated, Geneva saying briefly that she'd meet him in her room. She disappeared into the bushes before he could ask, not that he had to. She had found a secret way into the building, just as he'd expected her to, and, being Geneva, intended to keep that to herself unless he needed to know.

With a sigh that misted the very cold air, Grayson circled around the other way so that he could slip out onto the sidewalk some distance away and stroll unconcernedly toward the B and B, as if his late walk had taken him only in the logical direction of town, with its streetlights and two lone all-night convenience stores.

He almost wished he *had* gone to one of those stores, since he was willing to bet they offered hot coffee, no matter how strong and bitter. He'd barely noticed it while getting them off the mountain, but now he felt cold to the bone and was relatively certain a hot shower and something hot to drink, as well as the med that would allow him to sleep tonight, were probably still hours away.

His migraine would land sooner than that.

He was just about to turn into the pleasant, brick-lined, and winding walkway that led from the street to the front porch of the B and B when a crow alighted on a decorative lamppost no more than twelve feet from him. Shiny eyes caught the light as it turned its head this way and that, clearly watching him. Grayson paused, eyed the bird, and then continued on his way, hoping he looked as casual as he wanted to feel.

What the hell *was* it with those damned birds?

Since it was after midnight, he knocked softly to rouse the night porter, apologizing for getting back so late from his stroll, but the porter, who looked a lot like the same lean, casually dressed man Ms. Payton had briefly introduced as Jim, their handyman, said it was no bother and he hoped the night chill had helped Grayson's migraine.

Information certainly got around.

Fast.

Grayson wondered if the guy ever slept and made a mental note to check into his background, just to be thorough. And because even though he sensed nothing threatening from the man, he disliked the conviction that he was under observation all the time. But he responded only that the cold fresh air hadn't helped much at all—he knew his eyes were squinted against even the dim light of the lobby, something that would be visible to the other man—and that he was going to try a hot shower, a migraine pill, and a good night's sleep.

Then he waved a vague hand and headed upstairs, moving briskly but casually until he was out of sight of the night porter. He encountered no one else, and since he'd already noted there were no security cameras in the hallways or the main stairwell, he felt safe in passing his own small suite with only a brief pause to assure himself no one had gotten in during his absence, and then continuing silently to Geneva's.

THIRTEEN

Nellie had a hunch this was going to be one of those sleepless nights after the nightmare and . . . well, after. Even after she used the techniques she'd been taught for control, even after the faint rumbles of thunder died away and Leo relaxed beside her and she settled back on her pillows, she was still wide-awake.

There was control, and then there was *control*. She had tamped down so much inside her that she could almost feel it swirling around, looking for a way out.

Strange. And unsettling.

Automatically continuing to breathe slow and steady, she looked for some diversion. She channel surfed with the volume on low for a while but finally turned the set off and debated reading. But she'd taken off her gloves for the night, and experience had taught her that without them e-readers died on her long before she could finish even a chapter or two. She wasn't in the mood to reclaim the gloves.

She made a mental note to stop at the bookstore in town the next time she was out and buy two or three actual paper books to keep here for nights like this one. Because even if the nightmare no longer troubled her— as promised—she'd been a restless sleeper most of her life and that was unlikely to change.

It was after midnight now, and Nellie knew she needed to sleep. She couldn't lie here for the rest of the night just going over and over everything in her mind, especially after she'd worked so hard to calm herself down. The truth was, even with all her doubts about her father and what he'd told her, the lingering uncertainty about that voice in her mind after the nightmare, it was clear Finn at the very least knew quite a lot about her.

Maybe too much.

But no matter what he knew, like it or not, she was going to have to see Finn Deverell again, talk to him, and this time with plenty of her own questions she wanted answered.

But first she had to sleep. And she didn't want to dream. Even if the nightmare never returned, she didn't think she had the energy tonight for just normal dreams. Or maybe she had too much energy.

Control, that's what she had to have. And strong enough that it would follow her obediently into sleep.

She didn't know if she could do that without the gloves, although she'd had a certain amount of control before beginning to wear them. Not for the first time, she wondered if she used the gloves as a crutch more than a symbol.

She shook that thought away, made herself even more comfortable, patted Leo when he snorted softly, and closed her eyes, once again concentrating on the techniques she'd been taught. She'd never before used them to try to ward off dreams, but what the hell.

Bishop had told her that every individual psychic had his or her own limits and that she had no real idea what she could do until she tried. And this she wanted to try.

GRAYSON DIDN'T HAVE to knock on Geneva's door, slipping in as she opened it just as he reached it. A quick glance around told him that her suite had the same basic layout as his own but was larger, which made sense given her reservation and longer projected stay, and that it also had a kitchenette.

"Have you eaten anything?" he asked immediately.

"They left food and water in my cellar prison for me. Considerate gents."

He could still feel the weariness in her, and the hunger she was ignoring as well, which meant he couldn't let it drop. "What kind of food?"

"Protein bars and those premade, prepackaged sandwiches you get from vending machines." She paused. "I wouldn't recommend them."

"Okay, so you might not have been on starvation rations, but I doubt what they left for you was filling, much less satisfying. And knowing you, you hoarded what they gave you in case you were stuck there longer than they expected you to be."

She hunched a shoulder in that familiar way that said she had other things on her mind. "What I really want is a hot shower, but I'll take that later. I'll eat later too. We should compare notes tonight. From the look of your eyes, I'm guessing you've strained every sense, triggering the beginning of one of your migraines, and need to sleep as soon as you can or you'll be useless tomorrow."

Honors even, he thought wryly, not bothering to add the obvious retort that she looked tired herself.

"Any sign your suite was searched while you were gone?" he asked her.

"That happened the first week I was here. At least twice. And they were pros. I don't think anybody except you has been in here since I last left Wednesday night."

He didn't ask if she sensed he'd checked out her suite or simply knew he had. He was thinking about the fact that she'd been imprisoned more than forty-eight hours and that it must have seemed more like a week to her; he wanted to say something about that, but he knew her well enough to know she wouldn't have much to say about all the long hours spent alone in her prison.

Forcing his thoughts away from that, he said, "Well, grab a protein drink or something; my suite doesn't have a kitchenette. And we have to check in with Bishop; I told him I would as soon as we made contact."

She grimaced but went and did as he suggested, not commenting on the fact that he knew her habits as well as she did his; she virtually always stocked any room where she was staying during a case with protein drinks and energy bars, as well as a few favorite snacks, for the sake of convenience and because she had a tendency to skip meals whenever she worked alone.

Geneva got her small bottle of chocolate-flavored drink and followed him from the room, moving as quietly as he did.

Both their suites were on the second floor, but they passed the closed doors of several other rooms or suites along the way, and she paused at one closed door, staring at it fixedly, her gray eyes—unusual for a redhead—narrowed.

Grayson stopped as well, silent, watching her face, then opened up his senses a bit to pick up whatever might be in that room.

He thought there was a woman in there, calm, maybe sleeping, but the strongest sense he got was of a dog. And just as with the crows, those nonhuman emotions were distinctly disconcerting as they seeped into his own mind. He wondered abruptly if being able to sense those crows for whatever reason had opened another door into a new sense for him, or expanded the empathic abilities he did possess.

And whether that had been their idea or something in his own nature.

Either way, he didn't like it. At all.

The dog was drowsy, an ebbing dream of chasing a rabbit fading as he began to wake up, to feel more alert and watchful in order to protect his chosen human. Who was beside him on the bed.

Silently, Grayson caught Geneva's arm and drew her

away from the door and to his own suite, raising his own walls as well as he could at the moment, fighting nausea and the first faint throbs of the coming migraine. She didn't struggle or argue, but as soon as they were in his suite and he dropped her arm, she asked a quick question.

"You sensed something?"

"A dog waking up. I figured we didn't need him barking and rousing the place. Pretty sure I saw the woman who owns him checking in with him earlier today. Or yesterday, rather. It's after midnight, so Saturday." He paused, then added, "You were picking up something. What?"

"I didn't think you could sense animals," she said.

"I don't know that I can. Usually. Just the crows tonight, and now this dog. And no, I don't know why, though I wouldn't think animals would need shields or walls to protect their emotions. I also don't know why this is the first time I've sensed them, except maybe the weird . . . static around here. Gotta be energy, and we know it affects us. Gen? What did you sense back there?"

"I assume the dog's owner." She frowned, swallowed half the chocolate contents of the small bottle of protein drink without apparently being aware of it, then half pointed it at him. "Definitely a woman. I didn't get much, but it seemed like she was using some of those meditation techniques we were taught."

"Lots of people meditate."

"Not like we're taught, and you know it. This was all about control, drawing in threads and holding them tight. Weaving a shell around herself. A shell of energy.

Protecting herself, but more like it was from letting something out, something she was wary of. There was nothing about how she was being all Zen and going to her safe place."

"You saying she's psychic?"

"My guess is it's a strong maybe. If so, she doesn't have much of a shield, and what she does have is . . . unusual. Those threads of energy felt . . . almost alive. And her concentration was as much external as internal. Tied to something outside herself. Something physical, I mean real physical, like a barrier of some kind, or what she believes is one. An article of clothing, maybe. Don't know if she was wearing it, but she was using it somehow."

Grayson felt his eyebrows rising. "Never heard of anything like that."

"I have." Geneva was still frowning as she finished her protein drink and looked around for a trash can, spotting one and disposing of the bottle with a practiced and accurate toss. "It was years back, and I only heard a remark or two, but I pieced together that one of the psychics Bishop had found while looking for more of us for the SCU needed something outside herself, something she could see and touch, to focus on, turn into a barrier her own mind was always aware of and could believe in to protect herself. I think it was gloves. I remember because that's the only time I've heard of him using that technique to help a psychic build up a shield, and I wondered if it worked."

It was Grayson's turn to frown. "Does Bishop have

any idea just how much you know about stuff you really don't need to know?"

She ignored that. "I wonder if it's her. She didn't want to join the SCU is what I got, and it was before Haven really got started. She already had responsibilities, for one a very successful financial company of some kind she'd inherited and built on. And she wasn't real happy that she was psychic, hid it all her life."

"What kind of psychic?"

"Telepath with bells and whistles. The more dangerous kind. I got that was why Bishop tried something outside the box to help her to control her abilities."

"And you touched her mind just now? Gen—"

"It was a really brief and shallow touch, and I don't think she was at all aware of me. Really concentrating on those control techniques. Which, if I'm right about those bells and whistles and why Bishop thought outside the box, is probably a good thing."

"Bells and whistles of the more dangerous kind, inside a psychic who has to use a trick to raise any kind of shield. And she's here in Salem, where there's a weird sort of static that usually means energy being used or held under some kind of pressure or whatever the hell. Great. That's just great."

"I could be wrong," Geneva said, in the tone of one who knew she wasn't. "And even if she is here, she might have nothing to do with whatever's going on in Salem."

"Wanna bet? Bishop doesn't believe in coincidences, and neither do I. He also doesn't like wasting a psychic, whether officially one of us or not. If he found her, he kept track, and I'm betting he knows she's here. For whatever reason."

"What reason could she have?"

"Maybe we should be asking ourselves whether those three missings might have been psychic."

"Four," Geneva said.

"Four?"

"Yeah. Well, a body that didn't belong to the first three *or* the missing little girl. I'm guessing he'll turn up on Bishop's list soon, if he isn't already there."

"You saw the site?"

"Dump site. I'll show you the pictures later. I beat the militia there, but they cleaned it up quick. Nothing to see now."

"I'm still wondering about a psychic connection. All that static around here feels like energy to me. Psychic energy."

"Me too, to be honest. But would that be a reason to kill them?"

Grayson headed for the small desk where he'd set up his laptop. "I have no idea. But we've found plenty of psychics whose abilities could be used even unwillingly to harm others if they lack at least necessary control. If this woman has abilities on the dangerous end, maybe she disappeared the little girl."

"You said she just got here."

"Doesn't mean she hasn't been lurking."

"Jesus, you're more suspicious than I am."

"Just considering possibilities, though I agree that

one is unlikely, if only because of the timing. This little girl—"

"Bethany Hicks."

"Right, Bethany Hicks. So, she just vanishes into thin air. With the aid of some psychic ability enhanced by all this damned static?"

"Unless Bishop is hiding something absolutely *huge*, no psychic he's located can disappear people. Static or no static. And I haven't felt that kind of power since I got here. As for our fellow guest and psychic, what I got is that she can channel energy, probably a lot of it, in a very . . . specific way."

"Channel. And if all this static is from energy, psychic energy, that could be a likely trigger for her abilities, and even if she doesn't need or want it, extra energy to draw on."

"Maybe."

"And that doesn't sound scary at all," Grayson muttered, sitting down at the desk and opening his laptop. "Only a handful of us can do that on any level. Channel energy. Just tell me she can't channel lightning. That's spooky as hell, aside from being painful if you get caught in the backwash."

"I don't think she knows whether she can do that," Geneva said cautiously. "But there *is* something about her and storms I couldn't quite get."

"We both heard the thunder earlier. Not now, though."

"So maybe that's why she's practicing control techniques. She doesn't have to channel actual lightning to gather energy from a storm; all of us tend to be affected by them."

"And with all the granite in this valley, I'm betting storms are common even in winter."

"Been a couple of bad ones since I've been in town."

"Don't get too near," Grayson warned hastily as Geneva started toward the small desk where he'd set up his laptop.

She stopped with a sigh. "Bishop and his geniuses can figure out how to send and receive utterly secure messages between him and his agents practically anywhere on earth, but they can't figure out how to keep me from killing laptops with one touch."

"Maybe some mysteries are better off that way," Grayson suggested. "Want to keep comparing notes before I put through the call to Bishop?"

"Where is he?"

"No idea. But he got back to me quickly this afternoon." There was, after all, no telling where Bishop was, so times and even time zones rarely came into the matter. "Did you get a look at whoever grabbed you?"

"No, he put me down too fast."

"How did he put you down?" Grayson kept his voice cool and professional with an effort.

Geneva gave him a look, but all she said was, "Some kind of injection is my guess. A very quick-acting one. He didn't hit me or grab me or Taser me; I just went out like a light." She frowned a little. "I never did find an injection site, though. And I did go out awfully fast."

"Wake up feeling queasy, dizzy?"

"Not that I remember. One minute I was in the woods, staring at those damned crows and realizing I'd spent too much time in one place, and the next I woke up in that cellar prison." She shook that away, not as she would have a nightmare memory, but certainly something close. "But I know who at least one of them is. He asked me something just before he took me out, if I was out for a night stroll or words to that effect. Sarcasm of the first order. I recognized his voice."

"Somebody you'd been watching?"

"At a distance, since he seems to be high up in the local militia/deputy squad. I mean, I couldn't read him, but he was the one giving orders as far as I could tell whenever I saw him with one of the others I've tagged as likely militia. It's not like they wear uniforms, and even though some seem to be armed, it's an open-carry state and winter means coats and jackets. So it's taken me a while to recognize the players."

"But you think you know them now?"

"Most of the militia, I think."

"Most?"

"I think there's a top guy, the one really in charge, and so far I haven't been able to find out who he is."

"From one of the families?"

"Oh, yeah, bound to be. They aren't real obvious about it, but nothing of importance happens in this town unless someone from one or more of those five families is behind it, pulling strings."

"Speaking of pulling." Grayson sighed. "Gen, don't

make me feel like I'm trying to pull teeth here. Just tell me what you've found out. Do you have a report with specifics for Bishop or not? I haven't been here long enough to do much more than settle in, but it might help in understanding what's going on here if we had at least a few more puzzle pieces."

"That's about all I have, a lot of bits and pieces I haven't been able to fit together," she admitted frankly. "Not much to report that Bishop doesn't already know. Except that this place is strange in more ways than just the energy static, and he knows that."

"What doesn't he know?"

There was a faintly stubborn look in her eyes he recognized; Geneva preferred to make complete reports when she reported in at all, with all the *i*'s dotted and *t*'s crossed. But he waited, watching her steadily, and finally she shrugged.

"Well, like I said, there was that fourth body found up in the mountains earlier in the day before Bethany disappeared. Mutilated like the others. Tortured before death. Rocks ringing the body with nonsense symbols smeared in the victim's blood. Nothing occult I recognized, but it was designed to scare the shit out of anybody who saw it.

"Which is exactly what happened, and how I found out about it. A very shaken hunter was the first to stumble over the remains, and he was horrified almost beyond words. Happened to pass by where I was lurking in town, and I was able to get a general location from him. Found the remains myself a while later."

"I thought hunting was forbidden in Salem," Grayson

muttered, frowning over the new information that someone untaught might be using the occult to hide or disguise just plain old murder.

"For sport, yeah. Pretty sure he was hunting for food.
Something extra for the pot, I think was the gist.
Though I seriously doubt he ate anything that night."

Grayson looked at her for a moment, then shook his
head.

Geneva ignored his suppressed amusement. "And
something is behind the weird lack of curiosity or concern
in the townsfolk when stuff like that mutilated body happens, because as far as I could tell they barely noticed it."

"You said you checked out the dump site."

"For all the good it did me. The first time I was in
such a hurry I just stayed back and took photos, all I
could. Didn't dare get close enough to take a biological
sample, and I can't tell you exactly what killed the victim." She paused, a slightly odd look on her face for a
moment, then went on calmly, "By the time I got back
up there later, the militia had indeed been there, and
lemme tell you, they clean up a crime scene or dump site
like real pros, because I didn't find anything at all helpful, and I crawled around on my *knees*."

"Find anything not helpful?"

She frowned at him. "I could swear I smelled bleach
around some of the larger rocks at the scene, like somebody had been cleaning off that blood, which makes
sense. And scorch marks. It looked to me like they'd set
off a controlled burn to eliminate any signs of whatever
they'd found. No sign of a grave or that anything else

had been buried up there. And no sign of the body, in whole or in part."

"They do appear to know how to get rid of evidence."

"Oh, yeah. And they are quick. The hunter who'd stumbled on the remains was headed straight to report to somebody, but I didn't get a name. I haven't seen him since, and as far as I can tell, the militia put out the victim was a dead tourist hiking the Trail at the worst time of year, just a sad accident, and they'd taken care of things. As per usual. Nothing to worry about here, folks, move along. Whether they shared any of that with the county sheriff I couldn't find out. It's hell being undercover *and* unofficial in a situation like this one."

"Have we *had* a situation like this one?" he asked wryly.

"We haven't had a town like this one—I know that much. There aren't just undercurrents; there are *layers* of undercurrents, and all kinds of things moving in them. Look, Gray, along with the bits and pieces, I've got nothing more than a whisper here, a hunch there, the flicker of a thought. Nothing to hang your hat on. Nothing to report to Bishop, other than the latest death. Way too many questions I can't ask of way too many people who might have answers."

"You got the name of the missing girl. That's more than I knew when I checked in, so Bishop doesn't know it either. The name should help his people find her, if she can be found."

"Yeah, there's that." Geneva frowned and chewed on her bottom lip for a moment. "And maybe something else. The kind of walls I kept bumping up against are strong and solid. The woman down the hall here and us aside, there are definitely a lot of psychics in this town. Powerful ones. And given the balance of power here, I'm guessing—just guessing, mind you—that there's at least one psychic in each of the five families. Maybe more than one. And whatever's going on here, they're at the heart of it."

FOURTEEN

Bethany did her best to sleep, because she felt so tired it was an ache in her bones, but the cot was lumpy and she was just too scared to close her eyes for more than a few short minutes.

She thought.

Everything was a guess here. Everything except that she was alone, more alone than she'd ever been in her whole life, and she wanted a hug from her mom and dad in the worst way.

Did they know she was gone? Were they looking for her?

Was anyone?

She didn't think Jason would tell anyone he'd dared her to go up to the scary house and pick that flower to prove it. And even if he did, she knew he wouldn't tell a grown-up. He'd tell one of his buddies, and they'd laugh and tell him not to worry.

There hadn't been any more water or broth. The tray with the small cup and bowl lay just where she'd put it. The pinched feeling in her middle was worse, especially since she'd finally given in and used a corner of her small cage to empty her bladder.

She was so thirsty. So hungry.

Bethany rubbed her arms with both hands, feeling cold even though she was warmly dressed. Maybe that was the ache in her bones, or maybe it was because it was so quiet and she had an awful feeling she was going to die here, all alone, in this cold, dim place of rock and silence.

It was the silence that was almost the worst.

Maybe was the worst.

Because it added to her feeling so alone. It made her even more afraid to try to sleep.

And because she could almost swear there was something moving out there, past the point she could see. Something.

Something coming for her.

GRAYSON FROWNED. "YOU think that's why they're still in charge of things in Salem even after generations? A psychic edge?"

"Well, we know it can run in families, so why not?"

"Yeah, but even if, how could they be using it to stay in control of the town?"

"That's what scares me. They shouldn't be able to do that. Not even in a small town."

He coped with her extremely rare admission of being

scared, deciding not to comment on that part of what she'd said. "Mind control is pretty much a myth—we all know that. Oh, sure, minor things, unimportant things, definitely short-term. Maybe a bit more between blood siblings or other bonded psychics. But even psychics who can barely influence, far less control, another mind are rare. Control a whole town?"

"I'm not sure it's that clear-cut. A little psychic ability and a lot of superstition could have been the beginning. Customs form, and then just become the way of things. Over generations, what's normal is what you get used to. Habits, beliefs. So maybe if you're born under a kind of authority and grow up under it, how many are going to challenge it?"

"Especially if your life is an easy and comfortable one," he agreed, thinking it over. "The families make sure everybody gets a fair deal, good jobs with good pay, reasonable housing prices, no crime to speak of—if you set aside those mutilated bodies."

"Explained away as careless tourists or hikers and accidents, not exactly uncommon in the mountains, especially this close to the Trail," she added. "All evidence removed quickly and smoothly, so virtually nobody has to see the blood. *And* as far as I could find out, the one newspaper obediently reports just that. Probably because the owner is a Deverell."

"Ah. I didn't catch that."

"It isn't printed anywhere on the paper itself. I only picked it up by chance eating lunch out one day," she admitted. "Playing my part of being very visible and yet as unobtrusive as grass and rocks the way professional photographers have to be. I've been wandering around with my cameras and smiling at people until my face feels like it's going to break, and they're finally getting used to me. Relaxing. A little. Sometimes."

"Have you picked up another telepath? Besides our fellow guest, I mean."

"I'm sure there are psychics all around, like I said, maybe more than we've ever found in one small town. But what I've picked up is less about specific abilities and more about those damned solid walls. It's almost like . . . one wall. Pieces of something that fit together to protect or contain diverse abilities. Look, can you go ahead and find out from Bishop if they've had any luck in locating Bethany Hicks? She's only ten years old. I'm worried about that kid."

Well aware that she did indeed worry more about kids than adults tangled in a case, Grayson merely nodded, turned his attention to the laptop, and began typing.

She took a step closer and eyed him suddenly in a faintly hostile manner that he could feel was more automatic than real, because what he mostly felt from her was a chilled weariness and the need for sleep. "I better not see the word *rescue* appear on that screen."

"Right," he murmured, fingers flying over the keyboard as he established the connection and requested real-time communication. He was beginning to understand that he knew her a lot better than he'd realized, and it was an unsettling realization.

"I mean it, Gray. I got myself out of that cellar. Besides, you weren't even supposed to look for me; you were supposed to find Bethany."

Ignoring the first part of her comments, he said merely, "Bishop's got people searching data banks for info, and they're a hell of a lot more likely to find something than I am. Jesus, Red, there are twenty-eight girls under the age of thirteen missing within a five-hundred-mile radius of Salem, and I didn't even have a name. And the *Chronicle* isn't online in any sense, so I could hardly check their archives for info. Far as I could tell, nobody local was missing a kid. Or at least not talking about it or feeling about it if they were."

Somewhat mollified, she said, "I suppose you did your best."

He bit back the natural retort, saying instead, "I also didn't find any sign of the three people who mysteriously headed this way last month, and though I hate to assume, I think it's probably safe to assume they ended up like your supposed hiker."

"Which *maybe* means four people we haven't been able to connect to each other in any other way came to Salem, maybe were lured here—and died. I dunno, though. That's the problem. There's nothing solid to hang your hat on except disappearances we can't prove and one set of tortured human remains with only photographic evidence. No evidence at all to show if they were grabbed and if so by who. No evidence to show they weren't grabbed just like I was."

He turned his head to stare at her. "You think whoever grabbed you intended to kill you?"

Geneva was standing with her hands jammed into the pockets of her thick jacket, and met his gaze with no hint of fear in her own. "No idea. Possible, of course, and something I considered, even though they left me food and water, even candles and a mattress to sleep on. But I wasn't lured here and I wasn't asking any questions other than those I *would* ask, given my cover. So I can't see how I was even a possible threat to them until that night, when I apparently was someplace they didn't want me to be. So they locked me up until they could decide what to do with me. Just a guess, though. Didn't have much time to form an impression before they grabbed me, and never heard, saw, or sensed in any other way one of them in that house the whole time I was there."

"You think they grabbed you because you were in the woods at night when a photographer just wouldn't have been? Or *was* it where you were? Maybe getting close to something they didn't want you to find?"

"Yeah, either way, if they'd been watching me. Or if the crows were. I mean, the crows were there, I'd seen them before in the woods and in town, and nothing un-usual happened those times. And I'd been up there in the general area a couple times at night, though not too far. But, maybe . . . maybe that night I crossed some invisible line. The only thing I know is that I didn't have my cam-eras, and it was late. Too late and too damned cold for a casual hike up that mountain. Hell, *I* would have been suspicious of me."

"Then they knew or guessed you were looking for something."

"I would have, in their place. I have to assume that's what was on their minds."

"Then you *are* a threat to them."

"That," Geneva said, "depends on whether they're hiding something I could have found."

"You're thinking of Bethany."

Steadily, she said, "All the remains found so far, if we can trust what little information we have of the first three, and my evidence of the fourth, have been of adults. And as near as I can figure, the bodies turned up shortly after our missings *went* missing. So it's more than likely the first three bodies belonged to our missings. As for the fourth set of remains found . . . A young man, but a man. Could have been looking at thirty as his next birthday."

"And nonsense symbols painted on rocks in his own blood. So what's your take? Are we dealing with the occult, or just window dressing?"

"Off the top of my head, window dressing. We can study the photos later, but nothing about it looked like genuine occult signs or symbols to me. Though there were some weird things about what was left of that body." She paused, then added more briskly, "Where did you look for the other missings?"

"Haven't had much time to look anywhere. I did manage to check the register downstairs, but I had to be damned quick since Ms. Payton definitely hovers."

"Oh, you noticed that."

"Hard not to. Unless she's showing a newcomer to their room, she stays within sight of the front desk all the time; she can see it even from her office across that little hallway. So it's her during the day and their night porter the rest of the time."

"Then you found what I found. Zip. A whole bunch of people checked in back before Christmas, quite a few of them singles, our missings among them, and as far as that register goes, most of those guests stayed for a long weekend and then checked out and left as planned. With others coming and going before and after."

"Yeah. And they keep things old-fashioned; all the guest information I could find is in that old register. Payton has a computer in her office, but I couldn't get close enough to see if there's anything but an accounting program or Facebook or something."

"She likes to play mah-jongg on the computer," Geneva said.

Grayson wondered how she'd discovered that but decided not to ask. "Well, all I know is that the three guests whose names we know are in that register, checked in *and* checked out when they were supposed to, at least according to this B and B, and that the cars they drove had the correct license plate numbers. According to the register, again. And that their cars are definitely not here."

"So either they were grabbed after they left here," Geneva said, "or Payton is in on it."

"Yeah, but in on what? Wait—here's Bishop."

Gray?

Yeah. Found Geneva. She's okay. Somebody had been holding her prisoner in the cellar of an odd house up on the mountain, but she got herself out just before I found the house.

Glad to hear it. Was her prison guarded?

Geneva took a step closer and pretty much dictated what Grayson was supposed to type in response to that, and since his head was really beginning to throb and since it *was* her story, after all, he just typed as she talked.

No, she says she never saw, heard, or otherwise sensed anyone in the house or nearby once she woke up from whatever they used to knock her out. An injection of some kind, she thinks.

She's sure it wasn't a psychic knockout?

Grayson and Geneva exchanged surprised looks, and Grayson typed: We'd both heard you had a new recruit now in training who could put somebody down psychically, but she has to touch them, right? Geneva doesn't remember any kind of touch.

If touch can do it, and it can, then so can sheer energy if the psychic knows how to focus, Bishop returned. I'm guessing somebody is using plenty of energy in and around Salem. Reports from outside are that the static is getting stronger, much stronger, quite possibly building toward something, planned or not. And we all know that energy affects us, for better or worse. Both of you keep on your toes. Gray, did you have time to explore, either tonight or when you were coming down off the Trail?

Grayson had omitted a few things from his report before, largely because Geneva had been uppermost on his mind. Something he decided not to think about.

Coming down off the Trail. Found a set of parallel tracks, definitely not from a vehicle, mostly boots and shoes, a few indications of bare feet, that seemed to start in the middle of nowhere and led to the ruins of a very, very old stone building. Maybe a church, though why original settlers would have put one literally on the side of the mountain so far from where the town was sited is something I can't even guess at. I didn't get too close because my tracks would have been too obvious, but in the center of the ruins was what looked like a stone altar, hacked out of granite. And there were stains. Quite a lot of them. I'm guessing blood, violently spilled. Not recent, but not too long ago, I think. I took some photos and will upload them to you ASAP.

Even as he typed, Grayson was still a little preoccupied by the now virtual certainty of building energies he had felt earlier and his uneasiness at the changes—maybe slight and maybe not—he had experienced in his own abilities.

But before he could think much about that, Geneva was finishing her report for now, and he just continued to type. As per Geneva, the girl we're looking for is Bethany Hicks, Bishop. Age ten. Still no sign of her here, and nobody seems to even care that she's missing. Or possibly they just don't know. Weirdly, her family left with her two sisters, apparently on vacation, right after she disappeared. We don't believe there was ever a missing-persons report of any kind. And pretty much everybody we've encountered so far doesn't seem too worried about anything. Including missing little girls or the mutilated bodies of supposedly careless tourists or hikers. Gen says there's been another one found, just before Bethany disappeared.

Geneva, did you get a look at the scene?

Grayson continued to type obediently as Geneva reported what little she was able to, and he knew her frustration with the too-efficient militia came through the brief words.

Anyone see you two together? Bishop asked.

Grayson barely stopped himself from wincing, because he knew what was coming. No, he typed. Except maybe for the damned birds.

What birds?

Crows. A lot of crows. Gen and I both agree somebody's using them. Trained them somehow, or controls them. Spies, guards, I dunno, Bishop. They are very strange birds. Both of us have seen them, especially in the woods, but—he glanced at Geneva for confirmation—in town as well. Something else nobody in town seems to be bothered by. And even though it isn't my thing at all, tonight I got a strong empathic sense of the crows watching me in the woods just before I found that house. Very weird feelings in bird heads, let me tell you. At one point I could swear they were laughing at me.

"You didn't tell me that," Geneva observed as she watched the words appearing on the screen.

"Because it sounded crazy," he retorted. "But Bishop always wants everything, even crazy."

"Maybe especially crazy," she murmured.

What else did you get from them?

That they're . . . watchers. Guards, spies, like I said. Sentinels. Got the sense they report back to someone and, crazy as it sounds, I also got the sense that whoever they report back to is someone they're afraid of. Way down deep in a cold place I didn't think birds even had.

Evil?

It should have been a melodramatic query, but neither Grayson nor Geneva thought so.

Dark at least, Grayson typed in reply. Really dark. Really cold. And they felt . . . in bondage somehow. Trapped. But that was at a deep level, almost hidden or buried. If it was meant to be hidden, I'm not sure that was for my benefit, or . . . whatever. And I have absolutely no idea how I can suddenly read the deep emotions of goddamned crows. Do you?

"Cue Bishop nonanswer," Geneva said.

Try again when you have the chance. You need to know if it was a onetime thing or a genuine new ability.

"We could make a fortune," Geneva mused. "Except nobody who knows him would bet on a straight answer from him after a question like yours."

Grayson sighed. She was right. Dammit.

Copy. I'll get the photos of that odd building and the altar to you ASAP.

"Mine have to be uploaded too," Geneva said, frowning at what he had typed. "I'll slip the photos under your door if I'm up first so you can scan them in and send them."

"Up first? Tonight—"

"Tonight we both need to sleep," she countered flatly.

It was the *both* that got him. Grayson nodded and typed. We'll get Gen's photos of that dump site uploaded as well.

And was answered before he could say when.

Do it in the morning. In the meantime, get some rest, both of you. Keep your shields up and don't drop them entirely unless there's no other choice.

Copy.

Meet up at breakfast, if possible.

Do we know each other? Grayson made himself ask.

You have your camera, and it's loaded with pictures of the Trail back to Georgia. Geneva is a photographer. I imagine you can arrange a casual meeting. Or rediscover an old acquaintance. Up to you.

"Don't tell me you didn't see it coming," Geneva said. "Just because we've had . . . issues . . . as partners doesn't mean Bishop doesn't believe we work well together. And we both know he'll try more than once to match partners if he thinks they should be."

Grayson didn't bother to answer her. He simply responded to Bishop.

Copy. We'll upload all the photos and check in tomorrow in case you have news of Bethany Hicks or we have anything to report. And we'll see if we can gather a few more puzzle pieces.

Watch your backs.

Copy. Out.

Grayson closed the laptop and rubbed his eyes with both hands. They ached, and his head not only felt like it was stuffed full of cotton but was really beginning to pound. He was also still cold and hoped he could manage a hot shower before he made it to bed and the sleep he also needed.

"Breakfast is from seven to nine, right?" he asked Geneva, half-consciously keeping his voice quiet because everything was beginning to sound way too loud in his pounding head.

"Yeah. Let's make it toward the later end, okay? We both need sleep, Bishop was right about that." Her voice was also softer than normal. "I want a long, hot shower, and then maybe a snack or three, and I'm hitting the sack. Do you have your migraine meds?"

"Yes." He kept it simple.

"Both of them?"

"Yeah, but the doc said—"

"I know what the doc said. Not to take both at once unless it was one of the bad migraines and you could fall into bed and sleep immediately. Which is what you need to do."

She produced a second small bottle of protein drink from a pocket of her jacket, even though he hadn't seen her get it from her suite.

"I know you won't go out or even call down and ask for a glass of milk, so take this with the meds; you need something in your stomach." Her soft voice was brisk.

Grayson didn't bother to argue because she was right. "Thanks. We should plan to go down in the morning about eight thirty. That'll give me time to upload all the photos."

"See you there." She set the drink down on a small

table not too close to him and the laptop, waved casually, and left his suite.

Only Geneva, he thought a bit fuzzily, could emerge from the scary uncertainty of imprisonment by person or persons unknown and act like nothing unusual had happened. Only Geneva.

FIFTEEN

Miranda, well able to see and read the report and response glowing on the screen of the laptop on a nearby desk, waited until her husband returned to their bed before saying, "You didn't tell them about Nellie."

Bishop slipped into the warm cocoon of covers and drew her close. "I think they both know she's there."

"But not who or what she is."

"Nellie isn't even sure of that," he responded.

"You mean not yet." Miranda felt her body fit itself to his as though to her other half, which he was, very glad that they had this time together. They worked hard to carve out time for themselves and managed, for the most part, but the SCU tended to have a heavy caseload, and even though the unit was still expanding as new members joined, and Haven existed now to aid in their investigations as well as plenty of their own, it was still more usual that she was out in the field leading one team while he was leading another. Sometimes with thousands of miles between them.

But not tonight. Tonight, they had time for themselves. Still, their unit was very much a part of what they were, together and separately, so the teams working cases without them were always very much on their minds.

"You're expecting something to happen," she said, not reading him even though their connection was open, thoughts and feelings flowing easily and familiarly between them.

Just knowing him.

"Nellie's the catalyst," he answered. "And she turns thirty in a week. They're running out of time." He stroked the warm, silky skin of her shoulder and back, the physical touch as important to their connection as the easy mental link.

"It's an . . . oddly exact deadline," she mused. "I don't think we've seen anything like it before. Custom, or fact?"

"Custom made it fact."

Miranda lifted her head from his shoulder and smiled down at him, seeing his slightly amused expression even with no more than the dim firelight in the hearth beyond the foot of the bed to aid her. "Sometimes," she said, "I can really understand how you madden some of our team members. And why Hollis calls you Yoda," she added, referring to one of the more irreverent SCU team members.

His soft laugh was a sound very few people ever heard. "Beloved, some puzzles just *are*. I don't create them."

"No, but you revel in them."

"I like the Universe with mysteries still to be solved. If they can be." He sobered. "Salem is one of those mysteries, quite likely a bigger one than we know. When all is said and done, I don't know if we'll understand much more than we do now. It's hard to conceive of in this modern world, but some people and some places can be so isolated from the rest of our society that they almost . . . create their own reality."

"With the aid of psychic energy?"

He nodded slowly. "And determination, and will, and—a vision."

"Utopia?" Her tone was more wry than dry.

"Initially, I'm sure it was a group effort. They just wanted a nice, safe little town. And somewhere along the way, the five families took more of a hand in shaping it. Eventually one had to come along who wanted to shape it alone. Though in my experience and yours, one man's personal utopia is hell to most others. The never-ending lure of power."

Miranda settled back down, close, her head on his shoulder.

And that's what they're walking into. How long have you known? The mind talk was as easy to them both now as spoken speech, though it held far more layers of thought, idea, emotion, intimacy, and understanding.

Suspected since I met Nellie. She had no walls that really protected her then, and . . . her father left her far more than she was consciously aware of. Her mother left her even more.

And she has to find both in Salem.

Yes. Find. Accept. Control. And stop at least one hellish vision of utopia.

With Gray and Geneva to help her.

Yes. And one more.

Finn.

Finn. He holds the lock, Nellie the key. Gray and Geneva have the experience, the awareness and understanding of darkness, the strength and skill to push through whatever they have to, as they've already done.

We really have two teams there, don't we?

Bishop's rueful mental laugh was quicksilver. *Four people who need to find their own connections to each other. The Universe sets the place and time, puts them where they need to be, and puts their feet on the path. After that . . .*

Some things have to happen just the way they happen.

Yes, beloved. But every choice they make shapes the path each walks. It's something we've learned well.

We haven't seen . . . how it ends. For any of them.

No. And I don't believe we will until it's . . . all . . . over and done with. Perhaps because Salem really is out of sync with the world we know. Perhaps because those sent to search and understand face a kind of power we've never encountered before. Or . . . perhaps it's just the Universe reminding us again that our abilities are no more than the tools we use, the weapons when they have to be, but never to be used without understanding and the willingness to pay whatever price is demanded.

The Universe is a hard taskmaster, Miranda observed.

Which is why we train our teams to be tougher than even they know, to be more than even they know.

This time, it was Miranda's rueful mental laugh that was a quicksilver flash. *I think sometimes they wish they knew a little more about both right from the beginning.*

Some things have to happen—

—just the way they happen. Yes, darling.

SATURDAY

Geneva was up early despite—or because of—the first really comfortable night's sleep she'd had since being left in that cellar. The hot shower before bed had been blissful, both because it warmed her and because it got her clean; Geneva hated being dirty. In fact, she took another shower when she realized she was awake for the day a little before seven.

She doubted Gray was up yet. The migraines that tended to follow any extended use of his spider senses were the worst ones he ever had, and she didn't doubt he'd taken the knockout med the doctor had prescribed as well as the one that helped the pain and other symptoms yet allowed him to be functional. He hated giving in to what he thought of as a weakness to that extent, but he was neither stupid nor burdened with an ego that would demand he pretend to be okay when he wasn't, and he was a pro. She doubted he'd be awake before eight, if then.

They all paid some sort of price for their abilities, she reflected as she dried her long, thick, ridiculously red hair. She had trouble with electronics; she fully expected this dryer to short out before the end of her stay, even as carefully and briefly as she used it, and she'd already replaced the lightbulb in her bedside lamp three times. She'd simply unplugged the bedside clock radio within an hour of first arriving here, since it wouldn't have lasted long at all.

As for ATMs, computers, cell phones, or tablets, forget about it. To her, they were useful only as props of normalcy, plugged in a careful distance away from her touch, and strictly avoided until it was time to pack to leave.

And she'd learned the hard way not to stand too close to any clock, though the more old-fashioned the less likely she was to affect it. Hell, one of the reasons she carried and used the old-fashioned roll of film and view-finder sort of camera rather than a digital one like Gray's was because she had to; digital cameras in her hands lasted about as long as a cup of coffee.

With Gray, the price he paid was migraines. Virtually always when he was on a case, or was otherwise using his abilities, both empathic and the spider senses. Like her, he accepted the price demanded with resignation, though certainly not happily. It was common enough for quite a few members of the unit to suffer headaches, even black-outs, and so far the doctors and other specialists had found no preventative, only meds for the resulting symptoms.

But at least the meds worked, tweaked for psychic minds, Geneva believed, though nobody had ever said so.

As for Geneva's problems, Bishop had people constantly working to refine special casings for cell phones and tablets, and various protections for laptops, but the truth was that for a lot of psychics, tech they could reliably use was pretty damned low-grade.

An irony of the Universe that so many of those with "extra" senses often found communication over any distance at all to be a problem *because* of the useless sophistication of the communication tools they were given.

Bishop had, fairly recently, displayed a growing ability to reach some of his agents telepathically, and from quite a distance, but as with all their abilities, it had its limits. There were some rare team members he couldn't read even if they were in the same room—though most of those swore there was "contact of some kind" going on. As in many other things, Bishop had never explained whether his was a new ability or a natural evolution, a strengthening of his already formidable telepathic range, and his agents knew better than to ask.

If he wanted them to know, he'd tell them. Otherwise, questions would be ignored or turned aside with what Geneva considered one of his typical nonanswers.

Since she was one of those he could normally reach at a distance, and easily, Geneva knew that whatever weird "static" other psychics outside the area had picked up hovering in and around Salem, and the growing tingling discomfort she felt physically, which she assumed came from the same source, had to be blocking him somehow, because her normal faint, familiar sense of him was absent.

It wasn't at all intrusive, that sense. It was, she had

decided, rather like a ring one was so used to wearing that it was noticed only when it slipped off the finger suddenly and clinked on the floor.

Geneva caught herself grinning as she thought of Bishop clinking, then pushed that aside determinedly. She was, after all, a pro.

Now that she was out of her mountain jail and back in town, she was far more conscious of the "static" than she had been even those few days before. Even so, she didn't so much sense it as *feel* it. Like her skin was crawling a bit. Just a bit. Still, she had a hunch her current edginess was at least partly due to the probable buildup of that energy all around her.

Partly. The rest was due to Gray.

Not that she was about to tell *him* that, of course.

Any way she looked at it, the static/energy was worrisome.

Geneva killed as much time as she could before impatience drove her from her room at barely eight o'clock. She put a set of copies of the dump site photos in an envelope to slip under Gray's door so he could upload them to Bishop before he went down for breakfast. And she took only one of her cameras with her, its case hanging by a long strap casually on her shoulder.

Geneva had forgotten that the B and B usually filled up with guests on weekend mornings, drawn by the excellent breakfasts offered, so she was momentarily startled when she entered the big dining room to find every table occupied. The quiet murmur of conversation was accompanied by the occasional clinking of silverware against china, but they were peaceful sounds.

She knew Ms. Payton would appear within moments to efficiently conjure a table out of nowhere, but as she stood gazing around she saw suddenly at a table slightly apart from those around it a coal black Pit bull sitting quietly beside a petite woman with honey brown hair and a faintly preoccupied expression.

Even though she'd never seen her before, Geneva recognized the psychic she had sensed the night before. She hadn't thought much about making herself known to the other woman, hadn't weighed the pros and cons as she usually did, but even as that thought crossed her mind, a faint frown disturbed that very pretty face, and Geneva found herself meeting a pair of unexpectedly sharp brown eyes across the few feet separating them.

The other woman recognized exactly what Geneva was, static or no static.

Without realizing she was going to, Geneva went to the table, which was set for two, and said, "Busy this morning. Mind if I join you? I'm Geneva Raynor."

"Nellie Reed. And please do." She was maybe a year or two younger than Geneva, but those sharp eyes were older than her years and held shadows.

It didn't surprise Geneva; psychics rarely had an easy life, one way or another. She slid into the seat across from Nellie, hanging the strap of her camera case over one side of her chair. She met the intent gaze of the very large dog and smiled. "He's gorgeous."

"Leo," Nellie offered.

"Hey, Leo." Geneva leaned over to accept a paw suddenly waved in the air, aware of Nellie's surprise but not sharing it. Animals tended to take to her immediately, especially dogs and cats.

"I've never seen him do that before," Nellie said slowly.

Geneva settled back in her chair, still smiling. "I guess he knows I love dogs. Or"—she lowered her voice just a bit—"he knows I'm like you. Psychic."

Gray would have winced, Geneva knew; he was always more cautious about revealing psychic abilities, on a case or not. But Geneva had the sense of a clock ticking in the back of her mind, something that had begun the instant she'd met Nellie's gaze. And she was not a woman willing to waste valuable time, especially when there was a child missing and bodies turning up, however quickly they were swept from the view—and possibly the knowledge—of the townsfolk.

Nellie was saved from having to respond right away when a cheerful waitress appeared to fill Geneva's coffee cup and take her breakfast order. Having already discovered the pastries were to die for, Geneva ordered a large bear claw as well as bacon and eggs; she'd missed real food the last couple of days and intended to make up for lost time.

It wasn't until the waitress had gone off to get Geneva's order that she once again met Nellie's gaze. And found it, not unexpectedly, guarded, wary.

"We tend to recognize each other," Geneva said, her

voice low but casual. "Not always, but quite often. Recognize each other as . . . fellow travelers on an uncommon path. You recognized me, didn't you." It wasn't a question.

Nellie hesitated, one hand wearing a very snug, beautifully made, whisper-thin black glove toying with the handle of her coffee cup. Then, finally, she said slowly, "I just got the sense we . . . had things in common."

"Ah. Then I'm guessing you're clairvoyant. And a few other things as well."

"What do you mean?"

Geneva was good at reading all the layers of a question. "The way you phrased it told me probably clairvoyant; you tend to get a sense of things, flashes of knowledge. But that's not your primary ability, I think. A telepath, like me. That's always been the strongest ability, so it's the one you concentrate on tamping down. As for the other things . . . Well, don't freak out, but late last night when I passed by your door, I knew there was someone practicing meditation techniques of a . . . certain kind. Meant for control. If you were only clairvoyant, or even only clairvoyant and telepathic, you probably wouldn't have needed those."

Nellie was frowning now, but it was clearly thoughtful rather than angry. Abruptly, she said, "Bishop. You're one of his."

Geneva wasn't at all surprised by the guess—because she knew very well it wasn't a guess. And because she knew Bishop kept track of psychics he located over the years, whether or not they wanted to become agents or investigators, just as she'd reminded Gray the night before. "I'm a photographer; my job is to gather pictures of the gorgeous scenery around here for a proposed book." Geneva paused, grinned faintly, and added, "And yes, I'm one of Bishop's. Here very, *very* unofficially."

Half under her breath, Nellie murmured, "That's the one thing I didn't think of when I knew I'd come to Salem. I probably should have called him before I left home."

"To find out if he had people in place?"

Nellie hesitated. "To find out if he knew of any danger here. Anything . . . unusual going on. Though I guess you being here sort of answers those questions."

"Suspicions aren't necessarily knowledge," Geneva said, adding immediately, "and some answers aren't all that helpful. Did you come here to look for danger, or are you trying to avoid it?"

The blunt question widened Nellie's eyes, and for a long moment, she didn't answer. The return of the waitress with Geneva's order gave her an extra few minutes to consider how to answer.

It wasn't enough time.

Digging into her breakfast, Geneva said conversationally, "You'll have to forgive me if I don't dance around the subject very well. I'm not good at that. The truth is that I *am* here looking for trouble, danger. I've already found both, and I have a strong sense that time is short when it comes to finding answers. I need to know where you stand."

"Can't you read my mind?" Nellie asked steadily.

"Nope. I mean, I probably *can*, since I picked up on the meditation last night—we each tend to have a finite range, either distance or frequency—but I'm not reading you. I have my shields up. It tends to take most people, even other psychics, a bit of time to understand and accept that we telepaths aren't plucking your thoughts out of your head without so much as a by-your-leave. That would be an invasion of privacy, and we try to avoid that whenever possible."

"Try."

Honestly, Geneva said, "Well, sometimes the job forces us to be . . . impolite, especially when it comes to the bad guys. More often, though, the truth is that even the strongest psychic can't be on guard all the time. That's why you meditating slipped through my shields last night; I was tired, and when I passed by your door, your concentration on those techniques reached through. Probably helped by the fact that I recognized them. We've all been taught, and pretty much the same way."

"All of Bishop's people. The unit."

"Yeah. And others outside the unit. Psychics Bishop's been meeting for years who don't want to become feds or investigators or just aren't suited for the work. Still, he always does what he can to help psychics, whether they're his agents and investigators or just want to get on with their own lives as best they can. The gloves were his idea, right? To give you a visible, actual barrier you could focus on."

Nellie was silent for a moment, then drew a deep breath and let it out slowly. "Bishop is one of the few people I've trusted in the last few years. Since things got . . . stronger. Worse. And now . . . I need to know if I can trust you. Here. In Salem. Because I was sent here to stop something from happening. Something evil. And I don't even know what it is."

SIXTEEN

Grayson wasn't at all surprised that Geneva was already up by the time he dragged himself out of bed and took a hot shower to help clear away the last of the cobwebs the migraine sleep med tended to leave behind. It had at least been effective, pretty much knocking him out minutes after he'd fallen into bed, and thanks to both meds his sleep had been deep and painless. Now, the morning after, he didn't feel like turning his head too fast because even his neck felt sore, everything sounded a bit louder than it should have, and his eyes felt dryer than they should be, but those he recognized as aftereffects of the too-prolonged use of his spider senses.

Normal, for him. As the day wore on, things would improve. Unless they didn't.

The envelope with Geneva's photos had been slid under his door as promised, and Grayson took the time to scan them in and send to Bishop both Geneva's shots of the mutilated body left at a dump site and his own shots of the tracks he'd found on the mountain and the strange old ruins containing a bloodstained altar.

After that, he took a few moments to study Geneva's photos, frowning over them, convinced as she had been that the "occult" symbols painted in blood on the rocks around the body were nothing of the sort but likely left just to confuse or terrify whoever might have stumbled across the remains. Maybe the same reason . . . that . . . had been done to the skull, why the brain was so obviously missing, though he couldn't figure out how it had been accomplished.

Not that any of it made whoever they were after less dangerous. More likely their unsub was even more dangerous, smart enough to cover his trail or sick enough to believe that he had—or deserved to have—some supernatural abilities that justified his evil acts.

Or he was just plain evil.

None of the possibilities were at all reassuring.

Grayson didn't have to knock on Geneva's door as he passed just before eight thirty to know she was already up and about; she'd delivered the photos to his room. Even more, however, the thread of awareness he felt too often for his peace of mind was there, not a sense of her emotions, just a sense of her.

Just.

He went downstairs and into the large dining room, finding the weekend breakfast crowd beginning to thin out, two waitresses busily clearing several deserted tables and at least three others already cleared and set for the later risers such as him.

He also found Geneva sitting at a table with the woman and her dog he had seen checking in yesterday and they had both sensed last night while passing her door. The two women were sitting a little apart from the tables nearest them, and those were now empty of guests, but it still made Grayson uneasy.

They were talking very intently.

Knowing Gen, she had instigated the meeting, impatient as always to find whatever information she could to help her investigation, especially now with a kid missing, and she was talking to the other woman with an absorbed expression he recognized.

Sighing a little, Grayson went to another table some distance away, but at an angle where he could observe, and was soon eating his own breakfast.

His memories of the night before were clear—not always the case after one of his migraines—and one of them was that Bishop had suggested they find a way to meet up, team up in whatever way seemed best. Now he wondered if maybe Geneva had decided to avoid that. Then again, she could only be getting acquainted with another guest who just happened to be psychic . . .

Grayson sipped his coffee, his veiled gaze on their table. No. He hadn't been a big believer in coincidence even before joining the SCU; by now it was something he profoundly distrusted. He didn't believe it was an accident, fortunate or unfortunate, that another psychic with, Geneva believed, powerful abilities had shown up in Salem just now. Bishop believed that the energy static in and around the town was increasing, possibly building toward something, planned or unplanned, that could easily affect psychics in ways they could not predict. It could already be affecting the two of them in ways they weren't even aware of.

Like his apparent ability to sense those damned crows, and maybe even Geneva's "new" ability to tap into the residual thoughts left behind when people departed a place.

Her possible new ability sounded more useful to him.

A little girl was missing, three strangers they knew had been drawn here had seemingly disappeared into thin air, and there had been at least four bodies—or the mutilated remains of them—found over the past few weeks.

So where did this woman fit in?

For that matter, where did he and Geneva fit in? For the first time, Grayson had the uneasy suspicion that adding three outside psychics to an odd small town that had been virtually isolated for generations might well have upset some delicate balance. Especially if, as Geneva believed, each of the powerful five families could boast of at least one psychic and possibly more.

Was that why the "static" sensed by Bishop's monitoring psychics was increasing in strength? Because he, Geneva, and this unknown woman were here? Was it a defense mechanism, energy composed of the excess countless psychics were using to strengthen their shields because they consciously or unconsciously sensed a threat?

Grayson had belonged to the SCU too long to discount anything, and that possibility worried him. Many of them had experience with psychics creating or contributing to energy fields, and seldom was the outcome a positive one for the psychics caught up in those fields.

Pushing that aside for the moment, he opened his senses just a bit as he focused on that other table. He didn't try the spider senses again so soon, but even with just his empathic senses—and those dulled postmigraine, as usual—he could feel the tension at that other table and was pretty sure most of it came from the other woman. She was still wary but, more than that, she was . . . worried?

Afraid?

He felt another flicker, one of interest but curiously alien, and shifted his gaze to find that the dog was looking steadily at him.

Interest and . . . oh, yeah, disconcerting as hell. Not emotions he was accustomed to sensing or feeling from people. The interest was laser focused, and there was a curious weighing up of him by the animal that was more senses than anything else. How he smelled (woods and pine trees and bacon), the sound of his breathing, even his steady heartbeat and the faint throbbing behind his eyes.

Grayson knew a dog's senses were far keener than human ones, even those enhanced by spider senses and years of practice, but he'd never thought about what emotions might be behind those senses or how they were used. The dog even had a sense of his own identity. He was Leo. He was Leo, and he was curious about the man because . . . because the man was like Nellie.

Nellie?

Like Nellie and like . . . Geneva. Gen-ee-vaa. That other name was shaped tentatively, carefully, being committed to memory. And this other new name, this other new person, was Grayson. Gray-son.

The dog Leo felt friendly toward them all, because he knew they were alike in a way that made him feel comfortable and unthreatened. He was also certain they posed no threat to Nellie. Maybe they could help her; that was what he felt. But this place bothered him a bit, made the fur down his spine want to stir; even the air outside smelled just the slightest bit wrong and it baffled his canine mind . . .

GRAYSON BROKE OFF that contact with more effort than he expected and looked down at the pastry that was supposed to be the last of his breakfast. A flash of queasiness told him he would not be eating anything else for a while. In fact, he hoped he'd be able to keep the rest of his breakfast down.

That was a thought he pushed away quickly.

His head was throbbing, and he rubbed a thumb between his eyes. Hard.

Dumb. Dumb to try using any of your senses so soon.

But . . . First crows and now this dog.

Damn.

For the first time, he was getting more than emotions. And from *animals*. The crows and this dog, at least.

New ability, or evolution of what he'd always had? Same thing. Either way, it wouldn't come without a cost. Probably a painful one.

Because one thing he already knew was that picking up emotions from animals—crows and this dog, at least—forced his mind to work in a new way in order to somehow translate what was not human into something his human mind could understand. Alien emotions, concepts. Like looking at or hearing a new language that bore only a faint resemblance to his native tongue. And included hieroglyphs.

His mind seemed to be dealing with the chore almost automatically, if slowly and with an effort, the way a new ability triggered often did, and yet Grayson could feel the strain, like using a muscle he'd never known was there. The ache in his head was stronger, and this was the kind of ache he doubted any meds yet developed by science could touch.

It could, however, trigger another migraine. Possibly, at least. It was rare that one migraine followed hard on the heels of another, and he really hoped it wouldn't now due to these new senses.

That could definitely cause problems down the road.

The question was, was it something he could protect himself against by putting more effort into his shield, or something that would only worsen as time passed? Could he control it, or at least focus in order to use it? If the energy-static was indeed building, and that had been the trigger, he wasn't sure his shield would be able to hold steady against it. Though, presumably, keeping his shield up would keep him from sensing crows and dogs as well as people.

Or would it?

Most of the agents under Bishop had learned, sometimes at great cost, that conditions in the field could and did affect them in abrupt and unexpected ways. *And* that the shields many had come to depend on could fail them at critical moments.

It had also taught them that the side effects of using their abilities in new, different ways could easily worsen.

Great.

A steady series of migraines was daunting even to one accustomed to the occasional wall banger, but even more he seriously doubted that Bishop would keep him on this investigation—or possibly any other—if that proved to be the case. Not only because his effectiveness as an agent was bound to be lessened, but because Bishop did *not* take chances when it came to the health of his agents, especially when abilities and their side effects became unstable.

So far, none of the doctors and other geniuses the unit chief employed to monitor and frequently test his agents had been able to state with certainty that their abilities, with or without side effects, would not do some long-term damage to their brains. Especially since medical science had to begin with the unfortunate truth that they hardly understood how much of the brain even worked.

Doubly true of the brain of a psychic.

Before Grayson could gather his thoughts and make some sense of them, let alone ask himself some tough professional questions concerning just how effective he could be here if he couldn't even count on his usual control and shields, someone else was sending a message with the utter clarity that had always been able to cut through whatever shields he possessed.

Gray, we need to meet up, but a bit later. Nellie and I are going out to walk Leo. Nice new friends, casually met, with things in common. When we come back, we'll go up to my suite, because she's part of this too, and there are things we all need to talk about. Why don't you slip in there ahead of us and use your scanner to make sure nobody's listening in. I don't think anyone is, but best to be sure. Hang out your DO NOT DISTURB *sign. Nobody'll be surprised. You look like another migraine's coming. Better take at least that one med and maybe lie down to wait for us after you scan my suite.*

Grayson wanted to turn his head and glare at Geneva as the two women, the dog pacing beside his mistress, strolled from the room, because when she sent a stream of thoughts like that, they were a bit like sharp darts tossed into his already aching head.

And besides, who was the primary agent here?

He was.

Not that Geneva had ever been or would ever be subordinate to anyone else. She obeyed Bishop—mostly—because she chose to, because she deeply respected him, because she loved the work, and because she had been happy to find a use for abilities that had rendered her childhood miserable.

Not that she'd ever said as much to Grayson, but he'd caught her once or twice in vulnerable moments with her guards down, and he knew. He understood; it was the rule rather than the exception that people born with psychic abilities could not lay claim to memories of a happy childhood.

Still, he was supposed to be the lead partner here, dammit. Headache or no headache.

He pushed his plate away and fought the urge to keep rubbing his forehead. As if that would help.

Yeah, dammit, he needed the meds that would keep the worst of the pain and other symptoms at bay and allow him to function, and he needed to scan Geneva's suite if there was going to be any kind of discussion about what was going on in Salem. Maybe he even needed a nap. But most of all, he needed to get up and walk upstairs without falling on his ass.

Before he could even push his chair back, a professionally sympathetic voice spoke.

"I've heard migraines can be hell and last for days," Ms. Payton said. "Is there anything we can do to help?"

Grayson moved his head slightly, rather cautiously, so he could look up at her, and forced a smile. "No, but thanks. My fault. I didn't get enough sleep or give the meds time to work. I think this time I'll obey my doctor. Take a nap. Maybe even sleep longer."

"Probably best," she said, still professionally sympathetic. "And a good day to stay in anyway. It's even colder out than yesterday, and the forecast is for snow tonight or tomorrow."

"Looks like I came down off the Trail just in time," he murmured, pushing back his chair and rising to his feet, being careful of his balance and knowing she saw it.

"I'd say so. I hope you can get some rest, Mr. Sheridan."

At least she's not offering to have me carried upstairs.

"Yeah," he said, knowing that wasn't the plan. "Me too."

FINN DEVERELL WATCHED the two women and the dog walking slowly toward the park, talking intently. He was not surprised to see them, though he thought at least one of them might be surprised by his lack of it.

Then again, perhaps they had already figured out at least some of what went on here in Salem; Geneva Raynor had been in town long enough to have some ideas, especially since she was a trained investigator. And because he had the strong suspicion that she had located at least one of the dump sites, possibly more.

As for Nellie Cavendish, he wondered how long she expected the alias to hold. Not long, he thought, because she was a very bright woman—and a Cavendish. What she hadn't known when she got here she would be absorbing from the very air around her now, and so quickly he was certain it would surprise her.

He wondered if she even knew she could do that.

There were clairvoyants and then there were *clairvoyants*.

Probably, he thought, one reason the two women—and probably Sheridan as well—had connected so quickly. Nellie because she was more likely to trust visitors to Salem than residents, and the other two because they knew at least some of what had happened here, and perhaps even what threatened to happen.

Quickly. Events were moving quickly.

Finn had the sense that the urgency he'd been aware of for some time now was stronger than ever. Even the timing of what happened was not natural. He could almost *see* the strings being pulled, events being guided toward a desired end.

It wasn't his desired end.

Still, he'd been almost sure even before meeting Nellie Cavendish that there was no way to stop what was coming, not if it was just him. He had done what he could, hoping it would be enough, but by now he admitted to himself that without Nellie and the abilities he doubted she was even as yet fully aware of, there was no way to finally put an end to a horror that had already taken too many lives.

Nellie . . . and perhaps the other two. The ones who knew how to fight monsters.

Geneva Raynor had displayed the skill and cunning he had expected, escaping her prison with no help even from the man Finn knew was her partner, at least in this. And Grayson Sheridan looked to be a man capable of completing whatever task he set his mind to, whatever that might be.

Both would make good allies.

Finn had to talk to them, and soon. All of them. Less than a week now until Nellie's birthday, and he knew only too well that Duncan would not wait even that long to . . . test . . . her.

And so far his tests had proven lethal.

She didn't trust him; Finn knew that. He could hardly blame her for the natural distrust, but it made the situation all the more urgent that he find some way of convincing her they were both on the same side.

Her distrust of her father didn't help matters. Finn thought Thomas Cavendish had made a mistake in distancing himself from his own child, even though he understood the reasons behind those long-ago decisions and actions.

He wondered if Nellie would. If, perhaps, that was what she would need to hear from him in order to begin to trust.

Why her father had done what he had done.

As for the rest, those strings being pulled, Finn was in some ways hamstrung. He had to move cautiously, because a direct threat would be dealt with instantly; Duncan had too much at stake to risk anyone stopping him, not now. He wanted power, and he had found a horrific way of obtaining it.

Finn had his spies, loyal, long-standing, and well trained by him, even one of the militia Duncan believed was his own man. And having those others out and about would be expected since his family owned the *Salem Chronicle* and had their jobs to do. But there were some questions they could ask in pursuit of a good story or two and many more they couldn't ask.

Like everything else in Salem, all the important information lay beneath the surface, known only to a few. And virtually always protected by walls many generations of the five families had learned to build sure and strong.

Still, Finn knew far more than Duncan realized, and he intended to keep it that way as long as possible, even though the energy required to strengthen his own walls—now, at least—took more out of him than he wanted to admit.

Time. He needed more *time.* And there was so little left.

"Finn?"

He turned from the window to find his nephew Robert standing in the open doorway of his office. Finn didn't run the paper mill out on the river; an aunt was in charge of that business and doing very well with it. Finn had chosen to oversee the *Chronicle* and so kept his dual-purpose office here on an upper floor of the building housing the newspaper, right in the thick of things, where he needed to be. He could also take care of many of his responsibilities in the militia from this central position in town and this quiet office. As much of it as he could control, at least.

Robert, who should have been in college, had decided

to take a semester off, and even though he hadn't told his father why, he had told Finn.

He knew some of what was happening. Had a pretty good idea what was coming. And he was a Deverell. He was also one of Finn's best and most subtle spies and had been for years, patiently and thoroughly insinuating himself into the good graces of most of the younger five-family members.

"What is it?" Finn asked.

Robert came inside, closing the door behind him, and crossed to one of the visitor's chairs in front of Finn's desk and put his hands on the back, the grip a little tighter than casual. "Word is, Duncan wants everybody in church tomorrow. And the word wasn't exactly subtle."

Finn considered his nephew thoughtfully. Only ten years separated them in age, and they had been more like brothers since Robert's childhood. Especially since Robert had turned to Finn when he realized he had inherited the Talent that was solely of the Deverell family in Salem, a Talent Finn shared.

Robert had the Talent in spades.

He was an empath, strong enough to slip within the walls of others without even their awareness. And like Finn's, that ability had not been blocked in him from childhood, which made him both powerful and in possession of a great deal of control.

"Did he say why?" Finn asked finally.

"Not that I've heard. But people are getting edgy,

especially since that fourth body was found. I know his men in the militia tried to keep it all quiet, but word got out. Details got out. Some of the worst details. The kind that couldn't accidentally happen to a guy just hiking along."

SEVENTEEN

Finn wondered briefly if Geneva Raynor was responsible for that leak but dismissed the idea instantly. She was too professional.

"He didn't want townsfolk to know about that," Finn said. "All the ugly details. Or even that it happened."

"He never does, does he? Or about the other three. What was—done to them. Why it was. Still no idea who let it get out, but it's out. Just whispers so far, and that edginess. There are people arguing it can't be true, others who want to believe that. Plenty who just don't want to face it, like always. To pretend everything is normal here. But any way you look at it, people are getting jumpy. I'm guessing Duncan wants to clamp a lid on it, so nothing will interfere with his own plans."

"He'd want that. But the question is, can he do it?"

Robert frowned slightly. "The preachers will say whatever he tells them to—they always do. He's head of his family. And even if he *is* the only direct-descendant Cavendish with the Talent, he has it all."

"Does he?"

"Doesn't he?" Robert countered. "His clairvoyance is incredibly powerful when it's unshielded. He has the crows, and we both know they'd kill for him."

"At his command, not *for* him. There's a difference."

Robert nodded. "I know, but the end result is the same. And even if he's been cagey about it, we both know he has the other Cavendish Talents. He has a majority of the militia under his control, quite a few even among his devoted followers. And he has *them*. His . . . flock. The ones who believe every word he says like it's holy writ. Or unholy writ. They'll do whatever he tells them to; we both know that. Hell, we *all* know that, and I for one don't have to see the evidence to believe it. He has them convinced he can recognize evil, only he. That the evil threatens Salem, threatens them, and he can . . . draw it forth and send it to hell."

"Hence his little ceremonies," Finn said.

"Yeah. Look, I'm close to finding out where he holds them, or at least where the next one will be, but I don't have it yet. I can't even find out what goes on there, except that what used to be mostly chanting and sex and maybe a drop or two of some willing participant's blood mixed with God knows what herbs is something he's now built up to actual human sacrifice. I really don't think there's a question about that, Finn. Not now. Four tortured and mutilated bodies turned up is no coincidence. And if he's killing them, we both know he can gain power, grow stronger, from that alone. Especially if he's getting his own hands bloody."

"*Maybe* he can gain power through those acts."

"You don't think so?"

Finn was silent for a moment, frowning, then made up his mind. Robert was a strong empath and possessed strong shields, and he knew almost as much as Finn about what was happening and the dangers looming. In some ways, he probably knew more. He needed to know now that there were new players, that the balance was beginning to tip.

And the deadly danger of a single wrong move.

"Have a seat," he told his nephew. "We need to talk."

NELLIE SAT IN a chair in Geneva's sitting room at Hales B and B and eyed the two agents, still more than a little wary. She knew both were psychic—even though she was still wearing her gloves and thought her control was pretty good, at least for the time being—and she believed both were federal agents, Bishop's people, here to investigate. Not because of their IDs but because they'd talked briefly about Bishop and the SCU as strangers to either wouldn't have been able to.

And because . . . she'd just *known*.

She hadn't known people had disappeared, including a little girl only a few days before, and she had definitely not known about the bodies—or remains—found.

"How can that not be all over the newspaper? How

can it not be on the news, at least statewide? *Everything* makes the news these days. That or gets posted on the Internet, somewhere."

"One of the mysteries of this place," Geneva said from her position at the near end of the couch at right angles to Nellie's chair. "According to Bishop, we'd never have heard a thing except that it came through the usual un-official channels: Somebody who knew somebody who knew somebody who knew Bishop suggested they con-tact one of *his* contacts when the police refused to act, and he got the word. Since it was so unofficial, he prob-ably had a few people, maybe Haven operatives, talk to those who insisted their friends were missing, and then started them nosing around the area outside Salem. They didn't get much. Still only rumor and whispers, mostly, but it was enough to get us here. Unofficially."

Nellie didn't ask how that was possible. She didn't know Bishop well, but she thought she knew him well enough to believe that this was the kind of investigation he'd make possible, even if he had to go outside official channels to do it. "I know about Haven," she said almost absently. "The last time I talked to Bishop he told me about it. In case I might like that option."

"He hates to waste a good psychic," Grayson said. He was sitting on a chair across the coffee table from Nel-lie's, her big dog Leo sitting at his feet, and he was gently pulling at the silky black ears. And working very hard to keep his shields up. It had been Leo's idea to sit at his feet and gaze up at him steadily, and Grayson was still sur-prised and a bit unsettled by that, especially since he still wasn't sure if the . . . emotions and senses he could get from Leo even with his shields up represented a new ability or the evolution of his empathy.

Good . . . feels good . . . Graay-son . . .

"I got that impression," Nellie confessed, oblivious to the mental byplay between her dog and the agent. She was still frowning. "And he can be pretty convincing. But either the FBI or Haven is a step too far for me."

"You're not alone," Grayson said. "Plenty have turned him down, and all for very good reasons. Still, I think Bishop would make an even greater effort to recruit strong psychics like you, except that once he began putting the unit together, he discovered there were more of us out here than anybody had guessed. A lot more. Maybe because he was the first one to really go looking. To begin counting. Or maybe for some other reason."

"I always thought psychics were rare," Nellie said.

"Yeah, most people do, if they even believe in us. I know that's what even Bishop believed in the beginning, but he found out pretty quickly that there are a *lot* of us, all ages, both genders, all races, belief systems, professions. All over the world. Latent psychics who're adults when their abilities are triggered, and a lot born with them.

"Nobody really knows why, or why now. The docs and scientists who study us from time to time have lots of theories, everything from natural evolution to interference at the genetic level from all the electrical and magnetic energy mankind has wrapped us all in, especially during the last fifty years and more."

"That's a little scary," Nellie said, slowly now.

"Not their scariest theory," Grayson murmured.

A little impatiently, Geneva said, "Theories we can maybe discuss when all the shouting is over? Nellie, I know you're full of questions, and we hate to hit you with all this only a day after you got here, but bad things are happening and we need to stop them."

Nellie looked at her, then nodded. "So you guys believe the missing people are all dead?"

"Except for Bethany Hicks," Geneva answered immediately. Her voice was steady when she added, "I never touched her mind, so I can't be absolutely sure. But that body found last week certainly wasn't hers. My bet is he was a fourth person drawn here, maybe with fewer friends to worry and report him as missing right away."

"But you don't know that for sure."

"I think we'd better assume it. Also assume this one was grabbed en route somehow, because he was never registered here at Hales. The other three were."

"About that," Grayson said. "We had three missings, now maybe four, and we're reasonably sure they didn't get far from Salem alive. But we also have no crime scenes, no dump sites we could swear to in court, and that pretty much adds up to zip."

"I've been here two weeks," Geneva said, sounding disgusted now. "I should know more. But this town . . . these people . . . Everything seems just fine on the surface, better than fine. Nicely flourishing little town, good economy, citizens doing well and content. They have what appear to be excellent schools, a decent-sized hospital that's well equipped and well staffed, and trained first responders in EMS units, at least two fire departments—and the militia."

Nellie was watching her steadily. "But?"

"But . . . there are those bodies, probably belonging to the people drawn or lured here to Salem who never really left. The reasons for which we still don't know. A massive cover-up at the very least. And we have Bethany disappearing. And nobody in Salem seems very bothered, assuming they even know. About any of it."

"I can't believe her parents wouldn't know and wouldn't care," Nellie objected.

"Maybe Bishop can find out where her parents went on that supposed vacation. I felt a sort of residual energy in their home that day, and got a sense of panic and worry that became something cheerful and happy all of a sudden, and vague thoughts of Florida, but nothing more specific. I don't have a clue how that happened, or how reliable what I got is. Or what Bethany's family knows now."

"And then there's you." Grayson looked at Nellie. "Like the three missings we know about, and maybe a fourth one, you were . . . drawn to Salem shortly before your thirtieth birthday. We don't know what the others had as some kind of lure, but you had a message from your dead father, who by name at least belonged to one of the original five families here."

"A very strange message," Geneva said, having read the letter herself. "You're here to stop something, some kind of evil your father couldn't stop, and he made sure you could be here under an assumed name. From which we can probably safely gather that whatever this is about, it has something to do with those five families who founded this town and who basically run it, possibly the Cavendish family in particular, and that it isn't wise to identify yourself as such because you pose a threat to someone. Logically the longtime leader of the family, Duncan Cavendish, your uncle."

"And your father told you that you could trust Finn Deverell, that he's the only man who can help you," Grayson added.

"Which is also odd," Geneva said, "because he's pretty high up in the militia, and I'm positive he's the one who spoke to me just before I was grabbed." Her tone left the others in no doubt that she felt she had a score to settle with that gentleman.

"But he left you alive," Grayson pointed out thoughtfully, "with food, water, and light. Do you get the sense he knew you could find a way to escape sooner rather than later?"

"I didn't get any sense at all from him then; I told you that. It all happened too fast. And the few times I was fairly close before he grabbed me, I couldn't read him. At all."

Nellie was hardly aware of her fingers moving in her lap, compulsively smoothing the thin black leather gloves she wore. Reminding herself even unconsciously. Always reminding herself of what had to be controlled, contained. "He knows who I am. That I'm a Cavendish. He knows my father sent me here. He said he wanted to help me get out of Salem alive."

"Which," Geneva said, "would sound really melodramatic, except that we believe at least four people have been killed here in only a few weeks."

"Were they here under assumed names?" Nellie asked.

Grayson shook his head. "For the three we know about for sure, not unless they assumed them years ago. The names they used here when they registered were the ones they used before they left their homes to come here."

"Four people drawn here," Nellie said slowly. "People who disappeared here or near here. Now I'm here." She brooded a moment, then said, "I'm a Cavendish, and hiding that was important enough to my father that he made sure I could. Maybe the other four people were connected somehow to the other families."

Geneva looked at Grayson. "I don't see how Bishop could have missed that, even with different surnames. Unless . . . Suppose they were descendants, but through the female lines?"

"Possible." Grayson nodded. "That would take a lot more digging to uncover, depending on how many generations ago those original women left Salem, and assuming it happened at all."

Geneva muttered an oath under her breath. "I hate assuming anything. The more we speculate, the more questions we have. And damned few answers. Sometimes I really hate profiling. Look, even if those three, maybe four, missings were descended from Salem families, why call or lure them back here, each just before their thirtieth birthday? Why call Nellie? Were those other three or four also supposed to stop something they may or may not have known more about? Are they dead because they weren't able to do whatever was demanded of them?"

Nellie clasped her fingers together tightly in her lap. "I'm not finding any of this very reassuring." Leo got up from his place at Grayson's feet and went to sit beside her, eyes fixed on her face and a faint whine reaching their ears.

"He knows I'm upset," she murmured, reaching to pet her dog.

"Sorry." Grayson smiled faintly. "Half our job seems to be sitting around speculating, adding bits and pieces of information as we're able to find them. Until we figure things out. And usually we're under a clock."

"My birthday," Nellie said.

Geneva shook her head a little, frowning. "The letter said *before* your birthday. And I'm pretty sure the others went missing before their actual birthdays. So if anybody makes a move against you, I'm guessing it'll be sometime in the next few days."

"Great."

A faint rumble of thunder caught their attention, but before anyone could comment on that, Geneva, glancing automatically toward the nearest window, which was actually the sliders opening onto her balcony, said, "Don't look now, but we've got company."

Grayson looked, and since the sheers there had been pulled open, he could clearly see the crow perched on the balcony railing, looking shiny black even in the grayish late-morning winter light.

It was facing inward, gazing into the room, head cocked slightly to one side.

Nellie didn't look; she was frowning, automatically trying to tamp down the anxiety and stirrings of panic, draw in the threads of control. It was supposed to snow later, possibly not until Sunday, but lightly; there wasn't supposed to be a storm.

"The door's closed," Geneva murmured. "How good are bird ears? Assuming they report back to someone, that is."

"Just seeing the three of us together might put someone on their guard. Which might not be such a bad thing," Grayson said quietly. "It might slow them down, give them something to think about."

"Or push them to move faster, which *would* be a bad thing. Paint giant targets on our backs. There were crows about when Nellie and I went out for our walk earlier." Geneva kept her voice low. "I didn't notice if one followed us back here, but I wasn't trying to."

Grayson had done his best to shut out Leo's emotions, especially when he'd been petting him, even though he liked dogs; now he deliberately tried to touch the crow's mind, narrowing his focus as much as he could.

Stirrings in his own mind, and that sense of a new muscle being carefully tried. Curiosity. Interest. And something else, something Grayson couldn't quite define at first. Longing?

"I don't think he was sent," he said slowly.

Nellie looked up then, at Grayson, and when he met her gaze, even though he felt that her shields were up and her face was still, he also felt a kind of plea coming from her.

"You know what they're thinking?" she asked.

"It's . . . not that definite," he replied. "And new for me, so I'm trying to get it all sorted out in my head. But I'm an empath, so what I'm picking up are more like emotions. Different from people, more primitive or more attuned to senses, concepts, something like that. It only started last night, with a few crows up in the woods. Then—Leo. When we passed your door last night, then again this morning in the dining room. Last night, he was mostly sleepy. This morning, I got the sense that he liked us, Gen and me, because we were like you. I assume he knew somehow that we were also psychics."

That clearly surprised Nellie. "I had no idea he knew. Or—would understand if he did."

"I think he understands a lot more than most people would ever give him credit for," Grayson told her.

A little impatiently, Geneva spoke then. "What about this crow right now? What are you sensing that makes you believe he wasn't sent to spy on us?"

Grayson struggled to explain what he knew was an incomplete, hardly understood concept. "It doesn't feel the same as with those crows up in the woods. He's curious, interested, but I don't feel that same . . . watchfulness. But he wants something."

Geneva's eyebrows rose. "Wants something? From us?"

"From Nellie," Grayson answered without thinking about it.

Nellie, who had been listening intently, frowned. "What could it want from me?"

"Your help." Grayson spoke slowly, but with a certainty that came from God only knew where.

"My help with what?" That was almost snapped, in the tone of one who was holding on to something other than her temper.

"I think you know."

For a moment, it seemed she wouldn't respond. Her lips firmed, and those sharp brown eyes seemed to darken. But finally Nellie said, "You're wrong. I don't know. I've never known."

He knew what the answer would be but asked, "Have you ever tried to sense them?"

"They're birds."

"Leo's a dog, but you have a connection with him."

She looked startled for just a moment, then frowned again. "Dogs bond with their people. Everybody knows that."

"I somehow doubt all dogs can tell a psychic from a nonpsychic unless a psychic touches their minds to teach them the difference." Again, Grayson wasn't quite sure where the words were coming from, and it was beginning to bug him.

"I'm not an empath. And I don't—don't use the telepathy. I'm clairvoyant. If I . . . I pick up anything from Leo, it's like that. Not touching his mind, just knowing . . ."

"What's in it?" Grayson supplied dryly.

"It's not the same thing and you know it."

"Well, what I'm getting from that crow on the balcony railing is that he and his . . . feathered brothers and sisters . . . need your help."

"My help with what?" she repeated, less sharply this time.

"They're trapped somehow. You can free them."

EIGHTEEN

"I don't have any idea how to do that, even assuming you're right about any of this." Her voice was calm again, in that way that said she was forcing it to be.

Ignoring the protest, he said, "So you've never tried to contact another creature? Like that crow?"

Nellie drew a deep breath and let it out, then began speaking. Quickly at first.

"All my life, I've seen crows around. Not all the time, just now and then. Perched on something close enough for me to notice, but not so close that it bothered me. I mean . . . they were just *crows*. Just birds. Thought it was normal, until other kids started pointing and wondering. And even then—well, just a few crows. Then my father was killed more than ten years ago, and . . ."

Geneva leaned forward a bit, studying the other woman's oddly still face. "Nellie?"

"It was a single-car crash." Nellie didn't turn her head, and she was staring straight ahead, not looking at either of them or even, it seemed, anything in the room. Her voice was very steady. "No slick roads, no alcohol or drugs or anything like that. Nothing mechanically wrong with the car. The cops said—it looked like just a moment when his attention strayed, maybe, and he lost control. The car went off the road, hit a culvert, they said. Flipped. Rolled.

"But the thing I never understood, the thing the cops *really* couldn't explain, was that there were black feathers all around the wreck. No birds, dead or alive. And no feathers actually touching the car. Just . . . all around it on the ground. Hundreds of them. From crows."

It was Geneva who broke the silence, and with a characteristic remark.

"Now, *that* is what I call creepy."

Nellie turned her head, looked at her. Saw her. And a wry smile twisted her lips. "Yeah, well. After that, there were more crows around me. All the time. Didn't matter if I was in the city, at my office or condo. Even at the beach, or in another state. I'd see crows. Almost always more than one. And all watching me."

"If you don't try to sense them, what *do* you do?" Geneva asked.

"I've gotten pretty good at ignoring them. Only . . . on the drive here, I stopped at a motel for a couple of days to think, to ask myself one last time if I really did want to come here. And there were crows. Every time I took Leo out, there was one here and there. I think . . .

I think at night there were a lot. It was like they were waiting for me to make up my mind.

"When I finally checked out of the motel and got ready to head for Salem, there were crows everywhere. On the motel's sign. Streetlights. Tree branches. The fence between the motel and the road." She drew a breath, let it out slowly. "I loaded up the car, got Leo in. Got in myself. And when I pulled out of the lot, all the crows were gone. I didn't see another one until I got to Salem."

FINN DIDN'T DARE openly show his interest in Nellie, especially so soon after she arrived, by going to the B and B to seek her out. But from his office window he could see most of downtown Salem, and he kept an eye out all morning, fairly certain she'd at least bring her dog out for a walk and hoping she'd come toward town and the small park within the town limits.

If only because of the weather. Though light snow was forecast overnight and into Sunday, and thick gray clouds hung broodingly over the town, no snow had fallen as yet. God knew it was cold enough, he thought, but that was hardly unusual in Salem in January. The joke had long ago worn thin that everyone in town bought thermal underwear for January.

He had no plans to attend church tomorrow. He also had no intention of offering Duncan any excuses as to why he wouldn't be present. The older man had yet to directly challenge him, in part because Finn had made very sure there was no reason.

He'd been lucky in that only his own loyalist militia members had been with him on patrol that night and knew that he'd kept Geneva Raynor captive for a couple of days. That they were uneasy about that, and even more so now because she had escaped her prison, he knew. They expected her to, at the very least, file a complaint with the county sheriff.

She had, after all, been abducted and held prisoner.

The fact that she had not done so, nor had she packed up and left town, Finn knew also disturbed his men. But he had told them, quite calmly, that he had "taken steps" to make sure that all she remembered were the foggy bits and pieces of a really strange dream.

They believed him—but they were still wary, because very few of those with the Talent to alter memories had even been born in Salem in all its long history, and it was also not one of the usual Deverell Talents.

But he had made some small demonstrations of that particular Talent in recent years, little things he made certain his men were aware of. So they would, at the necessary time, believe he could.

They believed well enough now to keep their mouths shut about Geneva Raynor.

Restless, Finn moved to his window to look again down on Salem, and immediately spotted Nellie walking in his direction from Hales B and B with her dog.

Alone.

He wasted no time in getting his jacket and heading for the stairs, wondering *why* she was alone (except for Leo). He was a little surprised that Raynor and Sheridan, once they made contact, had not insisted at least one of them remain with her. They knew enough to take that precaution, he thought.

Then again, one or both might have been following her, and he doubted he'd see them if they were.

The building was nearly silent on this Saturday, with only a few hardy souls working since the *Chronicle* had a weekend edition that came out on Friday, and the work for the Monday paper was usually completed on Friday and Saturday morning. Mostly on Friday. It was a small town.

So there was no one to notice Finn leaving, and even if anyone had they would have thought nothing of it. Like all of the militia, he was apt to come and go abruptly, often at odd hours, and the people of Salem accepted that as normal.

They accept too damned much as normal.

He pushed the thought away, or maybe it was blasted away as the cold of the early afternoon hit him the moment he went out the front door. He didn't zip his quilted jacket—January in Salem meant layers like his flannel shirt and sweatshirt underneath jackets and coats—but instead just shoved his hands into the pockets as he set off toward the park. He could see Nellie some distance ahead of him, and he didn't hurry as he followed after her.

By the time he reached the fenced area of the park that was for off-leash dogs, she had unclipped Leo's leash and was standing near a bench, watching as he made friends with an Irish setter and a Rottweiler, both of whom seemed happy to have a new friend.

Their owners were standing some yards away near another bench, bundled against the cold and talking to each other.

Nellie also wore a quilted jacket and a knitted scarf, though her head was bare, brown hair gleaming even in the gray winter light. Like his, her hands were in her pockets; those black leather gloves hadn't been designed to keep her hands warm.

Finn let himself in, closing the gate behind him, and didn't waste any time in approaching her. "Hi," he said.

She didn't turn her head to look at him, saying merely, "I thought that was you behind me." She sounded resigned, like someone accepting the confirmation of a dental appointment.

In spite of everything, he felt his lips twitch. "Well, I wanted to talk to you." He kept his own voice casual, pushing humor aside. "Why don't we sit down?"

"It's freezing out here."

"You brought Leo out, and it's clear he wants to play for a while. We can talk while he does."

She glanced up at him finally out of guarded eyes, but turned and sat near one end of the bench, keeping her hands in her pockets.

Finn joined her but made sure there was a foot of space between them. He had thought about this more than once, what to say to Nellie, how to explain what she needed to know. But when he spoke, nothing that he had planned came out of his mouth.

"Your father was murdered," he said.

Nellie's head jerked around and she stared at him. "What?"

He thought there was shock in her eyes—but not as much as there might have been. Perhaps not as much as there should have been. Seemingly going off on a tangent, he said, "It all started with him when I was only a toddler, according to my father. The struggle, I mean."

"What struggle?"

"Within the Cavendish family. Thomas was the younger son in the direct line; we all have cousins, extended family, but there's only one direct male line in each of the families. Did you know that?"

"No, I didn't." He had her full attention now.

"Yeah, only one. And that's usually the one who has the strongest Talent in his family. Stretching all the way back to the people who founded this town. Of course there are offshoots, different, usually weaker, and sometimes highly unusual Talents from males and females both within and outside the direct lines."

"Is that supposed to make them superior?" Nellie asked. "Being in the direct line, I mean."

"All Talents are considered valuable, assuming the person holding them has some control. Which isn't always the case."

Finn shrugged. "At present, I'm the . . . designated head of the Deverell family. My father was the eldest son in the direct line. He has two younger brothers, my uncles, but neither was or is ambitious, so they didn't want to head up the family when he was killed about three years ago. And neither has the Talent."

"The Talent?" It sounded like a reluctant question. It sounded like she already knew the answer.

"Psychic ability." His voice was matter-of-fact. "It runs in all the five families; you must know that by now. You probably knew as soon as you reached Salem, if not before."

"My father never said—"

"Once you were here, you felt it. Clairvoyance was always one of the strongest of the Cavendish Talents."

"Talents . . . plural," she said slowly.

"In most of the families, it's only one Talent inherited by two or three in each generation, rarely more than that, and usually it's the same one, though occasionally something different turns up. The Deverells with the Talent, for instance, are almost always empaths."

"So you're an empath." It wasn't really a question.

He answered anyway. "Yes, I am. I also have a nephew with the same Talent, also in the direct line."

"Is he ambitious?" she asked somewhat wryly.

"Well, I'm not worried about a hostile takeover." He smiled. "Robert and I get along very well. Things haven't always gone so amiably for your family."

"Because of ambition. And . . . more than one ability?"

He nodded. "In a nutshell. Ambition can be channeled or even countered. But the Talent is more difficult to manage, especially if it's strong in someone. When you combine both, and the Talent comes in several forms . . . well, let's just say the Cavendish family has been . . . troubled . . . more than once because of that."

"Troubled? Like that struggle you mentioned?"

"Yes. Thomas's older brother, Duncan, was born with

multiple Talents. And ambition. A great deal of ambition."

Nellie was frowning. "But my father wanted to head up his family?"

Finn shook his head. "That wasn't what the struggle was about. There were . . . several reasons, but what disturbed Thomas most of all was that Duncan was ambitious for more than what he was entitled to. More than any one man in Salem is entitled to. He wanted . . . control. Wanted the other families to follow him, the heads of those families to defer to his wishes. He wanted power."

"And that had never happened before?" she asked slowly.

"In the early days, but not for a long, long time. For the most part, each family has what they want, the business they're raised up in and comfortable with. Everything balanced. One of my aunts runs the paper mill, loves the work, and she's doing well with it. I know business in general, the newspaper business in particular; put me on a dairy farm, or ask me to sell real estate, or to be in charge of producing electricity for the town, and I wouldn't really have a clue."

"How about finance?"

Finn had to mentally tip his hat to her. She was following his lead, rambling though it must seem to her, not breaking in with impatience to ask what any of this had to do with her but simply drawing the story out of him the way he wanted to tell it. He had a strong hunch that Duncan had no idea his niece was a hell of a lot smarter than she looked.

"Finance too," he answered. "I have an accountant to balance the books and a broker who invests for the family; my interest in finance other than knowing as much as I need to know in order to deal with both of them is nil."

She threw him a sudden curve. "Your broker doesn't live or work in Salem, does he?"

"No." Deliberately, he added, "Nor are most of my family's liquid assets on deposit in the Cavendish bank."

"Except for a personal checking account or three," she offered. "Maybe a business account to take care of payroll and other expenses. Just for . . . appearances. And common sense."

"Yeah. Except for those."

Nellie nodded, then returned the focus of the conversation to one overly ambitious man. "So everybody is happy with their particular place in Salem. Except for Duncan Cavendish."

He noted the present tense, but said, "According to my father, who had no reason to lie to me, it wasn't a question of leadership so much as it was goals. Duncan had his own ideas about what kind of place Salem should be, and in all those ideas he was in charge of everything. His word law. His leadership unchallenged. Centuries of history didn't matter to him, except that he recognized that the . . . insular nature of the town and its people could be used to his advantage."

"How?" She turned her head slightly to watch as a large crow landed almost silently on the fence a few yards to their right, then looked back at him, her expression of polite inquiry unchanged.

Bonus points. And he hoped her control really wasn't easily shaken.

"Superstition," he answered. "It's easily come by in these mountains, especially in places where present generations are descended from original settlers who had plenty to fear."

"Witchcraft?" She asked the question almost idly.

"Nothing so defined. What Duncan wanted everyone to believe was that the Talent wasn't just an inherent ability as natural to us as the color of our eyes and whatever physical or mental aptitudes we could boast of. He wanted them to believe it was God-given. And since he had more of it than anyone else—"

"They'd follow him. Where? To what?"

"Where every false prophet eventually leads his followers," Finn said without any particular emphasis. "To hell."

"STILL CAN'T READ him?" Grayson asked.

"From here? No way. Maybe if I'd been able to read him before, if there was some connection. But no. Walls. Thick ones. I wonder if Nellie has any sense of him."

"I doubt she's trying."

Grayson glanced again through the big window at their booth in the restaurant, from which they could see the end of the park with its fenced area for dogs, three of which were running and playing happily. One of the dogs was Leo. They could also see Nellie sitting on a bench, with Finn Deverell sitting at what Grayson judged to be a careful distance from her on the same bench.

The restaurant they had chosen for its view was beginning to get busy as people drifted in for lunch. Perhaps more than usual, Grayson thought, because of the forecast.

Whenever the forecasters promised "only a dusting" of snow, people in the Appalachian Mountains had learned to be wary and prepared for anything up to a blizzard. The weather could be very strange in the mountains.

"All this is taking too damned long," Geneva said in a low voice. She had mostly dealt with her lunch, eating what she'd ordered while all the time gazing with apparent dreaminess out the window. But, of course, intently watching Nellie and Finn Deverell.

Grayson kept his own voice low. "I know you're worried about Bethany. So am I. But even with both her father and Bishop vouching for Finn—and one of us should definitely talk to him about *that* once we're back at Quantico—she's the type who has to make up her own mind who she's going to trust. He's high up in the militia, and according to the letter from Nellie's father, he can help her. He can also help us. You found nothing in that house up in the woods, nothing in the Hicks house. And Bishop hasn't been able to locate the rest of the family yet. Lots of touristy places in Florida. We have no idea where to even *start* looking for Bethany. The militia is supposed to have eyes and ears everywhere; we need Finn on our side. If nothing else, we need to know what he does about the four bodies found."

"We need to know a hell of a lot more than that." Geneva kept her gaze focused on that distant discussion.

"Agreed. But it's like you said. There are undercurrents everywhere in this town, and we don't have the time to figure it all out on our own." He grimaced as she glanced at him with lifted brows. "No, I don't like that any more than you do, but it's the truth. Bethany is gone, we don't know where or why; Nellie, if she's in any way connected to our missings, and we *know* she is, has something very bad coming at her, probably in the next few days but maybe later today or tonight. We just don't know enough. We really don't have the first clue what's going on here except that people have gone missing and people have died."

"That about sums it up," she muttered.

"So, we wait long enough to see what Nellie finds out from Finn. We won't do anybody any good rushing around or sneaking around looking for clues like detectives in a bad novel. Especially when we don't even know where to start."

"She's been missing for *days*, Gray."

"I know that."

"I know you know that."

"And I know you know that some investigations get stalled, even early on, and we have to just keep following our noses until they lead us to a break."

Geneva looked at him finally, frowning. Her glance swept on, taking in the moderately crowded restaurant where people talked quietly and ate, relaxing on their Saturday afternoon.

"What do you suppose they'd do if I suddenly stood up and asked if any of them know where Bethany Hicks is?" she wondered as her gaze returned to his.

"My guess would be mostly blank looks, along with a few militia members making mental notes to report to their superiors." *Or if they really don't like the question, escorting your ass out of here.*

Geneva glared briefly, clearly getting that, then sighed and this time only glanced out the window before returning her attention to what was left of her lunch. "They're gonna freeze their asses off out there," she muttered.

"I'd guess Finn is acclimated, and Nellie's bundled up well enough." Grayson paused. "At least getting in touch with Bishop this morning told us a little more. The likelihood that the fourth body found the other day *was* reported missing just a little more than a week ago, and that his name was Mark Summers."

Grim, she said, "And do you honestly believe that *any* of the missings will turn up even as remains now? The militia took care of them, and I'm guessing the remains were either buried deep or cremated."

"We have to know who's behind it," Grayson said. "It can't be just the militia in general. Finn's part of that, high up in that, and Bishop vouched for him as being no murderer *or* one who would cover up crimes. That has to mean there are factions within the militia, or at least one faction under someone's influence or control and willing to at least dispose of remains—if not murder."

"I'm guessing murder," Geneva said.

"It takes a hell of a strong control to force someone to murder for you," Grayson pointed out. "More likely whoever is killing believes they're doing it for some . . . necessary reason."

"Like gaining power? Increasing his own abilities?"

"For whoever leads them, yes. And since Nellie's father sent her here under an alias, I'm betting the man is the longtime head of the Cavendish family, her uncle Duncan. As to what he tells those who help him commit the acts . . . We both know there are some insane reasons to be willing to murder someone else. Justifications that will never make sense to most people."

"Justifications for killing four people under the age of thirty, probably threatening Nellie with the same fate, and abducting a ten-year-old girl? I want to meet someone who can explain that to me, Gray, I really do."

And this time, her voice was beyond grim.

NINETEEN

Nellie didn't look shocked at that, but held on to her expression of polite inquiry. "Sounds like a cult leader," she said.

"I think he's become that," Finn admitted. "He crossed the line a long time ago."

"And you haven't done anything about that because—?"

Finn laughed without amusement. "Because he's managed to do much of what your father tried to stop. He commands the majority of the militia, and the county sheriff is one of his . . . followers. So are most of the town leaders. Except for the Deverells, he has the other families afraid of him. And rightly so."

"Why?"

Coming full circle at last, Finn said, "Fear. Because he murdered your father. And your mother."

That did shock her, clearly. "My mother?"

Finn chose his words carefully. "Nellie, you were only an infant when Thomas confronted his brother. According to my father, there was an actual physical—and psychic—battle for control of the family. I have no idea what that looked like; my father would never tell me. Just that it was ugly, and powerful, and when it was over Duncan was triumphant, that your father had literally burned out the Talent trying to stop him, and that within a week Thomas had taken his wife and infant daughter and left Salem. He never returned."

Slowly, Nellie said, "I wasn't born in Salem."

"Yes. You were."

"My birth certificate—"

"Altered. Thomas wanted to cut his family off from Salem. He had no idea Duncan's reach could extend as far as it did. I'm sure if he had he would have left the state, maybe even the country."

"And my mother?" she asked after a moment.

"I don't know how he did it, but I'm positive he contacted Sarah and threatened you and your father if she remained with you. Once she was away, with plans to lie low with a friend in another state, I'm just as positive that he had her killed. I don't have any proof, even Bishop couldn't find any, but he did find out that she never made it to her friend."

"I don't understand. Why would he care about my mother? If he had already—already defeated my father and driven him from Salem?"

"Two reasons." Finn kept his voice quiet. "Because Duncan had discovered he was sterile, that he would not produce a male heir, or any child of his own blood, and he knew that Sarah could still give Thomas a son. And because . . ."

"Because?" she prompted steadily.

"Because even though she hadn't been born to one of the five families, Sarah had her own Talent from her own powerful, long-lived bloodline, Nellie. Among other things, she could influence the weather, even call down a storm. A violent one."

Nellie blinked. Just that. Her face was expressionless.

Finn went on as if she had asked another question. "I don't think it was a Talent she wanted, and her control was erratic. My father said one of the worst storms ever to hit Salem hit just after the confrontation between Thomas and Duncan, when Sarah was clearly distraught. Once Thomas took his family and left, there were never any storms that violent again.

"I don't know if Duncan was sure it was Sarah, though he probably was, clairvoyance being one of the Cavendish Talents. Duncan was and is also a telepath. So he knew Sarah was a threat to him on two fronts. She could give Thomas a son, and she could fight Duncan directly if she had to. So he threatened you and Thomas; Sarah left, hoping to keep you both safe—and vanished before she could reach safety."

"I was a toddler," Nellie murmured. "I was told she just . . . ran away. Left my father without a word."

"Duncan made sure every sign pointed to no more than a runaway wife. Thomas always suspected him, but he could never trace Sarah, and never had proof that Duncan had killed her or had her killed."

After a moment, Nellie said, "He stayed in touch with your father."

Finn nodded. "They were of an age and had been more like brothers than friends. He stayed in touch. Confided in my father what he believed and feared. And one of those fears was that Duncan would come after you. So . . . Thomas deliberately distanced himself from you. He always had very discreet bodyguards around you, though I'm sure you never noticed them when you were a child."

"No. No, I didn't."

"And he never married again, because Sarah was the love of his life and because he wasn't willing to endanger another wife or another child he might have had from such a marriage."

Finn broke the short silence by continuing. "Duncan was, for the next years, busy building his power base here. Recruiting more followers, people who were willing to believe in him. Who believed he was what he claimed: chosen."

"A false prophet," she murmured.

"Yeah."

Nellie turned her head and gazed out almost blindly over the park and the still-frisking dogs some yards away. "You really believe he had my mother killed?"

"I believe he killed her himself. So did my father and yours. But none of them could ever find a shred of proof. And neither could I. Neither could Bishop."

"And my father's death? It was an accident."

"Was it? Why did he lose control for no apparent reason? A safe driver in a safe car he was familiar with? What about all the feathers, Nellie? All the black crow feathers around that wreck?"

She glanced over at the fence, where now half a dozen crows watched them with bright eyes, then looked back at Finn. "What are you saying?"

"Only a Cavendish born can command the crows. Your father could—before that confrontation with Duncan. Though Thomas never forced them; he was kind, interested in them. Sometimes he'd call one or another, and they always came. My father suspected he could actually talk to them, but Thomas would only laugh without confirming that."

"Do you believe he could? Talk to them?"

"Yes. But once he was gone, everything changed. Now Duncan controls them, and . . . rather brutally. He doesn't ask them to obey him; he forces them to, somehow. And whatever he does to them, I believe it hurts them at the very least. He may well have killed some of them. As examples, if nothing else." Finn paused, then added, "I imagine they'd much prefer you dealing with them than him."

"You're insane," she said. Her eyes were wide and without expression. "Nobody can control birds. Crows. Not like that. Not if you're saying he—he commanded crows to cause my father's car accident. Years ago and halfway across the state."

"I believe he did just that. And I believe that you're

half-convinced yourself." He heard a distant rumble of thunder and felt his pulse quicken. Both he and Bishop had been right. Nellie had inherited more than just the Cavendish Talents. She had also inherited her mother's.

Though there was so much danger if this particular Talent escaped her control . . .

"You're insane," she repeated, then frowned a little as a louder rumble of thunder reached them, adding almost mechanically, "I should call Leo and head back. It's supposed to snow."

"Snow rarely comes with thunder," Finn said.

She got to her feet and said, hurriedly now, "It happens. Rare, but more common in the mountains. Thundersnow. I've read about it."

He bet she had. He bet she'd studied it intensely, trying to understand how she could possibly trigger such storms.

And control them.

There was a louder rumble they could actually feel in the ground upon which they stood. The other two pet owners, after glances up at the gray, heavy clouds above, which seemed much more ominous by the moment, were calling their dogs, and Leo was coming toward Nellie, his ears up and eyes fixed on her face.

Finn, on his feet as well, could feel the dog's sudden concern, which surprised him. He had never been able to sense any animals—he'd certainly tried with the crows for years—*and* he had his shields up.

Nellie bent slightly, pulling a leash from her pocket, and clipped it to Leo's collar. "I have to get back," she said.

Finn looked at the black, skintight gloves she wore and wondered if they could help her at all now. "Nellie, you're in danger. Duncan is much stronger now as a telepath than he was back then. Stronger in all his Talents. Stronger than Thomas knew before he was killed."

She straightened and looked at him. He thought she was a little pale, but still expressionless. "You believe I might end up like one of those bodies nobody's talking about?"

"Maybe. Unless you can stop him." He met her gaze steadily.

She let out a little breath in what was not a laugh, the air misting in front of her mouth. "If my father couldn't defeat his brother years ago, when you say he was less powerful, what makes you think I can do it now?"

"Because you're stronger than you know. Because I'll help. And so will your new friends from Bishop's unit."

"He vouched for you. When they reported in earlier."

"He said he would, when the time was right. Once you were here, his team was here—"

"And a little girl had disappeared?"

For the first time, Finn was honestly shaken. "What?"

"You didn't know?"

"No. No, I didn't know." His mind was racing, considering and discarding possibilities, none of which he liked. At all.

"I thought you were high up in the militia."

He shook his head slightly. "There are . . . factions. I have a number of people loyal to me. But Duncan's faction has always been the largest, and always had access to information the rest of us didn't. Like the bodies. Some-how, they always seem to *find* those bodies first. And they've dealt with them as he ordered them to."

"You didn't find that suspicious?"

"Of course I did. That and . . . other things. It's why I got in touch with Bishop."

"You really knew nothing about Bethany Hicks disap-pearing?"

"All I knew was that her family went on vacation. We were notified to keep an eye on the house. It's a common request of the militia when a family goes on vacation." It was his turn to speak almost mechanically.

Thunder rumbled again, deep and rolling, yet seem-ingly right overhead. Flurries began to drift downward.

Control. I need to control this, dammit.

Nellie glanced up briefly, a slight frown drawing her brows, but her voice was matter-of-fact. "The family cer-tainly went somewhere. But without Bethany. She was taken. Near that house where you held Geneva impris-oned."

He didn't deny or try to defend or explain his own actions, but frowned and said, half under his breath, "He wouldn't go that far. Surely. He wouldn't abduct a child. A child born here in Salem, even if she doesn't belong to one of the Five."

"He has. If he's the one pulling strings in Salem. If he's the one behind all this. Then he has. Why would he have done that?"

Finn hesitated, then shook his head. "If she was in the woods, near anything he wanted to protect, and was discovered there . . . his men in the militia might have grabbed her."

"And held her, the way you held Geneva? Or something worse?"

Finn looked at her, his face grim. "I don't know," he said. "I honestly don't know."

GENEVA AND GRAYSON stood some distance outside the restaurant, far enough from the entrance not to be heard by people who were going in but mostly coming out and heading for home, eyeing the drifting snowflakes and talking in casual voices belied by their words.

"In two weeks you haven't been able to read anyone except a worried little kid and a shaken hunter, or to get anyone to open up to you in the normal way," Grayson said, and before she could take it as an accusation—as she likely would—he added, "and if you couldn't do it, I'm sure as hell not likely to. Especially since I haven't picked up a thing today except from Leo and those damned crows. Which means we really do have to count on Finn for information."

"I don't like having to count on one man I don't know," Geneva said. "Especially when he held me captive for days. And this is the oddest case I've ever been involved in. People start freaking out when bodies turn up; they just *do*. It's human nature. What is wrong with these people?"

Grayson shifted slightly, moving the strap of his very

professional camera—much like the one around Geneva's neck—a bit higher on his shoulder as he pulled his collar up to cover more of his neck. It was colder than it had been when they'd entered the restaurant.

"Maybe it has something to do with this energy that's still increasing, building. Dunno about you, but it's really making my skin crawl a bit."

"Yeah, mine too, but is it controlling a whole town?"

"You saw what Bishop sent, same as I did. And know what's been said within the unit. We've had experiences with energy fields, really wild ones, and not so long ago. Including people in an otherwise nice little town beginning to go nuts and kill their families and total strangers for no reason whatsoever. Focused energy can control people, if the mind controlling it is strong enough. You suspected one man was controlling things, the militia at least, and if he's psychic, as Bishop said he is, and powerful, he could be doing a hell of a lot of things."

Geneva turned her head slightly so she could better see the park, and said, "That conversation is turning into a marathon. And neither one of them looks very happy."

"I noticed. They're also beginning to stand out, with the snow falling. And so are we."

Geneva released a sound he didn't dare call a snort. "If the guy running things is so all-powerful, you can bet he knows about us already. Just because I wasn't able to penetrate his walls doesn't mean he can't get through mine, and without me knowing about it, dammit. As for his plans . . . I'm guessing he'd expect Finn to make contact with Nellie, but I don't know how he's going to react if we all four team up very publicly. On the other hand, I'm beginning to doubt we're fooling anybody."

Thoughtfully, Grayson said, "Nellie's alias hasn't protected her for very long; Finn knew who she was, and *I'm* guessing whoever is really in charge here also knows. Probably his people in the militia, at least some of them. Even though Thomas Cavendish clearly believed whatever Nellie had to do here could risk her life, I wonder if her father really had any idea what she'd be facing in coming back to Salem."

"And if he would have sent her had he known?" Geneva shrugged. "We don't have a medium here to ask him. But a lot can change in nearly thirty years. Even if her father was in touch with Finn or his father before he was killed, that was more than ten years ago. We don't have any reports of anything suspicious going on in this town in the years before that. Bishop didn't. The people lured here, probably murdered, that's all been recent. So something *must* have changed. Maybe because all these people were about to turn thirty, though I still can't figure that out."

"Descendants of four of the five families," Grayson pointed out. "Bishop confirmed that."

"Yeah, but what does it matter that they were about to turn thirty? That Nellie is? Does the guy in control believe they change somehow when they hit thirty, like it's not just a date on a calendar?"

Grayson, remembering Bishop's warnings about superstitious mountain cultures, slowly said, "Maybe he does. Maybe he's . . . created a culture where that's an important milestone, for whatever reason."

"Surely not for the whole town."

"No, I don't think it's the whole town. The five families. Maybe not even all of them, considering Finn. He can't be the only one— And maybe we're about to find out."

Geneva turned her attention back to the park to see that Nellie and Finn, with Leo pacing between them, were heading toward them. Nellie's face was impossible to read. Finn looked grim.

As soon as they reached the agents, Finn said, "Probably not the best way to handle this, but we need to talk, and now. The safest place is my office here in town. Very few are working in the building on a Saturday with bad weather looming, and nobody will be listening in."

Grayson exchanged glances with Geneva and said, "Lead the way."

DUNCAN CAVENDISH TURNED from the window, where he had watched the downtown sidewalk below, and said, "Is everything ready?"

His senior lieutenant in the militia, a Cavendish cousin named Aaron, nodded briefly, but said, "Moving everything up a day wasn't that difficult with the weather like this. But the moon won't be completely full tonight, and with the weather it probably won't be visible at all. Will that matter?"

Duncan waited out a slow roll of thunder, his expression thoughtful, then said, "We can't do anything about the snow. With the forecast calling for worse tomorrow, there was no choice."

He was a big man, quite imposing, with wide shoulders that could fill doorways and an almost visible aura of strength that was rare for a man in his sixties. Dark, like most of the Cavendish family, and with the brown eyes that could turn curiously sharp in one with the Talents.

Aaron didn't have them, though his younger brother Devin had a rare one: He was a Dreamer. Doubly rare because he was outside the direct male line of the family, where the Talent almost always lay.

Thinking of that, Aaron said, "Nellie Cavendish hasn't run; despite the nightmares she doesn't seem too shaken up. Now she's met up with Finn, even after Devin made sure she saw him in the nightmare. *And* the two outsiders you said would be trouble."

"They can't interfere with something they don't know is happening," Duncan said. "Or with something they could never understand. And after it's done, they'll never be able to touch me."

Aaron had learned long ago not to ask too many questions of this man, and simply nodded. "The snow is supposed to be light, tapering off before moonrise," he said, then paused to listen to another slow, deep roll of thunder. "Supposed to be. I don't think those clouds are going anywhere."

"We have the ceremony no matter what," Duncan said.

Aaron nodded in understanding and, recognizing the tone, turned and left the office.

Duncan looked at the clock on the wall—he hadn't been able to wear a watch in years—and smiled faintly. Hours to go. Plenty of time to prepare himself for what would be done.

Plenty of time.

TWENTY

There was a leather couch along one wall of the spacious office, where the two agents sat as they talked to Finn, who was half sitting on that end of his big desk. They had been talking for some time, covering much of what Finn had already told Nellie. She sat in one of the visitor chairs, petting Leo and trying her best to tamp down things trying to rise inside her.

And still, every few minutes, the thunder rolled.

"I could shoot Bishop," Geneva was saying in a tone more wry than angry. "All the time I've been here, nosing around trying to look like I was just taking pictures, and I could have been talking to you."

"Some things have to happen—"

She made a little exclamation that was more sound than word. "He has you convinced of that too?"

Finn smiled faintly, though the grim set of his features didn't alter by much. "It's a truth. He didn't invent it."

Geneva shook her head a little. "I'm not so sure, but never mind. It's practically the mantra of the SCU, has been from the beginning. Some things have to happen just the way they happen. Like all this, apparently. So you don't know *anything* about Bethany Hicks?"

"As far as I knew, she was on vacation with her family. Until Nellie told me, I had no idea she'd been taken."

Grayson said, "But you believe it was by Duncan Cavendish."

"Couldn't be anybody else. I'm sure he wasn't there. I'm just as sure it was done at his orders."

"Why?"

Finn hesitated. "I'm almost afraid to guess. That it was her, probably because she was convenient. Wandered into the wrong place at the wrong time. If he *had* planned to take a child, I think he would have looked outside Salem. Maybe far outside. To take a child living here, part of the town . . . Even for him, that's a line I wouldn't have believed he'd cross."

"What about her parents and sisters?" Geneva asked. "What could he have said to them to make them just pack up and leave on a supposed vacation?"

"I don't know," Finn admitted. "There are some with the Talent who can at least temporarily influence others to see what they're shown, and believe what they're told, though it seldom holds more than a few days or a week. Maybe that; I believe he has at least one among his followers. However it was accomplished, Duncan has a habit of getting what he wants, and it's been a very long time since anyone openly defied him."

"My father," Nellie said.

Finn turned his head slightly to look at her. "Thomas, yes. And all the other families know how that ended. With Thomas taking you and your mother and leaving Salem, his Talent burned out or somehow taken from him in the struggle against Duncan."

"You could all sense that?" Geneva asked intently.

"According to my father, yes. I was too young, but he said about Thomas that it was . . . like seeing a man who had lost an arm in some horribly traumatic way. That he was in shock—and something that had always been part of him was missing, gone forever."

Nellie looked down at her gloved hands and was silent.

Matter-of-factly, Grayson said, "We've actually seen something like that before, or at least the unit has. A psychic able to . . . steal the abilities of other psychics. It's rare."

"Thank the Universe," Geneva muttered.

Briefly, Grayson wondered if she even remembered the bitter resentment of her childhood and teenage years for the abilities that had made her different from those around her.

Joining the SCU always changed people. Always.

"He never said a word about—about Talents that I can remember," Nellie said. "Not that he'd ever had them, and not that I had them. The first mention I can ever remember didn't come until the letter. Then he said abilities, not Talents." She shook her head. "But I hardly saw him, growing up. And my mother was gone. I didn't know anything at all about her. That she had—"

"Talents?" Geneva suggested. "Maybe something to do with that thunder we keep hearing?"

Steadily, Nellie said, "It only happens when I'm upset. And it was really rare for a while. After Bishop taught me how to keep up a shield, how to . . . enclose it, control it. But today I can't seem to do that very well."

"Well," Geneva allowed, "it's been a very upsetting day for you, what with one revelation and another." She looked back at Finn. "But speaking of control, yours is damned good. I haven't been able to get through at all. An empath, huh?"

"All my life."

"Which, living in Salem, meant you'd one day head up your family after your father died."

"It isn't an automatic thing. One of my uncles might have, but neither really wanted the job. The other families work it out in their own ways."

"Except for Duncan Cavendish, who not only wanted to be the head of his family but apparently the lord high head of everybody else."

Finn half shrugged. "After Thomas left, there was really no one standing in his way. And I don't think the other families understood how much he wanted, not back then. That there was some struggle with Thomas everyone knew. They assumed it was just . . . a Cavendish matter. It wasn't until a few years later that he began controlling things outside his own family. In the town, in decisions being made about our lives here. Little things at first. It was gradual, insidious. It wasn't until I came home from college that I began to understand how far he'd gone."

"Cult?" Grayson suggested.

"For those who chose to listen to him and follow him, yes, more or less. He didn't push it too hard with the other families, the urge to control, I mean, but among his followers are members of each of the families. Except for the Deverells."

"And he accepted that?" Geneva asked, brows raised.

"None of us defied him openly, just went about our business. Until my father became aware of some very . . . unholy ceremonies taking place up in the woods."

"Satanic?" Grayson asked.

"Not exactly. Duncan was never willing to play second fiddle, so he always had to be center stage."

"Mixing your metaphors," Nellie murmured.

Finn glanced at her. "Sorry. The point being, he wasn't about to worship; he wanted to be worshipped. His followers apparently enjoyed the sense of freedom he offered them."

"Lots of sex with no strings," Geneva translated.

"I believe so, yes."

Grayson was watching him intently. "But you don't know for sure. You were never tempted?"

"I was tempted to try to find out exactly what was going on, but my father discouraged me from that. I think he knew a lot more than he said, and even that he confronted Duncan about it at some point, because—" Finn paused for a moment, then said steadily, "Just over three years ago, there was an accident out at the paper mill. My father was killed."

"A . . . bizarre accident?" Nellie ventured.

"Let's just say that none of the experts who run the machines could explain it," Finn responded.

"But you think Duncan was responsible," Grayson said.

"Bad things tend to happen to people who interfere with Duncan. That's enough for me to suspect. But I have no proof. And I have responsibilities to my family. I didn't want to run the paper mill, had no feeling for it even before Dad was killed. So an aunt runs that, and I more or less run the *Chronicle*. Doing so also gave me the time to join the militia, and to place a few loyalists to me there as well, eventually."

"To keep an eye on things," Geneva said rather than asked.

"To be . . . in the loop, as much as I could be without becoming one of Duncan's followers."

"Who were still periodically cavorting up in the woods," Grayson said.

"As far as I knew. The militia members loyal to Duncan are very good at keeping quiet about activities the rest of us aren't a part of. We all knew if we went looking for the site of one of those ceremonies, even signs of a past one, the crows would watch and report back to him. It didn't seem worth the risk, then. As far as we knew, no one was dying. That seemed to be it, at least for a while. Then last month, during what's usually a fairly busy tourist time for us, the bodies began turning up."

"You saw them?" Geneva demanded.

"No. By the time I found out, there was nothing to see. Tourists had come and gone, but no townsfolk were missing. The county sheriff, one of Duncan's followers, was blithely unconcerned when I asked him point-blank if he knew of any missing persons in the area. He said he'd seen no such reports."

Finn shook his head slightly. "I didn't dare cross Duncan until the odds were more in my favor. That's when I contacted Bishop, asked if he could do some checking for me. Unofficially, since I lack the authority to call in the FBI to investigate or assist in a local case."

"I guess," Geneva said, "it would be useless for us to ask you when and how you met Bishop."

"Do you want to tell your story?" he asked politely.

Geneva stared at him a moment, then said, "No. Dammit."

Finn nodded, unsurprised, and went on. "During the time I was initially in touch with Bishop, there had been, as far as I could determine, two bodies—or the remains of two bodies—discovered and disposed of. By the time Bishop very quickly uncovered missing-persons reports, he had three of them for people he was reasonably sure had come to Salem for some unknown reason. And the third body turned up, or so I heard."

"That's when he sent me in," Geneva said.

"Yes."

"And you knew about me." It wasn't a question.

Finn smiled faintly.

"Dammit," Geneva said again. And then, to Grayson, "Why is it that we all keep threatening dire things whenever Bishop does some kind of shit like this and yet none of us ever follows through?"

"He's our boss," Grayson said.

"That's not a good enough reason." Geneva shook it off and looked back to Finn. "Okay, riddle me this. Why is the thirtieth birthday the big deal it seems to be?"

Finn answered that readily. "It began as mere superstition, because of a succession of psychics able to hide what they could do for years. According to family lore— I wouldn't necessarily call it history—anyone in any of the families born with the Talent doesn't fully come into their abilities until their thirtieth birthday."

It was Nellie who spoke up then to say, "That's nuts. If you're born with it, it happens a lot sooner, and control comes when control comes. After a lot of work. I can testify to that, and I'm pretty sure the rest of you can too. It's got nothing to do with a date, unless abilities are triggered by some kind of trauma."

"I couldn't agree more," Finn said. "Note I said family *lore*. I have no idea when or how that started, but Duncan, like most would-be prophets, likes to claim he's all-knowing as well as all-powerful. And so, years ago, even before Thomas confronted him, he created the Barrier."

Geneva blinked at him. "Say what?"

"I have no idea how he did it, but it's real enough. He

said it was to spare those born with the Talent from the chaos of adolescence, and since we'd had quite a few problems from just that over the years, most of the elders in the families thought it was a good idea. The kids would come into their Talents only when they were adults—in the week or so before their thirtieth birthdays. So the elders, almost all of them, allowed Duncan to place a barrier in the minds of their children." Finn paused, adding grimly, "Few of them realized they were just handing him more power and removing the threat others with the Talent represented to Duncan."

"I still don't see how he could have kept anybody with abilities from using them," Geneva objected.

Finn hesitated, then looked at Nellie. "Another Cavendish Talent. Like your shield, Nellie."

She stared at him, expressionless for a long moment, then said slowly, "Bishop called it weaving. Lacing together threads of energy I could see in my mind, until I was wrapped in them. Protected."

"Damn," Grayson said, drawing out the oath. "I never heard of that before, not to build a shield."

Finn was nodding. "It's called weaving among the families, and it's a rare Talent. Very, very rare. Duncan had it, so he used it to help solidify his own position. And to prevent those young people with Talent from having the time to learn to properly control and use their Talent."

"You said almost all the elders agreed with Duncan," Geneva said. "What about the others?"

"At first, there were a few," Finn said. "Now only one family doesn't hand over their young to have a barrier placed around their Talents."

Nellie murmured, "The Deverells."

Finn nodded. "We prefer it to happen naturally. Some I believe you call latents never even realize they have a dormant Talent. Others grow up learning to contain and control as they should, their shields becoming stronger with time and practice. For most, adolescence is the most turbulent time, but those of us who've gotten through it help the others as much as we can. Still, several of us can point to at least one family member with the Talent who came fully into their abilities much younger, before adolescence. My own nephew Robert is in college, and both his Talent and his shield are quite powerful."

"Robert Deverell," Grayson muttered. "Huh."

"Yes, he was one of the two young men you encountered when you were coming down off the Trail," Finn said.

"He has a damned good shield all right. I didn't even sense he was another psychic."

"Which is one reason he's one of my best spies, my eyes and ears among the younger members of the other families and those following Duncan. He came to me when he wasn't yet into his teens and asked me how to learn to control his Talent. His father doesn't have it, nor his mother, so I was the logical one for him to turn to."

"But if they know," Geneva began, then corrected herself mid-sentence. "His followers believe what he tells them."

"Exactly what he tells them."

"And," Grayson said, "since he can do uncanny things like order the crows to spy for him, and report back to him, it just adds more to his mystique."

"Yes." Finn paused, then added deliberately, "The one Talent that has held true for hundreds of years is that only a Cavendish born can command the crows."

"I told you I can't do that," Nellie said a little tightly.

"You haven't tried. But there's a reason they've been around you all your life. A reason those here in Salem are drawn to you, even those held under thrall to Duncan."

"He's got them spying on me; that's all." She frowned a little, as if hearing the thought only as she spoke it. Then she met his gaze. "He has, hasn't he? Got them spying on me. Watching me."

"I doubt it was from childhood. Those that gathered around you then were simply drawn to you, because they knew, they felt an affinity with you. With Thomas gone from Salem, Duncan really didn't expect any trouble from you. Not from you as a child. I think he still considered Thomas a threat, and that some years later he sent his crows to eliminate that threat."

"How could he have done that?" Nellie demanded. "My father was in Raleigh when he was killed, returning to Charlotte from a business trip."

"I don't know how he did it," Finn told her. "I've never been able to even sense the crows. But he could and can. They obey him. I don't know what order he gave them, but I'm utterly certain they did something to cause that so-called accident. Remember all the crow feathers around the car?"

"Still creepy," Geneva muttered.

"Very," Finn agreed. "And potentially deadly. Still, Thomas was out of the way. But as the years passed, Duncan began to actually believe the notion that none with the Talent could come fully into their abilities until he, personally, *helped* them to break through the barriers he had built in their minds to keep their abilities dormant for most of their lives. In the week before their thirtieth birthday. One result of that, Nellie, is that the crows have been watching you more closely in recent years. And more of them. Right?"

She nodded silently.

"Most of those were probably his. He knew Thomas would never have placed a barrier in your mind even if he could have, and I'm sure he was curious to find out when you'd begin using your abilities."

"I tried not to," she said.

Geneva said, "We all try not to when we're too young. It just makes other people nervous."

Nellie glanced at her, then nodded.

Finn said, "I don't know if he had a plan to draw you to Salem if you didn't come yourself. He seems to have drawn the others somehow, though I don't know what means he used. I knew about your father's letter, and I knew when it was to be delivered. On your twenty-ninth birthday. But months passed, and I thought you had decided to ignore the letter."

"But you weren't surprised when I showed up," Nellie said.

"Well, in December I had told Bishop as much of the story as I knew, including about your father and his letter to you. He said you'd come, though likely at the last possible minute."

Nellie stared at him for a moment, then turned her gaze to the two agents. "I'm beginning to understand what you mean about Bishop," she said.

"Yeah, he's maddening," Geneva said, not without sympathy. "And right, too damned often."

Finn said, "He called me this morning, a while before I went out to meet you at the park, Nellie. Told me how the first four victims were connected to Salem. Ancestry, through female lines."

"So is that why Duncan wanted them here?" Grayson demanded. "They're descendants of women from the original families of Salem, and because of that they had to come here and die?"

With a slight shake of his head, Finn said, "I couldn't actually think of a rationale behind that. Until Bishop told me that dark energy can be . . . produced and gained by the commission of evil acts."

"Power," Geneva said slowly. "Duncan wanted more power. And *that's* how he decided to get it? By killing descendants of the original five families, family that wouldn't be missed because they'd never lived in Salem?"

"Blood from the bloodlines of the original Five," Nellie murmured. "Shed in torture and torment. And sacrifice."

"I never said he was sane," Finn returned.

TWENTY-ONE

Robert Deverell could act the lighthearted college student with the best of them, but he'd been born with an ability that set him apart from most other young men, and he was always aware of that fact. Here in Salem it was something normal, if not shared equally with everyone, but there were things about Salem that were not normal, and it was with those he was concerned now.

Especially after talking to Finn.

So Robert acted much as he usually did on that Saturday afternoon, out and about even after it began to snow, just as most of his friends were. He spoke to as many people as he could, and did his best to be casual. But each time he was with someone he knew didn't have the Talent, he opened a tiny window in his shield, a narrow beam of focus, just as Finn had taught him, and tried to sense what feelings he could.

Most of what he got was normal and unthreatening, a few things he really wished he didn't now know about, a few things that were revelations about people he'd thought he knew.

And then there was the dark stuff.

The really, really dark stuff.

When he began sensing that, he shored up his inner wall as much as he could to protect himself, but opened that tiny window a bit more and gathered in every dark, sickening bit of information he could glean from those seething emotions.

Once he was no longer forced to look at those smiling faces, he took a few minutes to regain all his control, then headed for Finn's office, keeping his own expression calm but walking quickly in the lightly falling snow.

It was nearly four, and the snow had tapered to flurries again when he reached the *Chronicle* building and let himself in. He went straight upstairs to Finn's office, not surprised to find it closed because Finn had told him about the people he wanted to talk to today.

He also didn't hesitate to knock, and walked in without waiting for an invitation.

"Anything?" Finn asked immediately. He was half sitting on his desk, talking to the two agents on the couch and Nellie Cavendish in one of the visitor's chairs, her dog sitting quietly at her feet.

"Yeah," Robert replied. "Oh, yeah."

"Good. Sit down and tell us what you've learned." Finn added quick introductions as Robert took the other visitor's chair, and he nodded politely to the agents and to Nellie Cavendish. She was pretty, he thought abstractedly, and wondered what Finn thought of her. Not that he'd ever know unless shown or told; his uncle was one of the very few people whose emotions Robert could never sense.

"Nice to see you again," Gray Sheridan said somewhat dryly.

Robert offered him a faint grin, then sobered and looked at his uncle. "If what I got was accurate, there is some really dark shit scheduled to go down tonight."

"Tonight?" That was Agent Raynor, sitting up straighter as she stared at him alertly.

"Yeah. And not what I was expecting at all. Finn, did you know they'd grabbed a little girl?"

"Not until Nellie and the agents told me," Finn answered. "That's what you were picking up?"

Robert had gathered everything together in his head on the walk here so that it made more sense than the initial jumble of sickening emotions, and was able to explain rapidly.

"What we thought was right. Duncan believes he's stronger now because of those people he killed—he and his followers—in some weird-ass ceremony that he *said* was intended to draw the evil demon out of those '*Children of Salem.*' Except the real demon is Duncan, because he tortured those poor people, Finn. Claiming to be the '*Chosen,*' with one duty: to purge evil from anyone from the blood of the original families. And purging that supposed evil calls for real blood, from them, and a lot of it. All of it, in fact."

"Sacrifice," Finn said grimly.

"Yeah, eventually. But I wasn't kidding when I said torture was first on the list. From what I was picking up, the whole horror show starts at seven o'clock tonight—moonrise—and goes on until nearly dawn." His mouth twisted sickly. "After they finish their sacrifice off, they have other kinds of perverted *fun*. Jesus Christ, Finn, how has this insanity been going on for weeks and we didn't know?"

"Never mind that now. We'll deal with guilt later. Are they planning to kill that little girl? Bethany Hicks?"

"I didn't get a name, but yeah, they are. They've held her someplace for the last few days, I think, and left her alone. A kid left alone like that must be scared half out of her mind, to say nothing of weak and hungry. As for his followers, Duncan's fed them some line of bullshit about evil wearing an innocent face, and how they have to deal with that before they turn to the true evil newly come to Salem." He looked at Nellie. "His own niece."

Her expression didn't change, but some of the color left her face. And he didn't blame her a bit for that.

"Where?" Finn rapped out. "Did you get where it's supposed to happen?"

"Yeah. I know exactly where it's supposed to happen."

IT WAS GENEVA who slipped back into the B and B by her secret way and retrieved her and Grayson's weapons.

He walked in the front door, brushing snow from his thick jacket and muttering to himself about how lunch had been a bad idea and he thought he'd take his meds and sleep until he woke up.

He made sure Ms. Payton was near enough to hear.

Then he went to his room, used his laptop to connect to Bishop, reported what was happening and what they expected to happen tonight, requested backup, but also asked that it arrive in Salem no earlier than eight p.m., and also that Bishop do whatever he could to ensure the legalities.

Calm as always, Bishop merely returned that he would do everything possible, and for them to watch their backs.

After that, Grayson hung out his DO NOT DISTURB sign, dimmed the lights in his room, and left to meet Geneva, finally learning her secret way in and out of Hales.

"You're a devious woman," he said as they stood out behind the B and B, just inside the shelter of the woods, and checked their weapons.

"That's not even conversation," Geneva told him. "But at least we know where to look, with Robert's info added to those pictures you took of the ruins somewhere up this mountain."

"I'm glad Finn recognized it," Grayson said, admitting, "With the cloud cover this heavy and snow falling, I'm not at all sure I could have found my way back there tonight."

Geneva, graciously, decided not to point out a failing.

As they waited for the others to join them, Grayson said abruptly, "Listen, you spent more time with Nellie than I did. Is she up for this?"

"She'll have to be, won't she?"

"I know we decided it'd be just us because of the time factor and the terrain—and because of what we believe is the only way to stop Cavendish. My question is, will Nellie hesitate to do what the rest of us believe she'll have to do? There's a kid involved, Red, to say nothing of who might get in our way."

After a moment, Geneva said calmly, "Bethany will be the key as far as Nellie is concerned. She will not let anything happen to that little girl if it's even possible for her to stop it. She'll tap every resource she knows about and—I'm guessing—quite a few she isn't consciously aware of."

Grayson checked his gun for the third time. "Well," he muttered. "This ought to be fun."

AS SHE FOLLOWED the others up the lightly snow-dusted mountain trail that would lead them to what Finn had described as the first church ever built in Salem, now only a ruin, Nellie tried not to think of what lay ahead, but found a moment to be grateful that Robert, though protesting his uncle's order at first, had stayed behind—and that he would be watching over Leo for her.

She was also glad that Robert was another empath, who had, seemingly in an instant, established a kind of connection with Leo that had allowed the dog to relax and not object to her leaving with the others.

Finn really hadn't had to point out to her that Duncan wouldn't scruple at killing a dog, and that at least some of the Cavendish loyalist militia members, those among his followers, were likely to be armed.

Grayson hadn't been happy at that reminder, and both he and Geneva had detoured by the B and B to claim their own weapons before meeting Nellie and Finn at a predetermined spot in the woods to the northwest of Hales.

Finn was also armed, clearly comfortable and familiar with his handgun. Nellie had decided not to bring her own gun, though she wasn't sure just why. Maybe because she wasn't sure she could shoot an actual person, even her clearly evil uncle. Or maybe . . . because a faint voice in her mind told her that was one weapon she wouldn't need.

It was still early, not much past winter-dark, and not really completely dark despite the gloomy sky, thanks to the dusting of snow and the peculiar light that sometimes showed itself in Salem. They were early because they wanted to get to the ruins well ahead of Duncan and his followers, and find the best spots to settle in. None of them wanted to take any chances with the life of Bethany Hicks.

"Listen to me," Finn had said to her. "I know you've spent your life trying to ignore some of your Talents and control others. I get that. I know this is all happening so fast you're telling yourself you haven't even had time to think, to make decisions you believe you have to make. I get that too.

"But, Nellie, you know as well as I do that you face whatever life throws at you the best you can in that moment. That's what matters, all that matters. How you face the hard things."

"Hard? Jesus, Finn . . ."

"This is not something any of us can soften or sweeten for you. Your uncle is evil, quite probably insane, definitely a serial killer, even if he dressed up murder to look like something else. The bald truth is that a little girl's life may well hang on your Talents, on your abilities to use what you were born to use. You can't hold back. Can't let yourself close off even a part of your mind *or* your emotions."

"Finn—"

"He'll send the crows ahead to scout. You have to be the one to command them, Nellie. You *have* to. Surprise is one of the few things we have going for us. After that, it's our guns and your abilities. Because Duncan will damned sure use his." He had glanced up as thunder rumbled distantly, and added, "And if it's necessary, *let* yourself call down a storm. It's one defense he can never match, never counter, and it could save your life and Bethany's—and ours."

But no pressure, Nellie thought more than a little wildly as she followed Finn and Grayson, with Geneva behind her, through a forest that was very still and very quiet, with hardly any snow dusting the ground. Then a rumble of thunder sounded, not so distantly now, and Nellie wasn't surprised.

Call down a storm. As if it could ever be that simple!

But she could feel her own fear and anxiety clawing at her, trying to escape the weaving of energy threads she had built to contain what was dangerous. She put out one hand to grasp a sapling and help herself up the path, and could feel the bark through her thin gloves.

The gloves.

It seemed to take forever, but was probably no more than half an hour or so of climbing in order to reach the ruins of a tiny church built hundreds of years before. Finn had said a wide mountain stream had once tumbled down this slope and had cut off the church from the town. After that, it had been swallowed up by the forest as the town itself shifted somewhat to the southwest to at least attempt to avoid the flash floods and mudslides that had early endangered the people of Salem.

Which pretty much explained both why the church had been built up here and why it had been allowed to fall into ruins so long ago.

But right now, tonight, the mountain slope brought them up to a flat area, probably no more than sixty feet across before the mountain began to climb again. In that clearing was a single standing stone wall that rose to a point, with the other walls that had once risen there to join it now only a tumble of stones. The original building had probably been no more than twenty-five feet from the entrance to that still-standing wall.

Now, in the semicleared space of the interior, someone had constructed a rough altar stone. Obviously hacked from a single larger slab of rock, the oblong was about two feet wide and at least six feet long, and laid across two big boulders beneath that brought the altar nearly to Nellie's waist.

That was a guess; they were careful not to go into the old church, because the clearing had allowed the snow to dust the inside of the space, and footprints would have been obvious. In fact, they stayed well outside the clearing as they circled warily, allowing the forest floor to mask their path.

They picked their spots, but then both Grayson and Geneva left their companions once again, scouting the entire area as soldiers would have, both of them moving soundlessly, and soon were lost to sight as well.

It was still, and bone-chillingly cold, but as she stood beside Finn just outside the clearing on the upward slope where they could see the tumbled interior of the church, Nellie tore her gaze from that and pulled her hands from her pockets, staring at the gloves.

"They're only a symbol of control," Finn said softly. "A reminder of weaving walls of protection and containment out of pure energy. They were never meant to stop your Talents, Nellie, just meant to be a symbol of your own control."

After a long moment, Nellie removed the gloves and put them into her pockets, though she kept her hands in the pockets and held the gloves for now, maybe for as long as possible.

"I hope I know enough," she whispered. "I hope I've learned enough."

"Trust your instincts."

Trust your instincts, my daughter. Listen to your heart.

Nellie caught her breath, suddenly aware that beyond

her pounding heart, that door had opened once more. She could feel the warmth and light that poured out. Into her.

"Nellie?"

For the first time she could remember, Nellie felt a strong and certain sense of utter control. She turned her head to look at Finn, his face clear to her in the odd light in the forest.

"I think I can trust my instincts," she said slowly. "Now I can."

He didn't question that. "Just remember, you have to command the crows when they come, because he'll try to use them to attack and distract us. Touch their minds. Let them know you can set them free of him."

It didn't seem strange to her now that he would say that, expect that of her. She knew she could do it. All she had to do was listen to what had always been inside her.

Finn said nothing more, and in the silence she felt the warmth spreading all through her, gloried in that sense of control, the feeling that she was *this*, this person she was meant to be. There was no need to struggle, no need to fight who and what she was.

Time passed, and Nellie calmly waited, vaguely surprised to realize that Grayson and Geneva were back. There were faint lights, they reported, coming straight across this slope from the east, obviously following the path Grayson had found now, and from whatever place they had kept and hidden Bethany.

"Where are the crows?" Nellie whispered, thinking of

Finn's certainty that Duncan would have ordered them ahead as his scouts, his sentries.

The whisper was barely out of her mouth when a very large crow alighted soundlessly on part of the tumbled wall on this side of the ruins. It was no more than twenty feet away, staring straight at them.

At Nellie.

Oddly, she didn't hesitate, but took a step toward the crow, listening to her instincts without question. Another step, then another, until she stood just above the clearing, her gaze locked with the bird's bright, shining black eyes.

A faint stirring in her mind. Muffled at first, but then clearing, as if she had always been meant to hear it. A question asked, tentative, but more out of caution than uncertainty. She felt . . . bindings. Unwanted bindings. No freedom with the bindings.

No freedom . . . There was great, overwhelming grief in that.

Somehow, without quite understanding how she knew, Nellie promised the bird freedom. All of them would be free. No bindings, no more bondage, ever.

She would set them free.

TWENTY-TWO

The crow raised both wings, beating them almost silently in the air, almost like a salute, something even brighter than before in those black, shiny eyes, then it lifted off with hardly more sound and vanished into the woods.

Nellie retraced her steps to join the others, feeling . . . very peculiar. And yet absolutely certain. The door now open in her mind was allowing her to see everything she had hidden from herself all these years. All her life.

How stupid she had been! Just as with the crows, this was freedom; that other had been bondage.

"She'll tell the others," she whispered. "They'll be nearby, but they won't obey if he tries to command them. Don't worry if they seem to come if he calls them. They won't be coming to him."

She thought she saw Finn smile slightly, saw Grayson

and Geneva exchange looks, and then they spread out to their previously chosen spots.

Finn remained with Nellie because, he'd said, he was armed. But she didn't think that was his reason. He was there to urge her on if necessary.

She didn't think it would be. And she was sure Finn was no longer worried about that.

How strange. I know what you're feeling, she told him in her mind. And she was again not surprised when he answered.

You always could. You just had to believe.

Nellie believed.

They stood, again, just outside the clearing, still above it so that they could see the doorway that had been cleared, and the area around the altar. There were several thick-limbed pine trees at their back, keeping them in shadow.

Sooner than Nellie had expected there were faint lights in the woods, dim glows that didn't really brighten but grew a bit larger as the people carrying the lights approached.

It wasn't until they came into the clearing that she could see, with a start of surprise, that they wore hooded cloaks like those she had seen in her nightmare. Though she wondered why she was surprised; at least one among those in the hoods had, after all, given her the nightmare. Trying to frighten her.

Nellie looked at the figures as they approached, not afraid. The hoods shadowed some faces, but not those who were carrying odd, round lanterns.

Duncan Cavendish was first, and as soon as she could make out his features, she felt a distant pang of relief. He did not look like the father she remembered mostly from a handful of pictures. There was a faint resemblance, and might have been more in the unforgiving light of day, but the features she studied intently were heavier, older, somehow more coarse than those that were more clear in her mind than she had realized.

And his eyes were burning.

Behind him, two hooded figures carried a sort of stretcher between them, and Nellie felt another pang, this one of stark sickness and a growing fury, when she saw a small, limp body, wearing some shapeless garment but with her wrists clearly bound as they lay on her thin middle.

Behind the two carrying the stretcher, perhaps a dozen or so followed in two lines, only the ones at the beginning and the ones at the end of the lines carrying the globe lanterns. There seemed to be a roughly even number of men and women, but Nellie wasn't sure of that. It was a smaller group than she had expected, and she wondered vaguely if only the most devoted of Duncan's followers were allowed to participate in this . . . ceremony.

She didn't hear them move but saw Grayson and Geneva close in on the last two in line. They moved with utterly silent efficiency and in perfect timing, and within seconds they were the last in the two lines, carrying the globe lanterns, shrugging into the robes they had removed from the two of Duncan's followers who lay unconscious, at the very least, on the cold ground back along the tracks.

Nellie had no idea how the two agents had managed to move like that, to do what they had done, but she was very, very glad she was on the same side they were.

She didn't waste much time thinking about that, though, because the stretcher-bearers were carrying Bethany into the ruins of the church, almost marching in a slow, stately manner, and she could hear a low murmur that might have been chanting.

As the angle changed slightly, the glow from one of the lanterns fell on Bethany's face, and Nellie felt the fury inside her burn hotter until it was a pure blue flame when she saw those thin, pinched features and the faint darkening here and there that looked like bruises.

What have they done to you already, poor baby?

Thunder boomed and rolled suddenly, directly overhead, causing the entire group below to start in surprise, some of them even stumbling.

Nellie didn't flinch, but remained motionless.

Duncan moved to the head of the altar, and she could see that he was frowning, saw those burning eyes dart upward as if he were questioning what he had heard.

The stretcher came even with the altar, and the two lines of people who had been behind separated, with two on the other side of the altar reaching to pull Bethany off the stretcher and onto the cold, snow-dusted rock.

Grayson and Geneva, Nellie saw with an automatic glance, were standing just a bit back, at the doorway, and she could tell both had their hands inside the robes and on their weapons.

Thunder boomed again, and a sudden flash lit the

gloomy sky, lightning skittering along the clouds, bright fingers probing in different directions as though looking for something. And the lightning was strange.

It was in colors. Blue. Green. Red. And blazing white. And it was continuous, pulsing as though it was being fed by some hidden energy source.

Nellie managed to tear her eyes from the motionless child as the stretcher-bearers moved away and discarded the stretcher, fixing her gaze on the uncle she had never met. He raised the globe lantern high for a long moment, then held it before him, looking over it at the child lying so still on his bloodstained stone altar.

Nellie knew the plan. She knew that three guns were trained on the group below, principally on Duncan, and that Finn would be searching what faces he could see to look for any of Duncan's militia members since they would be armed.

Geneva and Grayson were perfectly positioned at the rear of the group, their borrowed hoods allowing them to blend in, their training allowing them to mark targets before there was the need to even aim.

At the first sign of a threat against Bethany, Grayson and Geneva would act without hesitation, Finn would act as well, moving out of the shadows, aiming for any militia who could prove troublesome, making certain no one near the little girl could touch her, let alone hurt her.

And if this ended even close to the way they expected, Finn's authority coupled with that of the agents would stop this insanity.

The whole group was still murmuring, perhaps chanting, but Duncan's voice was louder, calling out words that were not English but perhaps Latin, or some made-up chant to impress his followers. He was summoning . . . demanding . . . calling on power to help him remove the evil from this seeming innocent . . .

He stretched out his arms slowly so that the lantern hung above her still body, and as he summoned, demanded, called, Nellie saw the light in the lantern change, its golden glow swirling suddenly with something darker, as though a black snake had somehow crawled inside and was now writhing in torment.

A gasp from the followers as they saw that apparent evil drawn from the child's body by their prophet.

A trick. A magician's trick, and he's convinced them it's real.

They began swaying back and forth, still murmuring as he began to raise the lantern and continued to chant hoarsely, his voice rising and rising—

Until it was abruptly overwhelmed by a tremendous boom of thunder and crackle of lightning over the clearing, the multicolored flash so brilliant it lit everyone within the ruins as though it were daylight.

In that light, the gleam of steel was visible, knives in the hands of those followers standing on either side of Bethany, while other hands froze in the act of reaching toward her, probably to tear open the garment they had dressed her in and bare her body to their gaze and their knives.

No.

Dimly, she was aware of Grayson and Geneva dealing with the next pair in line ahead of them, and now shouting, coming into the ancient ruins, the light of the entire clearing still seeming as bright as day. They held wicked guns in their hands now, and Nellie saw that two more of Duncan's followers fell to powerful, trained blows from both the man and woman.

Then their hands extended, guns pointed at those whose knives would have hurt Bethany, as they shouted for those frozen figures to drop their weapons. Nellie was dimly aware of Finn stepping past her, his gun extended steadily in expert hands. He fired twice, the sound oddly muted to Nellie, and she saw two followers stumble back away from the altar, hands clapped to bleeding shoulders.

She stared at her uncle.

No. I won't let you hurt anyone ever again.

And Duncan Cavendish seemed frozen in place, except that his face writhed like that snake of black in the lantern, something dark and ugly and evil twisting his features.

No.

His chant became a command, bursting from the thunderous sounds that had been overhead, and Nellie felt rather than saw some of the robed figures clawing the material that covered them, even then reaching for weapons despite the agents' and Finn's shouted warnings. Two more shots rang out, oddly muffled to Nellie's ears. Two more of Duncan's followers stumbled back, one falling heavily to the ground.

Those left still standing and unharmed cowered back away from the altar, their uplifted faces lit weirdly by the multicolored lightning still lacing the sky above the clearing, as if it hunted.

Duncan howled like some animal.

"No!"

She walked the few steps down the slope into the clearing, pulling her hands free of her pockets, her gaze still fixed on Duncan. She didn't even glance up when the sounds of what seemed a hundred wings beat the air and a shadow fell suddenly over Duncan. Only over him.

He looked up, mouth open, staring at the spiral of crows above him, the lowest one just out of reach, the highest one seeming to touch the clouds high above. Circling and circling in a tight black formation above Duncan, and then, with an eerily howling screech, the spiral burst apart and the birds were gone.

"You'll never command them again."

Nellie hadn't realized how silent the clearing had been in the moments after the crows flew away until her own voice sounded.

Duncan turned his head slowly, his gaze sliding past Finn and fixing on her. With studied calm, he said, "I've been waiting for you, Nellie."

"Have you? Well, here I am, Duncan." In that moment, she felt absolutely no fear. But thunder rumbled in the clouds above, like an echo of the earlier blast. Or like a reminder. And the lightning continued to lace the sky, still pulsing, as if fed constantly by a power no one could see. Perhaps the beating of a heart.

His eyes narrowed. "Do you really believe you can challenge me, girl?" His voice boomed.

Nellie felt herself smile. "Why would I challenge you, Duncan? I've already won."

His mouth twisted, opened—and froze.

"No, I can't let you say what you want to say. Or do what you want to do. It's over, Duncan. I won't let you hurt anyone else."

With what was clearly a tremendous effort, he began to slowly lift the globe, his mouth closing in a terrible snarl. It was clear he meant not to hurl it at her or away from himself, but to crash it down on Bethany's helpless body.

"No," Nellie said softly.

She raised one bare hand above her head, fingers reaching for the sky. Her other hand stretched out, pointing at Duncan.

Afterward, some of Duncan's former followers swore they had seen a bolt of lightning strike Nellie's raised hand, seen her entire body glow with all the colors of the rainbow, and then a bolt of pure white shot out from the fingers she pointed at Duncan, the flash so bright it nearly blinded those who dared to watch as it struck Duncan in the center of his chest and sent him hurtling backward to lie still among the tumbled stone of the ruins.

The lamp he had meant to use to kill Bethany Hicks had simply vanished.

Of course, the federal agents and Deputy Finn Deverell, in their official reports, said merely that Duncan Cavendish had been struck by lightning while attempting to murder what would have been his fifth victim. And when the coroner agreed he died that way, there really wasn't much anyone could say to deny it.

But there were whispers.

EPILOGUE

"I don't know about the rest of you," Geneva said, half hiding a huge yawn with one hand. "But I'm beat."

They were all seated in the front parlor of Hales, where they had retreated after all the shouting was over. Well, most of it. The wounded had been taken under guard to the town's hospital, Finn's loyalists in charge of both them and the others, who had been marched to the jail, all to be met by a swarm of federal agents.

It had taken hours, but still less time than it might have, to offer their reports, to confirm photographs. The other agents would be questioning Duncan's loyalist followers and his men in the militia, and when the weather broke there would be formal searches of homes and offices as well as the mountainside, but the agents were confident that more than one of Duncan's former followers would give them the information they needed to locate whatever might remain of Duncan's four victims.

Since they had at last been left in relative peace and it was snowing heavily now, they all welcomed the warmth of inside, the gas fire burning in the hearth—and the hot toddies that Ms. Payton had unexpectedly produced.

Geneva's opinion of Ms. Payton had improved greatly when she had tasted the clean bite of a very good brandy.

"When am I going to hear from you guys what happened up there?" Robert complained, but not as bitterly as he might have since he was working on his second toddy.

"It shouldn't be much longer," Grayson assured him. "Bishop and whoever he's bringing along to be absolutely certain we preserve the legalities of all this should be here soon, snow or no snow. Then most of us can make our brief preliminary reports to him and probably go to bed." He looked at Finn. "But I'm thinking you're up for the night."

"Probably," Finn agreed, but not as if the prospect disturbed him very much.

"What about Bethany?" Geneva asked, keeping her voice low even though the blanket-wrapped child sleeping on one of the couches in their group, her head pillowed on Nellie's lap, was clearly very deeply asleep indeed, with hot soup and cocoa inside her.

"My mother's on her way here," Finn told the others. He smiled as Nellie looked at him. "She'll take care of

Bethany until her parents come back. I have a hunch whatever was keeping them away and unaware will vanish now that Duncan's gone."

Nellie was gently stroking the child's hair. To the three in law enforcement, she said, "I hope you won't need her to testify to anything but having been grabbed in the woods. That's all she'll remember."

"Now?" Geneva questioned softly.

Nellie looked at her a moment, then smiled. "Now. She doesn't need to remember anything else. Does she?"

The big black dog lying at the other end of the couch laid his chin gently on the child's hip and made a little sound deep in his throat.

Robert said, "I think Leo has spoken. We should listen to him. Nellie, did you know your dog had a Talent?"

Finn said to him, not unkindly, "I think you'd better stop with that toddy."

"No, I'm serious," Robert said with utter clarity. "Pretty sure he's connected to Nellie. I bet I could describe to you what happened up there, because Leo knew. I'm just waiting for the official report to confirm it."

Leo made another sound.

Robert nodded seriously. "I know you told me stuff that won't be in their reports. Don't worry, it's safe with me."

"You're talking to a dog," Finn said to him.

"That's no dog; that's Leo. I think he's an angel or something. Definitely more than a dog."

Geneva and Grayson exchanged looks, and the latter said, "I think Bishop is going to want to talk to you about Leo—and about you—Nellie. At least one more time."

"I'm not joining the team," Nellie said calmly. "And neither is Leo."

"She has a bank to run here," Finn told them, equally calm. "And other things. Cavendish holdings."

Nellie eyed him. "What makes you think I want to stay in this weird little town of yours?"

"A little crow told me." He finally relented under her stare. "You're the head of the Cavendish family here now," he reminded her. "This is your birthright. The material part of it, to add to everything you found out in the woods tonight. You have to stay at least long enough to make sure everything is in order, right? Duncan had no children, which means the direct family line now passes through Thomas to you."

"I thought only a male could inherit."

"I never said that. I just said there was a direct male line going all the way back to the five families who settled Salem. Believe me, the women of the Five have every right the men do, and then some. You're officially head of the Cavendish family in Salem."

Nellie, her hand still gently stroking Bethany's hair, began to look mutinous. "I don't want to be."

Geneva spoke up to say, "Ask me, I think you should stick around long enough to see what there is to see. Now that the weird static is gone, as is Duncan, and his men are all wounded or locked up, this town may look and feel really different to you."

Leo lifted his head and made a rather odd series of sounds.

"Leo has—has spoken," Robert declared with less clarity, finally beginning to feel that second toddy.

Nellie sighed, avoiding Finn's amused gaze and refusing to allow his thoughts and emotions to touch her. For now, at least. "I'll think about it later. So much has happened in the last couple of days, I think I need time to let it all sink in."

To Grayson, Geneva said seriously, "It's not every day you see somebody summon a thunderbolt. Lightning bolt. Unless it's Zeus. Of course, I sort of had my hands full just then, so I'm not *exactly* sure that's what I saw."

"Me either," Grayson said, peering regretfully into the dregs of his toddy. "There was an awful lot of noise. And confusion. And the light was weird anyway. I mean, I've never seen lightning in all the colors of the rainbow before."

Geneva waved a hand. "Oh, you didn't see that. Your hands were full too. That acolyte of Duncan's took a swing at you and connected. You're going to have a lovely shiner tomorrow."

He eyed her. "What are you going to tell Bishop, you evil woman?"

Her unusual gray eyes widened. "Now, since when has one of us *ever* been able to tell Bishop anything but the truth? Eventually."

Placated, he nodded. "True. I wonder how much of it will find its way into his official report."

"The good guys caught the bad guys before they

could commit another murder," Geneva said succinctly. "That's all that matters in the end, right?"

Silently, empty cups were raised in agreement.

Leo woofed softly and laid his chin gently back on the sleeping little girl's hip.

Strange creatures, humans.

But curiously endearing.

CHARACTER BIOS

NELLIE CAVENDISH

Twenty-nine, petite, slender, brown eyes and brown hair. Very much tougher than she looks. Her father, Thomas Ryan Cavendish, leaves a message for her after his death saying she has to go to a town named Salem where his roots are, and trust only a man named Finn to help her do . . . whatever it is she's supposed to do. She has no idea who Finn is, why she has to go to Salem—or why it has to be before her thirtieth birthday, less than two weeks away, when she finally makes up her mind to go on that mysterious and quite possibly dangerous journey. Nellie is a rather extraordinary psychic, something she has hidden her entire life. She does not know what sort of situation she's walking into but feels driven to find out whatever it is her father wanted her to discover. To complete whatever it was he was unable to do. She is, among other things, clairvoyant.

Appearances: *Hidden Salem*

LEO

Nellie's black Pit bull.

Appearances: *Hidden Salem*

GRAYSON SHERIDAN

FBI Special Crimes Unit—thirty-four, six feet tall, black hair and blue eyes. Very athletic.

Job: Special Agent, profiler, sharpshooter, trained in mixed martial arts as well as other self-defense tactics and has a great deal of survival training and experience.

Adept: Empath, with a strong shield that helps protect him from the barrage of emotions from roughly sixty-five to seventy percent of all the people he encounters. Has to drop his shield to feel emotions. Except around one person.

Appearances: *Hidden Salem*

NOAH BISHOP

FBI Special Crimes Unit—thirties, six-three, black hair made more striking by a widow's peak and a shot of pure white at his left temple. Silver-gray eyes. Very athletic and physically powerful.

Job: Unit Chief, profiler, pilot, sharpshooter, and highly trained and skilled in several martial arts.

Adept: An exceptionally powerful touch-telepath, he also shares with his wife, Miranda, a strong precognitive ability, the deep emotional link between them making them, together, far exceed the limits of the scale developed by the Special Crimes Unit to measure psychic talents. Also possesses an ancillary ability of enhanced senses (hearing, sight, scent), which he has trained other agents to use as well, something they informally refer to as "spider senses." Whether present in the flesh or not, Bishop virtually always knows what's going on with his agents in the field, somehow maintaining what seem to be psychic links with almost all of his agents without in any way being intrusive.

Appearances: *Stealing Shadows, Hiding in the Shadows, Out of the Shadows, Touching Evil, Whisper of Evil, Sense of Evil, Hunting Fear, Chill of Fear, Sleeping with Fear, Blood Dreams, Blood Sins, Blood Ties, Haven, Hostage, Haunted, Fear the Dark, Wait for Dark, Hold Back the Dark, Hidden Salem*

GENEVA RAYNOR

FBI Special Crimes Unit—thirty-two, tall, very red hair, gray eyes. Determined, stubborn, independent.

Job: Special Agent, profiler. Highly intelligent, stubborn to a fault, and perfectly capable of working alone, Geneva is one of the few agents Bishop is willing to send into an investigation without a partner or backup of any kind in the initial, fact-finding phase of an unknown situation.

She can also handle herself in any sort of situation she encounters; she can live off the land as well as a highly trained military veteran can, and hard experience with some down-and-dirty street fighting taught her to use whatever weapon is near to hand when necessary to survive. Habitually carries about her person a number of small, concealed tools that can also be weapons.

Adept: Telepath, quite powerful, and with a solid shield. Has more control than many telepaths and can focus narrowly to read only one mind. Her range as a telepath is about sixty percent.

Appearances: *Hidden Salem*

FINN DEVERELL

Thirty-two, six feet tall, blond hair, blue eyes. The Deverells are one of the original five families that founded Salem, town leaders, and each owns and operates one of the major businesses that keep Salem not only viable but flourishing. In the case of the Deverells, the family business is a huge paper mill that produces not only the sort of paper people use every day but also beautiful, specialized paper that is still made by hand using tools older than the town. Employing workers skilled in operating the machinery to produce ordinary paper as well as dozens highly skilled in producing the specialized paper, the Deverells pay very well, offer generous benefits and bonuses, and are considered one of the best families to work for. Like each of the other families, the Deverells tend to have, in every generation, at least one family member with a psychic ability. Finn is an empath.

Appearances: *Hidden Salem*

MIRANDA BISHOP

FBI Special Crimes Unit—thirties, tall, with long black hair and electric blue eyes, strikingly beautiful, very athletic.

Job: Special Agent, investigator, profiler, black belt in karate and a sharpshooter.

Adept: Touch-telepath, seer, remarkably powerful; possesses unusual control, particularly in a highly developed shield capable of protecting herself psychically, a shield she's able to extend beyond herself to protect others. Shares abilities with her husband, due to their intense emotional connection, and together they far exceed the scale developed by the SCU to measure psychic abilities.

Appearances: *Out of the Shadows, Touching Evil, Whisper of Evil, Sense of Evil, Hunting Fear, Chill of Fear, Blood Dreams, Blood Sins, Blood Ties, Hostage, Haunted, Fear the Dark, Wait for Dark, Hold Back the Dark, Hidden Salem*

PSYCHIC TERMS AND ABILITIES

*(As Classified/Defined
by Bishop's Special Crimes
Unit and by Haven)*

Absolute Empath: The rarest of all abilities; this one causes the psychic to literally absorb the pain of another, to the point that the empath physically takes on the same injuries, healing the injured person and then healing herself.

Adept: The general term used to label any functional psychic; the specific ability is much more specialized.

Clairvoyance: The ability to know things, to pick up bits of information, seemingly out of thin air.

Dream-projecting: The ability to enter another's dreams.

Dream-walking: The ability to invite/draw others into one's own dreams.

Empath: One who experiences the emotions of others, often up to and including physical pain and injuries.

Healing: The ability to heal injuries to self or others, often but not always ancillary to mediumistic abilities.

Healing Empath: An empath sometimes has the ability to not only feel but also heal the pain/injury of another. It can be extremely dangerous for the healing empath, depending on how serious the pain or injury they attempt to heal, since it always depletes their own life energy.

Latent: The term used to describe unawakened or inactive abilities, as well as to describe a psychic not yet aware of being psychic.

Mediumistic: Having the ability to communicate with the dead; some see the dead, some hear the dead, but most mediums in the unit are able to do both.

Precognition: A seer or precog's ability to correctly predict future events. The SCU differentiates between predictions and prophesies: A prediction can sometimes be changed, even avoided, but a prophesy will happen no matter what anyone does to try to change the outcome.

Psychometric: The ability to pick up impressions or information from touching objects.

Regenerative: The ability to heal one's own injuries/ illnesses, even those considered by medical experts to be lethal or fatal. (A classification unique to one SCU operative and considered separate from a healer's abilities.)

Spider Sense: The ability to enhance one's normal senses (sight, hearing, smell, etc.) through concentration and the focusing of one's own mental and physical energy.

Telekinesis: The ability to move objects with the mind; a very rare ability.

Telepathic mind control: The ability to influence/control others through mental focus and effort; an *extremely* rare ability.

Telepathy (touch and nontouch, or open): The ability to pick up thoughts from others. Some telepaths only receive, while others have the ability to send thoughts. A few are capable of both, usually due to an emotional connection with the other person.

UNNAMED ABILITIES INCLUDE

The ability to see into time, to view events in the past, present, and future without being or having been physically present while the events transpired. Another rare ability, it seems to be a combination of clairvoyance, precognition, and sometimes mediumistic traits, though the ability is so rare it hasn't been studied in depth.

The ability to render someone else instantly unconscious.

The ability to "freeze" a person momentarily so that they are unable to move—or to move them using the force of energy alone, as if by a violent shove.

The ability to see the aura or another person's energy field, and to interpret those colors and energies. Through experience, trial, and error, the SCU has come to a tentative understanding of what the different colors usually mean:

White = healing/protective

Blue/lavenders = calm

Red/rich yellows = energy/power

Green = peaceful; unusual, tends to mix with other colors

Metallic = repelling or holding in energy from another source

Black = extreme negativity, even evil, especially if it has red streaks of energy and power

More than one color in an aura is common, reflecting the outward sign of human complexities of emotion.

The ability to absorb and/or channel energy usefully as a defensive or offensive tool or weapon. Extremely rare due to the level of power and control needed, and highly dangerous, especially if the energy being channeled is dark or negative energy.

The ability to hide or disguise an object or person.

The ability to communicate with animals, which is part telepathy and part empathy—and part something else.

AUTHOR'S NOTE

The first books in the Bishop/SCU series were published back in 2000, and readers have asked me whether these stories are taking place in "real" time and if, at this point, more than twenty (!) years have passed in the series. The answer is no. I chose to use "story time" for several reasons, one being to avoid having my characters age too quickly. Roughly speaking, each trilogy takes place within the same year, with some overlaps.

So, from an arbitrary start date, the timeline looks something like this:

Stealing Shadows—February

Hiding in the Shadows—October/November

YEAR ONE:

Out of the Shadows—January (SCU formally introduced)

Touching Evil—November

YEAR TWO:

Whisper of Evil—March

Sense of Evil—June

Hunting Fear—September

YEAR THREE:

Chill of Fear—April

Sleeping with Fear—July

Blood Dreams—October

YEAR FOUR:

Blood Sins—January

Blood Ties—April

Haven—July

Hostage—October

YEAR FIVE:

Haunted—February

Fear the Dark—May

Wait for Dark—August

Hold Back the Dark—October

YEAR SIX:

Hidden Salem—January

So, with the publication of *Hidden Salem*, the Special Crimes Unit has been a functional (and growing) unit of agents for barely six years. Time to have grown from being known within the FBI as the "Spooky Crimes Unit" to becoming a well-respected unit with an excellent record of solved cases. A unit that has, moreover, earned respect in various law enforcement agencies, word quietly passed from this sheriff to that chief of police that they excel at solving crimes that are anything but normal using methods and abilities that are unique to each agent, and that they neither seek nor want media attention.

An asset to any level of law enforcement, they do their jobs with little fanfare and never ride roughshod over locals, both traits very much appreciated, especially by small-town cops and citizens wary of outsiders. They regard both skepticism and interest with equal calm, treating their abilities as merely tools with which to do their jobs, and their very matter-of-factness helps normally hard-nosed cops accept, if not understand, at least something of the paranormal.